LOVE

it's wild

JEANNINE COLETTE

For Tara McCormick and Nicole Parsons

one

I AM DANCING WITH the most handsome guy at the wedding.

Brown hair, matching eyes, a devilish grin, and patent leather shoes that are currently stepping on my toes. I'd be annoyed, but when you're dancing with an eight-year-old, you let it slide.

"You're a good dancer, Tara," Hunter says as he raises his arm to twirl me.

I duck between our joined hands. "Not so bad yourself, kid."

"This is our fifth dance in a row. You sure you don't want to dance with a grown-up?"

"Why would I want to dance with any of these fools when I'm already with the coolest person here?"

I'm not kidding.

I look around the lavish reception of my best friend's wedding and sigh. It's no surprise that the bride and wedding planner extraordinaire, Melissa Jones, has transformed a barn into an elegant affair. She and her groom, William Bronson, paired their tastes perfectly. The room is rustic chic with twinkling lights and extravagant florals.

And while it's ripe with romance, there isn't one to be had for me.

There are plenty of handsome single men here tonight. At the bar is Todd, Dick, and Kyle—all friends of the groom. Todd and I went out once, but the night ended when he asked if I wanted to go back to his place and play video games. No, that wasn't a euphemism. He literally wanted to play Romp the Sack—a two-person battle where you fight each other's avatar on the latest gaming system. Dick and I had a coffee date, where he berated the barista. I left with my full latte in hand. And Kyle and I chatted at a party once, but there was no spark.

Seated at a nearby table is Kent, a sergeant I dated, but his fear of intimacy had us parting ways. Standing by another table are a few single gentlemen I've met through Melissa and Will. I've scouted them all and even kissed one or two. Instead of princes, they all turned out to be frogs.

My dating history is longer than Taylor Swift's, and I don't have the cool songs or Easter egg–laden music videos as a bonus to each romance ending horribly.

"You know what your problem is?" Hunter states. "You're picky."

"I'm a successful, gorgeous thirty-six-year-old woman with an amazing sense of humor, and killer taste in style—I mean, have you seen these shoes? More importantly, I know my fucking worth. Let that be a lesson to you, my fabulous godson. Never settle for anyone less than what you deserve!" I declare and then add, "Oh, and don't tell your mom I cursed. I promised I'd watch my language."

"Your secret's safe with me."

It's not usually my style to come to an event stag. As a woman on the hunt for a man, I know better than to attend a wedding or engagement party without a date. Women tend to eye the single gals with skeptical glares. They hang on to their man's arm like a mama bear protecting her cub from a circling vulture. It's as if going to a wedding is supposed to make me extra horny and want to sleep with every man whether he's taken or not.

For the record, I've never ever taken another woman's man.

After a series of dead-end relationships, bad dates, and a thumb that hurts from swiping left, I decided to just enjoy the evening of my best friend's wedding on my own.

Melissa's laugh from the dais sounds over the music. She's seated beside her now husband and is positively glowing—and not just because she's in her third trimester of pregnancy. It's because of the man whose eyes she's staring into, the ones that are lit up with a smolder as he looks at her like she's the most magnificent being on the planet. It makes me smile, and a warmth runs up my arms and swirls in my chest.

When Melissa's first husband left her, she never thought she'd find love again. Will had to bang down the door to her heart, and she's now happier than she's ever been. While I'm still searching for my one and only, this bitch was lucky enough to get it twice.

Yes, I can call her a bitch because she's my soulmate. My sister. The one I would kill for—and almost did when her swine of an ex had an affair. I had the shovel in my hand, ready to bury the body.

Alas, she opted to move on.

The best of us do.

I'm living proof.

"Mind if I cut in?" a young voice I know well asks.

Hunter and I turn to Ainsley, the six-year-old daughter of my other friend, Jillian—another one who found love this past year. Jillian fell in love with the same man not once, but twice. Luke had stolen her heart years ago, broken it, then put it back together after discovering they had a child together. It's a complicated story but a good one.

I'd even settle for a love like that … angst and all.

I turn to the little girl in a sparkly dress and smirk. "Actually, I do mind if you cut in. Hunter's dance card is full."

She places her hand on her hip. "Dancing all night with a second grader isn't a good look for you, Tara."

"It makes me look like the sweet aunt who's spending time with her nephew."

"It makes you look desperate."

I match her snark. "Watch your mouth, young lady, or I'll have to tell your mother."

"She'll yell at you right back. She says I'm turning into a mini you."

"What did you say in return?"

"That if I grow up to be half as classy, sassy, and badassy as Tara, I'd be a lucky girl." Ainsley snaps her fingers and gives a flip of her hair.

LOVE...IT'S WILD

I laugh and then release Hunter's hands so I can throw mine around Ainsley. "I love you. You are a sweet, silly, and *sassy* little thing. Don't ever change." Taking a step back, I sweep my hand toward the vacant space. "Have at it, kids."

I glance around the dance floor that is full of couples, hands joined, cheeks touching, and eyes gleaming.

Izzy—Melissa's teenage daughter—is gyrating, cell phone in hand, with the teens and young twenty-somethings as they film their entire life for social media. Melissa's aunt calls me over to come dance with the over-sixty crowd who have made a circle on their section of the dance floor. I politely decline and step away.

It's time for a drink.

A very tall drink.

I sashay through the crowd with my shoulders back, tits up, and my chin held high as I sway my hips.

As my grandmother always said, "Walk into a room like you own it," and own it I do every time.

As I sidle up to the mahogany bar, I lift a dainty wrist and call over to the bartender.

Beside me, a gentleman in a dark gray groomsman suit looks my way. I recognize him from pictures I've seen at Melissa's house. I have been quite curious about Cade, the youngest brother of the groom and an elusive bachelor.

We lock gazes, and he finds this as his invitation to approach.

"Can I buy you a drink?" he asks.

"Sure, at the hotel bar after the wedding because the drinks here are free, and I don't talk to men who like to pawn off free cocktails to get in my pants." I wink and then turn to the bartender. "Pinot grigio, please. Make it a generous pour."

The bartender leaves, and Cade places an elbow on the bar.

He has a wicked gleam to his eye. "You're attractive and feisty."

"I heard you were a lady charmer."

"You've heard of me?"

I lift my now-poured glass of wine and turn to him.

"Where do I start? Cade Bronson, world traveler, bedder of woman, and often in trouble for not showing up to family holidays. Left home when he went to college and hardly ever returns to his hometown of Castleton, yet makes many appearances on social media, where he posts Pinterest-worthy photos of himself in various cities and often with a different half-naked woman on his arm."

"Guilty on all counts." He has a Cheshire grin.

"Word also has it, you call your mother every day, so we all know you're not the total bad boy many think you are."

He laughs. "Also, guilty. That must mean you are Tara Parsons, the bride's best friend, who is known as a stunningly beautiful troublemaker who's looking for love."

"Only trouble if you get caught."

"Trouble is when you're doing something wrong."

"Depends on whose rule book you're reading."

"I like you."

"Touché, little brother."

He places a hand on his chest and winces. "Ouch. Little is never a good thing to be called when you're flirting with a woman."

"You don't stand a chance with me." I take a sip of my wine and eye the handsome bachelor. Light hair, dark eyes, and all the features that would make any woman swoon. Too bad he's not my type. "There are only two reasons a man would stay away from his hometown for as many years as you have. One is because he's running from the law, but your brother is a sergeant in this county, so I know that's not the case. The other is running from unrequited love. I'd be a fool to flirt with a man whose heart is already taken."

His brows rise with an impressed grimace. "You're good."

"I know."

"What's your story? Why hasn't a catch like you gone for a walk down the aisle yet?"

My stomach churns momentarily, and my breath hitches, but not in a good way. It's funny how your body reacts to situations before your brain has a chance to catch up.

I lift my chin and smile with my cheeks tight. "Why walk down an aisle when I can run down the freeway?"

I raise my glass, and Cade clinks his with mine.

"It's a pleasure meeting you, Tara. Enjoy your evening."

I drink more of my wine as I watch him walk away. My fingers run along the smooth wood of the bar as I let out a deep breath, giving myself a moment to let that uneasy feeling in my stomach subside.

A teenager takes Cade's place beside me at the bar. I turn my back slightly to have a moment to myself as I numb my nerves.

"Beer, please," the teenage boy asks the bartender, who shakes his head.

"I don't think so."

"I'm older than I look."

"Let me see an ID."

The teen scoffs. "I'm at a wedding with my family. Why would I ask for a drink if I'm not allowed to have one?"

The bartender doesn't appear to like the rude tone. "I'm not losing my job over some kid. You want a beer? Ask your parents to come up and get you one."

The teen looks at me and then back at the bartender, motioning his head in my direction. "She's my mom. She says it's okay."

I blink a few times as it dawns on me that he's referring to me as his mother.

I squint my eyes at the teen. "Excuse me?"

"You okay with that, ma'am?" the bartender asks me, and now, I'm staring at him with narrowed eyes.

"I'm not old enough to be his mother," I declare and then do the math in my head. Damn, actually, I could be.

And when I was his age, I most definitely was stealing drinks from Melissa's parents' liquor cabinet and imbibing in the neighbor's tree house. Now, I'm about to tell a kid he's too young to do the stupid thing I did when I was his age.

"You have any Athletic Brewing Company back there? Get me a Wit's Peak."

The bartender does as I asked, and I place a tip in the nearby jar. I hand the beer to the teenager, who looks at me like I'm handing him turpentine.

"You got me nonalcoholic beer?"

"You're lucky I got you anything at all. Where are your parents?"

"My mom's not here, and my dad's an asshole."

"If you're gonna play the moody bad-boy role, you at least have to pretend to be charming. If you walked up here and complimented me, I might have gotten you a beer."

"Really?"

"I said, might have. After the flattery wore off, I would have remembered you're about five years too young to be drinking. Now, go dance. Have fun. It's a wedding."

He sulks off with his booze-free beer, and I commend myself for acting like an adult. It's not often I make good decisions, so when I do, I give myself a mental pat on the back.

The band leader announces it's time for the bouquet toss. Young women sprint toward the dance floor.

Melissa's aunt calls me over. "Tara, you're still single. Get on out there!"

I smile and tip my glass at her. This is my cue to step away.

I'm walking toward the ladies' room when I nearly collide into a burly man who stepped into my path.

"Tara, I've been looking for you," he says, to which I do a double take.

I vaguely remember meeting him at Melissa's engagement party. "Hello."

He takes a handkerchief out of his pocket and dabs his forehead, which has light beads of sweat along the brow. "Sorry, it's hot in here. Great wedding!"

"It's amazing. Enjoy your evening." I try to walk around him, but he sidesteps in front of me, forcing me to give him my attention.

"So, um, my wife and I were wondering if you wanted to … you know … hang out after the wedding?"

He nods his head toward a table not too far away. A woman is seated there with wide eyes as she watches our conversation.

"Yeah, sure. The hotel bar is where most people will probably be hanging after the wedding. I'll see you there."

I start to walk away, but he moves to block me.

"Actually, we were thinking of something more … intimate."

My feet feel like lead, and there's a heavy sensation in my gut. I tilt my head as I look at him. "Can you explain what you mean by intimate?"

The handkerchief makes an appearance again. This time, he swipes the side of his head. "My wife and I have been talking about expanding our interests for a while, but she hasn't been comfortable with anything yet. Tonight, she agreed that if you said yes, she'd do it."

I pull my lips inward as I try to comprehend what I think he's asking. "Do what?"

"A threesome."

My jaw nearly hits the floor. For a gal who always has something to say, I find myself temporarily at a loss for words. "Wow. You don't know me. I'm not that kind of girl."

"That's not what I heard," he states, dumbfounded.

My eyes narrow into fierce slits. "What exactly did you hear about me?"

"That you're a whore."

A wave of shock, annoyance, and mortification slams into my chest, nearly toppling me over. Adrenaline surges through my veins, boiling beneath the surface, like a volcano on the verge of erupting. My fist clenches, and I fight the urge to punch him in the face. Instead, I do what any lady would do.

I knee him in the balls.

"Asshole," I spit as I walk away from him and toward the exit as he winces in pain.

His wife jolts up from her table and starts to sprint over.

Luckily, no one else seems to have noticed the scene because they're all gathered around the dance floor. Melissa is standing with the bouquet in her hands, ready to throw it as the eager singles wait with reaching hands.

I pick up my pace.

My pulse quickens.

My hands open and close as I try to find a way to not crawl out of my skin. That's what I want to do. I want to bolt right out of my bones and fly somewhere else. Be someone else.

The blood pulses in my ears as I walk quicker toward the exit. There's a tightening in my ribs, restricting my ability to breathe.

I need air.

I need space.

I need a damn Valium.

I run outside, bursting through the door. There's a group of people having a smoke. My wine sloshes as I dart to the right and head toward the back of the building and down a stone path. I'm not one to run away from a situation, but my heels click loudly on the ground as I scurry away, desperate for a moment to collect my thoughts.

It's dark on the side of the building. The only light comes from the full moon. It's large and bright and so close that I feel like I could touch it. I want to, so much so that there's a tree at the end of the path at the back of the property, calling my name. It's the kind of tree Melissa and I used to climb as kids. The kind where we'd share our dreams of the future, back when we had decades ahead of us and were excited to see what would happen.

I sprint to the tree.

Out of breath and out of my mind, I slam my hand into the bark. It's coarse against my palm. Earthy. Cool. Reliable.

I place my glass on the ground, slide out of my shoes, and hoist myself onto the bottom branch.

I climb.

Why am I climbing a tree exactly? Like I said, I don't always make the best decisions, and apparently, being indefinitely single at yet another romantic wedding, continuously awaiting my Prince Charming, realizing I could be the mother of a teenager, and being called a whore makes me want to climb a tree.

Limb by limb, I hoist up my dress and lift myself up, nearly slipping a time or two, until I'm as high as I can go. On a wide, sturdy branch, I settle myself against the bark and look up.

I breathe.

My breaths are long and hard, the inhales so deep that my lungs hurt. I allow myself the time to calm down up here, about fifteen feet off the ground. I rest my head against the hard trunk and wait as my heart composes to a subtle beat.

The moon appears through the leaves. I give a small wave to the moon, and it glistens back. It's like it's blinking hello to me, day after day, as it peers down and says, *Hi, Tara. Have you found your happily ever after yet?*

I shake my head. *Not today, moon.*

Hunter says I'm picky. I've heard that before, and usually, it's from judgmental idiots who think procreating with a man because some ticking time clock is about to alarm is a reason why a woman should give up her priorities.

I don't want any man. I want a real man.

One who values the woman in his life. Who treats her with honor and doesn't take advantage of her weaknesses or use them against her. A man who recognizes she's different from him and respects that. A man who I, in turn, can love, support, and above all, bust his balls to high hell because whoever ends up with me will have to have a sense of humor and a whole lot of patience.

We'll dance in the kitchen at three in the morning, drink coffee in the afternoon while talking about celebrity gossip, and travel the world together, placing pins in our corkboard map we keep in the dining room. It's not just the activities that will make our relationship amazing; it's also the fact that we'll want to do them together.

We'll be in love.

"I know it will happen for me." I speak into the night sky. "My fairy tale will come true. Doesn't matter if I'm eighty years old and in the nursing home. I know I'll meet him someday."

A breeze whispers strongly through the leaves, and it nearly knocks me off the branch. I grip the thick wood and catch my balance. My head spins at the idea of falling.

The cheers of the bouquet and garter toss and the loud music that follows echo out of the barn. I don't want to go inside yet, but I should get out of this tree.

My stockings make it harder to get traction on the way down. I try to hold my dress while bracing my weight as I get my foot on the next limb. The space between   branches feels farther apart than they did when I was climbing up. I stretch my toes to find the next one. When I do, I lose my footing and start to slip.

"Ahh!" I yelp as I quickly grab onto the branch, catching myself and dangling from the limb.

Looking over my shoulder, I'm still about ten feet in the air. If this were a social media post, it would be captioned "Dumb Ways to Die".

With desperate grips, I claw at the branch. I'm crazy strong from regular workouts, but my arms burn, and my hands can't grasp the loosening bark as it scratches at the pads of my fingers.

I slip even more and panic.

This isn't good. I haven't even met the man of my dreams, and now, I'm going to die from falling out of a tree. Okay, maybe I won't die, but this can't end well.

I grasp and scratch and try with all my might to help myself, but it's no use.

My fingers slide down the bark, and I lose my hold.

I fall fast and far down the tree.

Falling …

Falling …

I yelp again loudly and then gasp as I land on something hard.

I'm not on the ground.

No, I'm in the strong arms of a man who caught me with a step back and a steadying of his body, hoisting me up with his rugged and tanned hands peeking out of the sleeves of a gray suit.

I grab on to his titan-like shoulders. My heart is beating a million miles an hour. My breath is coming out in heaving pants.

I thought I was going to crash onto the hard ground, yet here I am, cradled against the chest of my hero.

I turn in the man's arms to look at him and find myself face-to-face with rich almond-shaped eyes, darkly peppered stubble, and the concrete jaw of the one man I never ever in my life would have thought would play hero to my damsel in distress.

Robert Bronson.

Fuck my life.

Two

"YOU SAVED ME."

I look at my hero.

Rob Bronson, oldest brother of the Bronson clan, has a roguishly handsome face. His thick, dark hair and prominent cheekbones, add a sense of masculinity and strength to his appearance that his brothers don't have. It's a sculpted, chiseled look that's severe because he's always glaring so seriously.

While I've noticed this man before, I've never been this close to him to appreciate his chestnut-colored eyes—warm in color yet there's a harshness to his gaze. If I wasn't in his arms, I wouldn't feel the buzz that courses through his body with the rush of testosterone. His parted lips let out the faintest sound of hurried breaths.

He doesn't say anything. Instead, he just stares at me.

"Thank you." I swallow hard.

He grunts a deep, gravelly sound that vibrates through his chest. It would be sexy if it wasn't the only form of communication this man has had with me. I'd think it was just his way, but I've observed him speaking with other people. He has a voice. A nice one too—a low timbre that's kind of sexy. For me, he just makes these animal sounds.

It's not sexy. It's rude.

I put on my best dramatic damsel-in-distress voice. "You know,

Rob, if we were in a movie, this is where the heroine would kiss the hero for rescuing her from uncertain peril."

Another low grunt escapes his hard-lined mouth. There's something about his displeased aura that makes me push further.

"Have you come to rescue me and then carry me out into the sunset? I am now forever in your debt and will serve you all the days of my life. Marry me, Robert Bronson, and let me love you forever!"

"They told me you were crazy," he mumbles, and my face lights up with joy.

"He speaks!" I declare dramatically. "I knew you could do it, big boy. You can let me down now."

"I will as soon as you let go of me. You've got a damn vise grip around my neck."

"Wuss."

I loosen my hands from his neck, and he places me on the ground roughly.

With my feet now firmly planted, I brush my dress down and make sure I didn't tear it. "Nice to know you have verbal skills. Every time I'm around, you grunt at me and walk away."

I look up at Rob as he just stands there, sliding his hands in his pockets and assessing me. His dark gaze starts at my face and then trails down my body in an unnerving way. The widening of his eyes could fool me into thinking he likes what he sees, but his deep scowl shows he's completely bothered by my appearance.

I fold my arms and give him the staredown right back.

He's hard and steely. Like the kind of man who would get his knuckles bloody just for fun. His demeanor is a stark contrast to the way he looks tonight, dressed in his gray suit that tapers at the waist and accentuates his broad shoulders and the definition of his thighs. He's dressed like a humble groomsman who just stood by his younger brother's side at the altar, but his attitude exudes annoyed party guest.

We stand like this for a few moments more, our eyes glued to one another. While he can maintain this standstill of quiet, I don't know how to keep my mouth shut.

"Why are you back here? Are you stalking me? I'm very stalkable, so I'd understand if you followed me, but it's giving serial-killer vibes."

He runs his tongue along the back of his teeth.

I continue, "You didn't have to catch me. I would've landed just fine. I'm agile, like a cat."

He lowers his gaze. "What were you doing, climbing a tree?"

"I was being impulsive. Haven't you ever done something on a whim because it felt right in the moment?"

He doesn't answer immediately, so I place my hands on my hips and wait for his response.

With a rise of his chin, he narrows his eyes before simply stating, "No."

"You should try it sometime. Life's too short to just wait for exciting things to happen."

"Hardly consider nearly killing yourself, falling from an oak tree, exciting."

"I liked it better when all you did was grunt."

My comment is rewarded with a light laugh. It's quick, but there nonetheless. I'm confused by this encounter. When I say Robert Bronson has ignored me the three times we've met, I mean he flat-out ignored me. No words, no eye contact. I've seen his back more than I've seen his face. Lucky for me, he has an attractive backside to watch walk away.

"I'm Tara, by the way."

"I know your name. Surprised you weren't inside with the other hopeful romantics, trying to catch the bouquet."

"I'm not ashamed of my single status, but playing eager beaver to some rose petals being flung in the air is not my cup of tea. Sure, it would be romantic if I caught the bouquet and my knight in shining armor caught the garter, placed it on my thigh, and we fell madly in love. But based on the cast of characters at tonight's wedding, my knight is most definitely not here."

Rob kneels to the ground and picks up his glass—a lowball filled with amber liquid. He leaves my wineglass on the ground. If I waited for him to hand it to me, I'd be here until I was dead. I bend down and pick up my own glass, which is still half-full.

"You can tell a lot about someone by what they drink," he remarks.

I look at him from over the rim of my glass, confused as to why, after a year of knowing me, he chose tonight to communicate with me.

"Let me guess. White wine makes me dainty and incapable of making hard decisions."

"From the way you were struggling to hold yourself up on that tree, I'd say the dainty part is right."

"I'm hella strong. I teach a kickboxing class twice a week. Why are you so mean?"

"Why are you still standing here, talking to me?"

"Because I don't cower to assholes."

He gives that low laugh again. For the life of me, I can't figure this guy out, and I don't know why I'm intrigued by him.

"White wine also means you're curious, sarcastic, and a perfectionist," he adds. "After tonight, I think I'll add headstrong."

He's not wrong in that assessment. "What's that in your glass?"

"Bourbon."

"I bet that makes you serious and pensive. A fortress of steel as you assess those around you with a cautious attitude."

His brows crease as he drinks. His tongue darts out to lick his lips. "I like the burn. You should try it. It'll bring you back down to reality."

"What's that supposed to mean?"

"Aren't you a little old to be daydreaming about happily ever afters?"

I should storm off and leave this broody jerk alone in the dark. That's what any sane woman would do. As we all know, I'm not a typical woman. Instead of walking away, I get in his face.

"I'm not ashamed to be a grown woman who daydreams. It's called being hopeful and imaginative. I'm also a great conversationalist and hardworking, and people love spending time with me, yet every time I walk into a room, you walk the other way. And now that you are speaking to me, everything is rude and condescending. You don't even know me, and I demand to know why you've decided to act the way you do around me."

Stroking his chin, he regards me carefully. There's a pensive shimmer in the shadow of his eyes.

"I was told you're on the hunt for a man. I didn't want to give you any false impressions."

My hand flies to the top of my head as I stomp on the ground. "I am really fucking tired of this false narrative going around that I'm some floozy who will throw herself at any man because I'm looking for love. When did the message go out that I was desperate? Just because a woman is actively and openly trying to find someone to spend the rest of her life with doesn't mean she's easy. It doesn't mean you have to run away from her because you think she'll attack you. It doesn't mean she wants to sleep with every Todd, Dick, and Kyle just because they're single too. And it most certainly doesn't mean you can go up to her and proposition her for a threesome at her best friend's wedding. It doesn't mean she's a whore!"

Rob takes a purposeful step forward. "Wait, wait, wait. I did not say that." He closes the gap between us in two more steps. There's a tightness to his jaw, and his eyes darken. His voice is stern. "Did someone hurt you tonight?"

"Not the point. It's fine. It's no big deal."

"You're right. It's not a big deal. It's a huge fucking problem. Who was it?"

"Calm down there, Hercules. I'm a big girl. I can take care of myself, and I did with a swift knee to the groin. I'm fine. Don't repeat that story to anyone. It's embarrassing enough, and I don't feel like rehashing the reason why I kicked some douche in the balls."

"He doesn't need his reputation protected."

"Yeah, but mine does. I've fooled around quite a bit. It's the happenstance of dating for twenty years. A man would get a high five. A woman gets labeled easy and loose. For the record, there is nothing loose about me. I'm perfectly tight."

I down my pinot and then hand him my empty wineglass. He takes it and then looks shocked as I grab his lowball out of his hand and drink that as well. The amber liquid is harsh and stings as it slides down my throat.

I start to cough.

"Wow, that does burn." I hand him his glass and wipe my mouth with the back of my hand. "Why does anyone like drinking bourbon? Cruel and unusual punishment. It's like smoking cigars. No one could like either of the two. They just do it because people tell them it's the sophisticated thing to do, yet all they do is hit your larynx and make it impossible to breathe."

LOVE...IT'S WILD

He places the empty glasses on a nearby rock. When he turns back, he has an almost-amused look on his face. "Did it help?"

"Kind of."

I stumble slightly. Rob moves swiftly and catches me by the small of my back. His hand is warm against the satin of my dress, and I move toward his chest so as not to fall backward. My hands grip the lapel of his jacket and then claw at his back. It's enough for me to feel the hardness beneath the suit. This man is not just steel emotionally, but physically as well.

"Can you be trusted not to fall to the ground? That's twice in one night I've had to catch you."

I look up at him and instantly become mesmerized by the magnetism of his stare—an intensity that burns stronger than the bourbon I can still feel in my chest. It's not just his eyes. It's his mouth, jaw, and the commanding stance he gives with his entire body. His full lips part as his chest rises with a quick inhale. There's no mistaking the musky smell of him as he presses against me.

My imagination would love to say this is a romantic scenario.

I'm smart enough to know this is far from it.

This man has been avoiding me for a year because the thought of being with me is repulsive.

Message heard loud and clear.

I step away from him. Nay, I push him away. "I don't need to be rescued. I'm okay with falling because I always get back up. If you weren't here, I might have landed on the ground, but I know how to dust myself off."

"Maybe you aren't the damsel I thought you were. You're better off," he drawls. "People aren't as good as they seem, and that happily ever after bullshit is overrated."

"No way, Bronson. I might have just had a shitty encounter with some douche, a mishap with a tree, and too much bourbon, but I'm not changing. You can put on this crude facade to keep women away, but I'm not giving up."

"You might not be desperate, but you're determined. Too determined."

I take a step toward him. "Well, I am most definitely not interested in you. I have standards. High ones. Now, will you stop being a dick and quit ignoring me? I don't want a romance with you, I promise.

You're too damn moody for me."

"And you're too damn unpredictable for me."

"Someday, I'm going to find my soulmate."

"I never want to be married again."

"Good," I state with my chin held high.

"Good." He closes the gap.

An uneasiness weaves through me as a conversation Melissa and I had a while ago pops into my head. Rob was married, but his wife left him. Makes sense why he's so bitter. It's most likely why he's out here in the dark and not inside at his brother's wedding.

Little does he know, we have more in common than he thinks.

Without my shoes on, I'm much shorter than he is, so I must look up to make eye contact with him. "Some romances end, but it doesn't mean it's not worth trying for another chance at love. I'd rather have forty days of blissful happiness than spend the next forty years alone."

His forehead creases as he looks down at the ground and absorbs my words. There's a slight pinch to his lips and a heaviness in the scowl of his brow. When his eyes meet mine, I'm so seared by the intensity of his gaze that it makes me inhale deeply.

"Why are you so afraid to open yourself up to love again?" I ask.

"I don't share my personal business with the rest of the world." He shifts in an almost-uncomfortable manner. "While you can flit around life, looking for Prince Charming, I have kids to think about. They're more than a handful to keep me from needing anything else in my life."

"Funny, some kid earlier tried to pawn me off as his mom in order to get a beer. The bartender believed I could be his mother. I might be old enough to be one, but I do not look it."

"Did the kid have brown hair that could have used a haircut about three months ago?"

"Yeah, and a cocky-ass attitude."

"Fucking Jesse," he bites.

The similarities between Rob and the teen I met at the bar are strong. I didn't realize it until now. Same chestnut eyes and dark hair and an equally displeasing demeanor on a first impression.

"I take it, that was your kid?"

Just like that, Rob tenses, and that impenetrable steel wall of emotion is put back up.

"I have to make sure my idiot son isn't up to no good." Rob storms down the path and then stops a few yards away and turns around. "You should come inside too. I don't want you outside alone."

"What kind of trouble could I possibly get into out here?"

"You could try to climb that damn tree again."

I lift my shoulder and bat my lashes. "Will you be back here to save me if I do?"

He looks like he's about to say yes. Instead, he purses his mouth. "No."

"Liar." I scrunch my nose at him.

"God damn crazy woman," he mumbles as he heads down the path to the wedding.

I lift my shoes off the ground, slide them on, pick up the glasses, and then look up at the moon.

It's glaring down at me, asking for my thoughts, so I tell it exactly how I feel.

"You know, when I said I wanted a fairy tale, I didn't intend for you to send a dark knight. Try again, moon. Tomorrow's another day. And make it someone other than Rob Bronson."

Three

I MIGHT NOT HAVE been successful in love, but career success has come in spades.

While I moonlight as a kickboxing instructor, my main job is as an accountant. My job has allowed me to stay in my hometown of Newbury and work for the same accounting office that has been on Main Street since before I was born. I've been filing taxes for the working class for twelve years and made quite a name for myself. People in this small town gossip about my love life, but they know when it comes to their tax returns, they're in good hands.

I'm a little bit of a local celebrity, if I do say so myself.

Another perk of the job is the hours. As long as I get my work done, no one cares where I am, and that bodes well for my free lifestyle. During the week after Melissa's wedding, I stayed at her house and watched Hunter and Izzy while she went on her honeymoon. I got a lot done from my laptop since I had to be available for the kids after school.

Today though, I happen to be in the office. I have paperwork on my desk from clients who need extensions. I dive into my files, reading through the papers and making sure what I need is here. Then, I sift through emails, respond to client inquiries, and schedule appointments.

Around noon, I head to a local bakery shop, whose owner has a question about payroll. Our conversation is quick, as I came prepared with answers to what I already knew he wanted to know.

At the end of our meeting, I'm packing my computer into my bag when the bakery door chimes as someone walks in. I do a simple peek up and then look down to my bag. My head shoots back up quickly because the man standing in front of the eclairs and looking at me like a deer in headlights is one I didn't think I'd see in this town again.

"Tara," he says as if he just ran into an old high school buddy.

Here's the thing: we're not high school buddies.

We were once engaged to be married.

The engagement didn't end early either. It ended with me in my wedding dress and him having second thoughts while the guests were already in the pews. I still have a hard time digesting champagne, remembering what it felt like to be sipping on mimosas while taking pictures when he called to apologize that he got cold feet.

I hate champagne.

More than I hate champagne, I hate Patrick Murphy.

"Patrick," I stutter momentarily and then mentally smack myself. "Surprised to see you in Newbury."

"I just moved here."

I'm positively baffled by this news. "You? You moved to the town I live in?"

"I assumed you'd have moved to the city by now. Surprised to see you're still here."

"Not as surprised as I am to see you. Here. In Newbury."

"Wow," he breathes like he's looking at a meteor floating through the sky. "You look great, by the way. Really, really great."

I don't miss the way his eyes skim down my dress that highlights my curves. "Did you think I'd gotten fat and ugly because you left me? Nope. Still smokin' hot."

"Same sense of humor too." His grin is wide as he extends a hand toward a woman who is about five feet away, near the bakery case. "Victoria, come here. I want to introduce you to someone."

The woman walks over—blonde, svelte, and dressed in a brown maxi dress.

"Darling, this is Tara Parsons. Tara, meet my wife, Victoria."

"It's a pleasure to meet you." Victoria extends a manicured hand, and I take it. "It's so nice to meet a friend of Patrick's. I didn't know he knew anyone in town. This is wonderful."

I swallow down the rage bubbling in my gut. Patrick Murphy has the audacity to act as if I were a friend he wanted to introduce to his new wife, and she thinks we're gonna be chummy neighbors, sharing recipes and having game nights.

My total shock and aggravation of the situation quickly morphs into laughter. Honestly, there's no other reaction to have in this moment. Sure, I could punch him in the face, but I have more decorum than that. Instead, I place my hand on my hip, throw my hair back, and lift my shoulder playfully.

"Old friend? More like former lovers! Patrick and I were together for two years before he put a ring on my finger. Yours is much nicer though. Probably why our marriage never started. As they say, the bigger the rock, the longer the marriage."

"Jeez," Patrick says to himself, and Victoria releases my hand.

"Oh. You're that Tara." She has the nerve to look uncomfortable. "I'm sorry—"

"No need to be sorry at all." I wave off the notion of being upset that the man I loved deserted me while I was throat high in lace and wearing my grandmother's pearls. "Looks like it fared well for all of us."

"Are you married?" Patrick looks down at my left hand.

"No. Once I dodged the first bullet, I raised the bar dramatically." I turn to Victoria and whisper loudly, "You know what I mean."

Two young girls, who look to be about four and three, skip over.

"Daddy, can we get the cookies now?" the older of the two asks Patrick.

She has his small upper lip and freckles on the bridge of her nose. I might not want children, but there was a time that I considered it, and they looked like the cherub-faced girls in front of me.

My bravado falters as I blink over at Patrick. "You have children?"

Patrick's demeanor shifts as he takes the girls' hands and brings them in front of him. "Tara, these are our daughters. Lemon and Clementine."

The chortle that falls out of my mouth is unintended. I quickly rein it in with a clearing of my throat and smile kindly. "The fruit of your loins are beautiful."

Patrick, who seemed delighted to see me when he first walked in, now appears uneasy. Glad he caught up to the energy in the room.

"My family and I just moved to Newbury," he explains. "The girls will be starting school here in the fall. We just closed on our house, so this is our little celebration. Cookies for the girls."

My heart sinks, and I look at the family of four—Patrick, his Stepford wife, and their fruit. The realization that I will be seeing them often, running into them, is a knife to my belly.

Of all the towns on the planet, why, oh why, would Patrick be so cruel as to choose mine? Perhaps I'd have known he was a family man and would be attracted to a town such as this one if he'd had social media and allowed me to cyberstalk him properly, like an ex would do.

I often wondered what had come of Patrick Murphy in the years since he left me.

Now, I know he was pruning.

If I could tell him to go fuck himself, I would, but there are children present.

My only other option is to smile bigly and declare my excitement for them. "Congratulations!"

Victoria drops her shoulders in relief. "Thank you. I hope to see you around. It would be lovely if we could be friends."

"Nah, I'm good," I reply with a courteous smile.

I wiggle my fingers at the kids, lift my chin, and put an extra sway into my hips as I walk out the door, knowing the two of them will both be watching me leave. I know it's not Victoria's fault her man was a cad before they met, but it doesn't stop me from disliking her for the mere point that she exists. In my town. Where I'll be seeing her out and about for the rest of my pathetic single life.

Am I angry? Yes.

Could I possibly cry when the nerves boiling under my skin try to find a release the moment I'm out of their field of vision? Double yes.

Am I going to ignore both emotions, go to the bar, and drown myself in the flirtation of men?

You know it.

Four

"FILL HER UP TO the top. I want that wine to hit the rim."

Lone Tavern has been one of my go-to places to meet men the past few years. I started coming here when I was dating a man I'd met on the internet, and when that relationship ended, I kept swinging by.

Located about thirty minutes from my house, the bar has a cowboy vibe with rustic everything—decor, lighting, music, and men. Wrangler jeans and steel-toed boots are the norm here, and it fulfills every *Yellowstone* fantasy I have—not that there are any ranches within twenty miles of this place. No, the men and women here are playing a role. Me included.

Dressed in my tightest jeans and a formfitting top with lace trim around the revealing neckline, I slid on a pair of cowgirl boots and came out to get my flirt on.

My outfit seems to be doing the job because I am currently talking with Jason. He works for the electric company, has good teeth, and just asked to buy me a drink, which I refused before ordering my own.

The bartender slides my glass to me.

"My friends and I come here for the music. Can't get a live band at any other bar. What kind of music are you into?" Jason asks.

"I have eclectic taste, but this country music works for me."

"That doesn't answer the question. What music do you listen to when you're alone in the car? That's the real tell."

I like his question. You can tell a lot about a man based on the questions he asks in the *getting to know you* stage.

"I've been known to listen to some '90s and 2000s pop. Does that scare you off?"

"Of course not. That's the Backstreet Boys era, right? I can dig that."

I cross my legs in his direction, angling myself a little more toward him.

"If you can tell me at least one name of a Backstreet Boys song, then maybe I'll let you buy me my next drink," I challenge him.

The smirk on his face, paired with the side-eye glance before he looks back at me, shows I just caught him in a teeny-tiny lie.

He bows his head in defeat. "You caught me. I can't name one. Did I just lose points?"

I laugh. "If I rated every man's desirability based on if he knew the names of Backstreet Boys songs, then I'd never go on a date again."

Jason places an elbow on the bar and leans into me. His spearmint breath lingers in my face as he declares, "When you told that bartender to fill 'er up, I thought you were talking about yourself. I was thinking, if she wants to be filled up, I could certainly do the job."

He adds a slow wink and glances down the front of my shirt.

And that's where the fun flirtation ends.

"Unfortunately for you, my tank might be filled tonight, but it won't be by you. You should take a moment to go find another girl to flirt with because I'm no longer interested."

"Just like that?" he asks, perplexed.

I nod. "Just like that."

"Tease," he mutters, and I'm unaffected by his unoriginality.

Jason sulks away, and I'm a little disappointed. I'm disappointed in him for trying to turn this into a one-night stand and disappointed in me because there once was a time I would have been intrigued by his comment. We'd have talked some more at the bar, had a few drinks, danced, and then we'd have made our way back to his place or mine. I don't sleep with every man who's talked to me, but I have quite a few regrets. Men who are attractive, easy to talk to, funny, and seemingly interested in my stories—I convinced myself they could be the one. I learned the hard way that sex didn't equal love. Now that I'm well in my thirties, I'm far more particular about the type of man I'm willing to talk to these days. Jason isn't one.

I spin around and lean against the bar. One nice thing about Lone Tavern is, it isn't just filled with twenty-somethings. There're some thirty-, forty-, and even fifty-year-olds sprinkled throughout, making it a comfortable place to meet new people. I'm casting my visual net around the room, seeing who I want to catch and reel in for my next conversation, when I'm nearly thrown off my stool when I see a man seated at the far end of the bar.

Robert Bronson.

The gorgeous man of steel-plated emotions is sitting alone and drinking from one of those lowball glasses, in which I can only assume is his bourbon. He doesn't notice me, nor does he appear to truly be noticing anyone else.

A girl in a crop top shirt approaches him. She has her breasts in his face as she angles her body between the bar and him. For a moment, I think this could be his date, yet from the disdain   on his face and the way he's shaking his head, I can see he's refusing her advances. He's that opposed to love that he won't even give a few moments to that sexy thing trying to get into his pants.

I know I just turned down Jason, but I'm looking for something serious. According to Rob, he'll never get married again, so a one-nighter with a pretty girl should be right up his alley.

The girl walks away, and he resumes sitting by himself in the loud, crowded bar, sipping his bourbon.

I call over for the bartender. "I'd like to send a strawberry daiquiri over to that gentleman in the brown shirt down there." I point to Rob. "Bonus points if you have one of those bendy straws and a tiny umbrella."

The bartender makes the drink just as I asked and brings it over to Rob. Rob's eyes lock on mine as the bartender explains just who ordered the big, frilly cocktail for him. I lift my fingers and wiggle them in his direction.

Rob lets out an exasperated sigh.

I take that as my cue to get up and walk over toward his end of the bar.

LOVE…IT'S WILD

There's a man seated in the stool beside Rob's. I tap the man on the shoulder, politely interrupting the conversation he's having with his friend, and pout my lower lip.

"My feet are so sore from dancing all night. Could you be a peach and let me take this seat, please?"

"Absolutely, sweetheart." The guy stands up, and I take his seat. "I'd be happy to buy you—"

"No, thanks. Just the seat will do. I'm here with someone." I motion to Rob as I lift my shoulder with a cutesy wink and then swing my entire body in Rob's direction to let the guy know that I have my sights set on a particular man this evening.

Rob leans his forearms against the bar and looks straight, offering me a view of his profile.

I give him a nudge. "Don't worry, you big romantic. I already told you I'm not into your broody ass. I'm just surprised to see you here, riding solo. Or are you meeting someone? You know, I used to come here to meet a date from the internet. Oh my gosh, are you online dating? Please let me see your Tinder page!"

He growls, "I don't date, and I'm certainly not on any dot-com. I just came out for a drink tonight."

I tilt my head, and my long hair dances down the side of my arm. "If you want to sulk while having your cocktail, you go to a quiet tavern on the other side of town. You don't hit up the hottest nightlife in all of Castleton. Come on; be honest. We're both adults. You came here to meet a woman."

"Is meeting someone all you ever think about?"

"That beautiful brunette who was just over here would've made a fine catch for the evening. I can't believe you let her walk away."

"She's too young. I can't bring home a woman who is closer in age to my son than me."

"Fair enough. What kind of woman are you looking for?"

He narrows his eyes, circumspect. I roll mine in return.

"Stop looking at me like that. I'm not hoping you'll say a gorgeous raven-haired girl with striking blue eyes and an exquisite personality." I bat my lashes and look up toward the ceiling.

"You forgot to mention crazy," he says with his glass in his hand. Just before he takes a drink, he adds, "That and curly hair. I almost didn't recognize you at the wedding. It was straight and up in one of those fancy updos."

He drinks his bourbon.

I'm momentarily taken aback. I didn't know he'd paid attention to me before the wedding. I guess when you're running from a woman you think will try to jump your bones—or worse, want to marry you—you remember what kind of hair she has.

"You're diverting from the question. What kind of woman are you looking for, Mr. Bronson?" I wait for him to answer. When he doesn't, I lean my elbow on the bar, place a hand under my chin, lean closer, and widen my eyes.

His mouth twists. After a few beats, his brows rise, and he lets out an exasperated breath, turns to me, and gives me his attention.

"Crazy and persistent," he mumbles and then starts. "I don't know what I'm looking for. I was married for sixteen years, separated for two, and now after a year of being divorced, I'm out on a Thursday night because I dropped my kids off at their mother's and didn't quite feel like going home. It's my first night out in a long time."

"And?" I pry further. "What do you think?"

"I haven't been here that long."

"Someone must have caught your eye."

"Not really."

"Liar."

He turns back to his drink, as if the liquid will give him all the answers. "I saw someone earlier who caught my eye, but she was talking to someone else."

"Bummer. The good ones are usually taken."

Rob pushes the strawberry daiquiri my way. "I'm not drinking this. You should take it."

"I knew you'd refuse a pink drink. Such a typical man. It's a vacation in a glass. Not a declaration of your masculinity. Only guys with small penises would be afraid to have a daiquiri in public."

I wait for him to comment on how his penis isn't small. All men do it. Make one comment on the size of their package, and they go on the defense.

To my surprise, he doesn't say a word.

He just stares at me as I suck down the frozen beverage. His nostrils flare, and he pulls in a breath.

I swallow and clear my throat. "If you're back in the dating world after two decades, we're gonna have to get you up to speed."

"I'm not looking for a date."

"You will be soon, which means you need to know what it's like out here. It's a battlefield. When you were last out here, you were in your early twenties. Everyone was beautiful, and the single-to-dating ratio was heavily in our favor. Now, we're in our thirties. If you're fortunate enough to find someone you're attracted to and is single, they come with serious baggage. Ex-spouses, kids, crazy work schedules. They are also steadfast in their ways, so where people once tried to put on their best attitude in their twenties, in your thirties, it's more of a *fuck it, if they don't like me the way I am, they can leave* attitude."

He lifts his glass. "I believe it."

"If you want to date someone young and beautiful—say, late twenties—you run the risk of having nothing in common. Trust me, it's not fun until you realize there's an entire generation that doesn't know what a pay phone is."

His mouth tips up ever so slightly. "You have war stories from this battlefield?"

"Too many. This one time, I was being picked up for a date. I didn't know where he was parked, so I called him. He said, 'See that fatty by the crosswalk, wearing the belly shirt she shouldn't be wearing? I'm the car in front of her.' I never left my apartment."

"Dick."

"Insulting a person's physique, especially a stranger, is a definite red flag. That and the fact that he drove a Hummer. Second red flag."

Rob lets out a gruff, incredulous snicker. "You rate men based on the cars they drive?"

"Don't act all self-righteous. You judge people based on the liquor they drink." I take a long sip of the daiquiri. "A Hummer meathead doesn't care about the environment and has no respect for money, other people's safety, or personal space. A Prius dude is practical and less emotional than the Tesla guy, who is flashier and likes to have a good time. If I see an ultra-expensive sports car, I run the other way. He has lots of money and is probably overcompensating for something; plus, he wants someone much younger than me. A Jeep Wrangler means he's gay, and a compact car dude is your mild-mannered, run-of-the-mill Joe Schmo, who is either twenty years too young or twenty years too old for me."

"Glad to know you're not judgmental. What is a good car for a man to drive?"

"A truck. That's a man who isn't afraid to get his hands dirty and is far too cool to even care what you think about him. He works hard, plays harder, and enjoys the simple things in life," I state easily. "What kind of car do you drive?"

He smirks. "A Maserati."

"You're full of shit. How old are you anyway?"

"You were close in your assessment. I just turned forty."

"Looking good for being over the hill. Now I get why you don't want to date too young."

He places his now-empty glass on the counter. His eyes aren't on me when he asks, "What happened with that guy you were talking to before?"

I look at him quizzically, having momentarily forgotten about Jason. "I am all for fun sexual innuendos, but R-rated small talk five minutes into meeting a man at the bar is where I draw the line. If a guy can't have a conversation with you for longer than two minutes without bringing up sex, then he's not worth the next two minutes."

Rob's mouth turns down, along with a surprised yet impressed tilt to his brows.

"You look intrigued."

"Tara, there's little about you I don't find intriguing."

"Aww, I think you're starting to warm up to me."

"That's not a good thing. You worry me. Soon, you'll learn the perfect man doesn't exist, and you're gonna be crushed."

"At the end of the day, I don't want a perfect man. I want someone who is tough yet sincere and honest, who loves to travel and makes a good cup of coffee. A man who will break the headboard and not my heart."

His eyes fall shut as he sucks in a deep breath. It's as if he's bothered by the fact that he might enjoy my company. It's unnerving yet completely satisfying.

"Let's do some people-watching, shall we?" I offer.

"No." He motions to the bartender for another drink and is promptly served.

I slide my chair around and look toward the dance floor, pulling on Rob's hand for him to face the room with me. His palm is warm and callous, and I hold on to it for a moment too long because there's something sexy and rugged about his hand that I like.

"What about her?" I point toward a girl dancing with some friends on the dance floor.

She appears to be in her late twenties or early thirties. Dark hair, a pointed nose, and a killer body.

"She's very attractive."

"Get up and talk to her! I'll give you some tips. You might not want to date, but she might go home with you tonight if you play your cards right."

"I don't need help with bedding a woman."

My chest rises with a zing and hardens my nipples. The thought of Rob in bed with a woman is quite the visual. A good visual. White knuckles on the headboard and an animalistic passion. He could probably fuck that anger right out of his system.

"I find the men who captivate me the most are the ones who are themselves. Introduce yourself. You're crazy hot, so you don't have to worry about her finding you attractive even though you're really old." He looks at me from the side of his eyes, but I keep on talking. "Just don't grunt at her. Women don't like that."

He grunts at me, and it makes me laugh.

"The bar scene isn't for me."

"That's fine if you don't want to get married again, but everyone needs to get laid."

"Believe it or not, some people have more important things to worry about than getting laid. You wonder why you have a reputation. This kind of talk is what makes people think you're easy even though you're not."

I slide off my seat and stand in front of him, angling my body between his knees, which are opened wide on the barstool. "I'll forgive you for being a dick if you explain that comment about having more important things to worry about."

He runs his hand down his face. His expression is pained, as if him explaining his troubles to me is the last thing he wants to do.

I inch closer.

"Fucking persistent woman." He sighs and takes a swig of his drink, placing the glass roughly on the bar, and then tilts that clenched jaw at me. "Summer vacation is coming up, and I want my kids to come stay with me at the ranch, but my ex says it's impossible since I work too much."

"You have a ranch?"

"That's all you heard?"

"Ex-wife. Kids. Summer. I heard the other stuff. I just got caught up on the word *ranch*."

"It's not a working ranch. It's an abandoned one and about an hour's drive from this town. My ex and the kids kept our house here in Castleton. All I wanted was my land and my truck."

"You sound like a walking country song," I kid, and his scowl in return has me clearing my throat. My cheery smile morphs to one of seriousness. "Go on. What's the problem with the kids?"

"I'm entitled to my kids for the summer, but she's giving me shit because I can't leave them in the house alone while I go to work. She's planning on traveling all of July, and she may have to take them away with her. If she does, I'll never see them."

"Where do you work?"

"I'm a commercial contractor. I'm building an outlet mall, so I can't take off too much."

"How old are your kids?"

"Sixteen and ten."

"Have the sixteen-year-old watch the ten-year-old. I was way younger when I started babysitting."

"No way. I can't trust that kid to spit out a piece of gum. He's gotten into more trouble this year than you can imagine. He's coming to work with me."

"Take the ten-year-old too."

"The construction site is no place for a young girl, and it's definitely not a way for her to spend the summer. My ex wouldn't allow it."

"Don't you have a bazillion family members? Ask your mom."

"The ranch is far. No one wants to stay out there for a full summer."

"Hire a nanny."

"Absolutely not."

"I bet you could find a hot one. And who wouldn't want to live on a ranch with beautiful green pastures and horses roaming around, ready to eat out of the palm of your hand?"

"It's not that kind of ranch, and there's no one I trust. Plus, I wouldn't even know where to find a nanny. I'd have to interview them and do test runs. By the time I settled on someone, the summer would be over."

Rob's hand tightens into a fist as he brings it to his mouth and thinks. It's bothering him, not being able to see his children.

It's sweet actually—a man who wants his kids to live with him for the summer. I'd find it sexy if he wasn't so standoffish. I might not want children of my own, but I like kids … a lot. It's why I wasn't too harsh on Patrick earlier when I saw him at the bakery and realized his young daughters were around.

Fuck. Patrick.

I nearly forgot about him and his fruit. I'll be seeing the four of them around town, and I'm gonna have to get used to it. I don't want to. If I had known he was moving to Newbury, I would have sabotaged that housing deal. Trust me, I would have, and my money's on the fact that I'd have been successful.

But he's there, and I'm stuck there too.

Or am I?

Over the years, I've done plenty of babysitting for Melissa and Jillian. Hunter and Ainsley aren't just close to me because I'm awesome. It's because I've cared for them more times than I can count. I can watch a ten-year-old girl easily, all while meandering on a ranch as I decide how to get Patrick and his family to move out of Newbury so I don't have to watch him live his happily ever after while I'm still desperately trying to find my own.

"I'll do it," I state. "I'll watch your daughter while you work this summer. I'll be the hot ranch nanny."

"No, you won't."

"I'm awesome with kids. I watch your brother's stepkids all the time. I had them for a week while he was on his honeymoon with Melissa, and that was seven overnights, where homework was done, after-school activities were accomplished, showers were given, dinner was on the table, and the house didn't burn down."

"The answer is no." He rises from his stool, takes his wallet out of his back pocket, and throws two twenties on the bar.

I stagger backward. "Why not? I'm a completely capable grown-up."

"You're a grown child."

"Says the man who is as stubborn as a toddler. You're a moody son of a bitch, and you should be happy someone—namely, me—is offering to help." My words force him to turn around. "And tighten up on the way you talk about your son. You make it sound like he's a heathen when he's merely a teenage boy."

"Jesse and Molly are good kids. They're just … going through a lot. What they need now is stability. Not someone who is doing something on a whim because it sounds cool to hang out on a ranch."

"You don't always have to be so cynical. And stubborn. You'd rather not see your kids all summer than let me—someone who might be too free-spirited for your liking—hang out with you guys. You can't be so close-minded that you'd spite yourself and your kids. Live a little. Take a damn chance, or you're gonna end up miserable and alone forever!"

Thank goodness for the music because my voice is loud, as I can get a bit overdramatic sometimes. Still, I mean every word.

Rob doesn't know me, and while I might need this for a personal benefit, I'm very much putting myself out there to do him a solid in a sticky situation.

He rubs his jaw as he looks down at me—staring, assessing, taking in my offer, and deciding if it's complete bullshit or not. I grab my purse and start to walk away.

"You'd move to my ranch for the summer?" he asks. I halt.

"Why not? You need help, and I don't mind assisting. Plus, I love kids."

"You love kids?"

"Yes. I don't want any of my own but I like being with other peoples'. I'm a modern-day Mary Poppins."

"What about your dating life?"

"I assume I'll be able to go home on the weekends. I do have to get back to Newbury from time to time for my actual job."

"Almost forgot. You're a kickboxing instructor."

I roll my eyes at him. "I'm an accountant. Kickboxing is what I do on the side."

His face twists in confusion. "You're an accountant?"

"You don't always have to seem so surprised by the things I say. Trust me, if I wanted to make up a career, accounting wouldn't be one of them."

"Why would an accountant, who also teaches kickboxing classes and apparently babysits her friends' kids all the time, want to add summer nanny to her already-full schedule?"

It's a valid question with a valid answer. Rob needs help, and I need some breathing room from Newbury before I do something stupid, like egg Patrick's new house or give it a termite infestation.

"Maybe I just want a change of scenery for the summer. Plus, I have these boots and nowhere else to wear them."

He groans. It's not a grunt. It's a sound of submission. "I think I've had too much to drink because I'm considering this."

"Question is, do you trust me enough to watch your kids?   "

"I don't trust anyone."

Add this to the top of the list of bad ideas I have and seem to follow through on even though the red flags are waving vibrantly in my face.

"Start with me," I say, as if conceding and begging at the same time. "Let's do a trial run. Maybe I'll regret even offering this. You might hate the notion of me being at your house all summer, but is it worth not seeing your kids?"

The sides of his eyes turn down as he moans. "Okay."

"Wait, seriously?" I jump up and clap my hands with giddiness. The thought of spending the summer on a ranch seems fun and so very convenient. No Patrick. No fruit. A chance to figure out my next move because if the Murphy family is infiltrating Newbury, Tara Parsons is moving out. "This is so exciting. I have the cowgirl boots, but I'm gonna need a hat, some spurs, oh, a lot of those cute floral dresses and jean jackets. I must raid my closet. I don't have a ton of ranch-chic looks."

"I already regret this."

Looks like I'm going to live with Rob on his ranch for the summer. What could go wrong?

Five

WHEN I THINK OF a ranch, I picture a rustic yet modern estate sitting on sprawling acres of lush greenery. Trees should hang over the long road creating a tunnel-like feeling. Fences line the pastures, keeping the cattle from escaping. Chickens and hens roam, and men on tractors drive through to maintain the growing grass. There should be an oversize wrought iron sign above the road leading up to the property with the name of the ranch.

And there should be cowboys. Lots of hunky cowboys on horses with Stetsons and straw dangling from their mouths.

This ranch has none of those things.

The drive here was scenic. Houses spread far apart and a farm or two that had me turning my head. About five miles from the house, it became nothing but wheat fields and the occasional deer crossing the road.

My navigation gives out, as it doesn't even register the road I'm on. I look at the directions Rob sent me and follow them to a metal gate, rusted and weathered, and make a right.

I drive up a long dirt road toward a blue house at the top of a hill. There's plenty of land for sure, but it's more dead grass than grazing pastures. There's an old truck parked on the side of the drive. It's faded and full of rust with a tire leaning against the fender.

As I get closer to the house, I notice a large barn-like structure way past the house. It's brown and red, and it looks dingy next to the house that is freshly painted with white trim and a matching deck.

I park my car between a shiny black pickup truck and an SUV—not an oversize monstrosity, but a solid American-made family car.

Today is supposed to be a trial, so I only brought a tote bag with me, along with my laptop that I always travel with. I'm taking my things out when the screen door opens, and a young girl stands at the top of the steps. Her brown hair is long with flyaway strands, like she just got out of bed.

I place my hand over my eyes to shield them from the sun as I look back at her. "You gonna stand there or give me a hand?"

The young girl walks down the stairs and up to my car. "Are you the babysitter?"

I hand her a grocery bag. "Sure am. Although I don't like the term *babysitter*. Just call me Tara."

"Dad says we should never refer to adults by their first names."

"Well, Mrs. Parsons is my mother. I'm just Tara."

"First names are for friends. It's respectful to call you Miss something. If I don't, I'll be in big trouble. Can I call you Miss Tara?"

"God, no. That sounds like we're in the South and I should be wearing a corset and living on a plantation. Just call me Tara. I'll deal with your dad. It's only disrespectful if you don't have my permission."

"Yeah, he won't go for that. Other adults have tried."

I close my trunk, place my hand on my hip, and then concede. "Fine, you can call me Madam Amazing."

She lets out a laugh. "That's funny."

"Is it formal enough for you?"

"I guess. He's still not gonna like it."

"Well, it's my name, so I'm the one you should worry about. Okay, now that you know who I am, will you please tell me who you are?"

I extend a hand, and she takes it with a grin.

"Molly."

"That's the sweetest name ever. I would've thought the grumpiest man in the world would have named you something cold and serious. Is it short for Mildred or Maleficent or something?"

Molly giggles. "Nope. Molly Bronson. Although I'm starting not to like it. Molly is a baby name. I'm gonna be eleven soon. Everyone treats me like my name. Like I'm a toddler."

"I bet you and I can take care of that. Building up women to have badass attitudes is what I do. You're okay if I say ass, right? I tend to curse sometimes."

"Dad says cursing is for those who don't have proper vocabulary. He curses all the time though. Pretends we don't hear it. I can't repeat it, or I'll get grounded."

I snicker to myself. I've most certainly heard her father curse. I guess he has a different persona around his kids. Saint Rob. This should be fun.

Her eyes widen as she takes in my car—a cute little sports convertible. "Is this your car? Can we go for a ride in it? Dad lets me go in the tailgate of the pickup truck, but there aren't seats. This is much cooler."

"Maybe. Only awesome kids who listen to me are allowed to use my stuff. What kind of kid are you?"

She twists her mouth. "I'm just Molly."

"Okay, just Molly, today is the day we see if you and I are compatible enough for me to spend some time with you this summer. Why don't we start with you showing me around?"

Molly takes the grocery bag up the stairs, and I follow behind with my stuff. The front porch is bright white with two rocking chairs looking out to the front yard. We walk inside, and I'm pleasantly surprised. The house is quaint yet cozy. A living room is to the left with a stone fireplace and two oversize couches. A wagon wheel light hangs above with a coffee table of a similar shape below. The floor is polished in a shiny lacquer. To the right is a staircase that leads upstairs.

I follow Molly down a wide hallway toward a kitchen in the back. It's a massive room with a large island in the middle. Red brick lines the backsplash and an adjacent wall, where a farmhouse-style dining table is. The house doesn't have many rooms, but the rooms that are here are very big.

Molly places the bag on the counter, and I leave my belongings on a seating area in an alcove off of the kitchen, where two wing chairs are placed in front of a picture window.

"I brought ingredients to make cupcakes. Do you like to bake?" I ask Molly as I take the flour and eggs out of the grocery bag.

"Cupcakes are my favorite. I've never baked them. I'm not allowed to use the oven."

"You said you're ten, right? When I was ten, I was practically living on my own. Not really. My parents just gave me a lot of responsibility and freedom at a young age. Are you allowed to cross the street by yourself?"

She looks up to the ceiling, as if she's puzzled by the question. "I think so. I mean, I don't really have to cross streets. My parents just drop me off at places, and I get out of the car."

"Man, how times have changed. If things work out between us, we'll be working on you having some responsibility, starting with learning how to use an oven. Where's your dad anyway?"

"He's probably out in the shed, getting his equipment for the day."

As Molly and I put away the supplies, Jesse comes into the kitchen. He's wearing black jogger pants, and his hair is sticking up like an upside-down head of romaine lettuce, which I think is the style.

"Hey," he grumbles as he saunters in with his head down and his shirt half over his head. When he sees me standing here, he does a double take. "Who are you?"

I smile. "Don't be coy, kiddo. We're old friends. Here, I brought you something." I reach into the bag of groceries and hand the moody teenager a six-pack of nonalcoholic beer. "Thought you might be thirsty."

He rolls his head back and groans. "Oh, fuck. It's you."

"Jesse!" Molly admonishes him.

"I can say whatever the hell I want when Dad's not around," he hisses back to his sister and then looks at the six-pack that I'm still holding up with a bright grin on my face. "Why are you smiling like that?"

"Just offering you some fucking beer."

His brows scrunch as he looks at me like I have seventeen heads.

"I thought you two weren't allowed to swear. If cursing is cool, then I want to be the one to curse the most," I explain. "Are you going to take the fucking beer out of my fucking hands, or would you like me to throw it into your fucking lap and wait for you to say thank you?"

Jesse hesitantly takes the beer from me. "Thanks."

I pat him on the cheek. "You're very welcome."

The back door opens and closes, and Rob comes walking in.

When I said this ranch had no hunky cowboys, I was wrong.

Faded denim jeans and a crisp white T-shirt that molds his chest, outlining the definition of his rippled torso. I must lift my eyes up from the fine definition of the man before I drool all over the kitchen floor.

Okay, Rob's no cowboy, but he certainly has the workingman thing down, including extra scruff, as if his hands have been so busy building that they don't have time to put a blade to his chiseled face. A face, bronzed from working in the sun, bearing those chestnut eyes. Eyes that clearly don't know they sit on the perfectly fine specimen of a man that is Rob Bronson. If they knew, they wouldn't be looking at me with a hard scowl and appearing so utterly annoyed.

"Why is my son holding beer?"

"It's safe. A little joke between us. Right, Jesse?" I smile.

"Sixteen-year-olds shouldn't be drinking alcohol of any kind." Rob steps toward me with a direct stare.

I turn my back to him and open the refrigerator. "Please. Like you didn't try to sip a brew or two when you were a teen." My hand runs over the fruit crisper drawer as I explore its contents. Rob keeps a tidy refrigerator with a ton of fresh produce. "Jesse just needs adults like us to keep him in check."

Rob takes the beer from Jesse and walks up to me at the refrigerator. "This isn't a joke. It's only seven in the morning, and I already don't see this going well."

I take out an apple from the drawer and bite into it. "Exactly. It's already seven. Go to work and let me do my thing."

"What exactly is your thing?"

I swallow. "Being spectacular at life."

Rob crosses his arms and glares down at me. "Ground rules."

"What kind?"

"No swearing."

"Why? You swear all the time."

"Says who?" he growls.

Molly gasps on the other side of the kitchen. Rob turns toward her.

She shrugs in defense. "I told Madam Amazing that I can hear it, but I can't say it."

Rob lifts a brow. "Madam who?"

"Amazing. That's what she wants to be called," Molly explains.

Rob slowly turns back to me. He opens his mouth to speak, but I place a finger against his full lips and halt him from saying anything rude.

"You raised a good-mannered kid. If you won't let her call me Tara, then she calls me by my chosen moniker." I bat my lashes up at him.

He grunts in return. It's long and deep. "Molly, you can call her Tara, but only because I refuse to have you call her Madam Amazing."

I smile.

Swaying over to the island, I take the paper grocery bag and fold it up. "All right, boys. Time to get to work. I didn't wake up at five in the morning to drive out here so I can stare at your sourpusses all day. My girl and I have a day planned."

Rob closes the refrigerator door with a huff. "Call me if anything happens."

"I will," I say, taking another bite of the apple.

"I was talking to Molly. I have a feeling she's gonna be the more responsible one." Rob starts walking out of the kitchen with Jesse in tow.

I laugh sarcastically at his comment. "I'll have her call you after her pole dancing lesson."

The two men stop in their tracks and turn around, Jesse with a mischievous smile on his face, like he's trying not to laugh. Rob hits him in the chest.

"Let's go." Rob grips Jesse's shoulder and pushes him toward the front door, then points a finger at me. "You just try to behave for the next ten hours."

I give him a soldier's salute as I follow him. "Yes, sir!"

Gruff mumbles are said by Rob, which I'm vaguely sure are laden with colorful words that should be heard yet not repeated. I blow him a kiss as they go off for a day of work on one of Rob's construction sites.

With the door closed behind them, I lean on it and look at Molly. "Okay, kid. What kind of trouble can we get into around here?"

Six

"UNFAIR ADVANTAGE. You own this game!" I shout as I launch half my body across the air hockey table.

"I hardly ever play because Jesse is a jerk who refuses to go up against me."

"That's because he knows he'll lose. People never want to participate in things they're not good at."

Molly smacks the puck with her pusher. "My friend Nicole does that to me too. We only play what she wants, which is fine because I like playing everything."

"Pushover," I call her. "It's cool you're amenable, but don't let a friend boss you into playing something you don't want to play. What are you into?"

"Air hockey. And slime. I love to make it, but my friends aren't into it anymore. They like their phones and iPads. We just play online stuff when we're together."

"You can play that stuff when you're apart. Your idea of slime is way cooler. Back to this Nicole chick. Is she a good friend?"

"My best friend. We do everything together. I even pack her favorite snacks in my lunch box."

"Super cute." I block the puck from getting into my goal. "What does she pack for you?"

"She doesn't. It's just what I do."

"Huh? Does her mom not buy cool snacks?"

Molly huffs as she moves quickly to play offense. "Nicole has a ton of cool snacks. Her mom gives her Nutella. She doesn't share because it has nuts."

"Sucks you're allergic to nuts."

"I'm not allergic to anything."

"Then, why doesn't she share? Your friend sounds like a user. We're gonna have to discuss this further." I rip the puck across the table. "Score!" I shout as I sink the puck into her goal.

My day with the ten-year-old has gone well. We started off by going on a tour of the house. Four bedrooms, three bathrooms, all recently renovated by Rob in the last year. The only room in the house that doesn't seem complete is a small room off the downstairs bathroom, which has mint-green walls and a sofa that looks like it once lived in a college dorm.

We spent an hour in Molly's room, being ultra girlie and giving ourselves makeovers. Then, I helped her find a preteen-approved outfit for a party she's going to. After, we baked, played basketball, had lunch, went for a walk, did some fishing in a nearby pond, and now, we're hanging out in the basement game room.

Molly is an easy kid to hang with. She's a tomboy, having spent most of her year on a sports field and less watching television. She has an iPad limit of one hour a day, which she didn't even try to take advantage of with me as the quasi-nanny. I had to open my laptop to take care of something for a client, so that one hour of iPad entertainment for her helped a ton.

Overall, it's been a good day.

Especially since I'm kicking her butt at air hockey.

"This room is great. You've got enough games to occupy a party of twenty ten-year-olds. You must be down here a lot."

Aside from air hockey, there's foosball, Skee-Ball, and darts.

"When Jesse went to high school, he became too cool for school. All he cares about are his dirtbag friends."

I line up my air hockey puck for another round. I hit it toward her. "What's a dirtbag friend like?"

"The kind that shoplifts at the mall. Jesse was arrested last month for stealing a shirt from Hot Topic. Dad had to pick him up at the police station inside the mall. Did you know they have those there?"

"It's just a room where mall cops take you while you wait for the real police."

"If they're not real, how can they arrest you?"

"It's called shopkeeper's privilege. It's a rule that allows mall security to detain a suspected shoplifter long enough for the police to come. The police are the ones who make the arrest. Was Jesse arrested by the actual police?"

She swipes at the puck, giving me a good run for my money. "I don't think so. I think he confessed so they let him go."

"Oh man. Do not confess even if it is to a mall cop. You can walk yourself into a criminal conviction in exchange for avoiding a few hours of bother if you just wait it out at the mall. Trust me, I learned the hard way."

Molly bolts upright, leaving her goal defenseless and letting the puck slide in. "You were arrested?"

I rub my forehead as I realize what I said. "No. Not me. A friend," I lie. "She stole a lip gloss when she was twelve because someone had dared her, and the cop on the scene tried to make an example of her and took the whole ordeal overboard. Never ever do something just because some idiot dares you. If they're daring you, it's because they're not brave enough to do it themselves, and there's probably a reason for it."

Shoplifting at twelve was not a high point in the life of Tara Parsons.

Molly raises a curious brow. "If you weren't the one arrested, were you the one who made the dare?"

"Nice try, kid." I score on her again and do a dance. "Victory!"

She tosses her handheld pusher dramatically. "Doesn't count. I wasn't paying attention. Besides, you're supposed to let me win."

"You want to win? You need to earn it."

I spin around and walk toward the counter where I left my water bottle. What I'm learning today is that while the ranch's property might not be pristine, the house is meticulously updated. Every room features fresh paint and is adorned with expert craftsmanship. The basement showcases a long wall of shiplap, running alongside posters of iconic moments in sports. I'm currently looking at a photo capturing Muhammad Ali standing triumphantly over Sonny Liston. It's a timeless image that evokes memories of my dad—a sports enthusiast who took me to numerous boxing matches during my childhood.

Rob put a lot of thought into the design of this room—industrial ceiling, paired with rustic features. Either he loves gaming or he wanted his kids to have a nice space to hang out.

At the far end of the room is a door. I open it and find a bathroom, kept neat and tidy. Beside it is another door. It's locked.

"What's in here?"

Molly looks up from where she's playing on a miniature Pac-Man arcade game. "That's Dad's workshop. We're not allowed in there."

I turn the knob again, but it doesn't budge. "What does he keep in here?"

"I dunno. Never been inside."

I look at the child funny. To have a room in your home, but to never have seen the inside is baffling to me. I'm the nosiest person on the planet. When I was a kid, I was a thousand times worse.

"How long have you lived here?"

"We've had the house a few years, but Dad just redid the basement."

I put my hand on the molding at the top of the door, looking for one of those key pins that come with doors. There isn't one.

Yes, I'm aware attempting to break into a room in someone's house is wrong, but if I'm going to be staying here this summer, I need to know if he's secretly a serial killer and keeps his dead bodies in the basement. Maybe it's his room of torture. The deadliest people hide in plain sight. Then again, this house isn't exactly in plain sight. It's in the middle of nowhere, and there isn't a neighbor to be seen.

Molly continues to talk while she plays. "Mom hates this house. She says it's a money pit. Dad always wanted her to come out here for the summers, but she refused. Jesse and I love it. That's why when Mom said she would take us traveling with her this summer, we begged Dad to find a way to allow us to stay with him."

I give up on the door and walk back to her. "Why did your parents buy it if your mom hated it so much?"

"That's a good question. I'm not entirely sure. I'm not sure why my parents did a lot of things." She drops her hands on her lap and sighs. "They fought a lot. It sucks. I know I'm not supposed to say that, but having divorced parents is the worst."

"It's okay. Sometimes, you need to use a bad word to get the annoyance out. It does suck. Say it. It sucks."

"It sucks!" she says.

"It sucks big, hairy, sucky ass."

"It sucks hairy, sucky dog ass!" Molly yells at the top of her lungs and then laughs.

I follow suit until we hear heavy footsteps barreling down the stairs, caused by the large boots worn by a towering man with a mean mug on his face.

"What the hell is going on down here?" Rob bites as he walks into the game room.

I clear my throat to gather my giggles. "We were just letting out some steam. Sometimes, a girl has to get it out."

"What could a ten-year-old possibly need to scream *hairy, sucky dog ass* for?"

Molly straightens her face and looks at me with a pleading not to tell her dad what she was saying.

I turn at Rob. "I apologize. I won't allow her to verbally express herself again."

Rob groans as he looks at me and then to Molly, his head swaying with annoyed confusion. "What the hell is on your face?"

"Makeup," she states demurely.

"You're too young to wear makeup. Your hair looks ridiculous."

"Rob!" I scold, walking toward Molly and putting my hand on her hair, which we spent a long time curling. "She looks beautiful. We had a makeover party. I styled her hair and put a little blush on her cheeks. It's no big deal."

He walks over to Molly and grips her shoulder. "You cut her shirt?"

I don't see what all the fuss is about. "We made a funky one-shouldered shirt for her out of an old sweatshirt."

With his eyes trained on me, cold and indifferent, Rob glares. "Molly, go upstairs."

She hurries up the staircase, leaving me and her father alone in the room that's meant to be for fun, yet right now, I feel like I'm about to get a lashing from my parent.

"Tara, I left you alone with my daughter for one afternoon, and I return to her looking and speaking like a harlot."

"Harlot? No one says that word unless you're an ancient Victorian."

"Please grow up and be serious."

"I am being serious, Rob. We were having a talk about ..." I stop, wondering if Molly would want me telling her dad she was talking about his divorce or the issues she's having at school, being seen as a toddler and not a preteen, or even her friend—who I don't think Molly quite realizes is a user and not a giver. I have a feeling Rob would be mad at her for talking about their personal family business and then be dismissive with her friend issues. "We were talking about clothes. It's hard for a ten-year-old girl. She's stuck between two places. She's not a girl. Not yet a woman. All she needs—"

"If you start quoting Britney Spears's songs, I'm kicking you out."

I jump up with glee. "You know Britney! There's hope for you yet, Bronson."

I walk past him and head up the stairs from the basement, toward the foyer. My tote bag and laptop are in the kitchen, so I turn to the right and walk down the hallway. Rob's heavy footsteps are behind me.

"What the hell happened in here?!" It's not a question. It's more of a loud rant.

"You say *what the hell* a lot—you know that? Molly and I baked." I'm confused by what he doesn't understand by the mixing bowls, spatulas, cupcake tins, and empty boxes of cake mix and frosting on the counter. As if to further explain, I point to the large platter of cupcakes.

"This kitchen is a mess. No one needs six bowls to make cupcakes!"

"We decorated them all the colors of the rainbow. Well, we left out indigo because it was redundant with blue and violet. You can't mix colors in the same bowl."

"Did anyone teach you to clean up?"

"Yes," I answer slowly, as if this is a trick question. "I was gonna clean. We decided to play games first. You're getting red in the face, and while I think the brutish attitude is kind of sexy, I have to say, it doesn't feel good since you're practically spewing venom out of your eyes."

He places his hands on his hips and looks down, shaking his head. "This isn't gonna work."

"What are you talking about?"

"I can't have you watch Molly all summer. The language, the makeup, cutting up clothes, making a mess of my kitchen … and that's only what I've seen in the ten minutes I've been home."

"You're not serious."

"I need someone I can trust."

"You don't trust anyone, remember?" I lift a finger to make a point, yet I think better of it. "Never mind. I have plenty of things I should be doing other than helping you out."

"So, you're quitting already?"

My hands fly to my head, ready to pull out the strands. "You're the one who just—" I scrunch my face and let   out a growl. "Never mind. Please tell Molly it was awesome hanging with her today and I wish her luck with everything because she's a great kid."

I grab my tote and laptop and storm toward the front door, open it, and then spin around to face him.

"And make sure you tell her that Nicole girl isn't a good friend. If someone expects you to give them your snacks at lunch, they should at least give you Nutella in return."

I'm marching out the door and down the stairs as I also add, "The shirt we made today should be worn with a colorful, thick strapped, tank top underneath, or people will think it's a bra. Trust me, if she does, no one will make fun of her clothes again."

Nearly out of breath, I swing open my convertible door, toss my bags on the passenger seat, look up, and point at Rob. "You know, Rob, you have real potential to be a great guy. A hero even. You get in your own way. You're mean and course, and you don't give anyone a chance to explain."

To give him a taste of his own medicine, I get in my car and close my door before he can say a word, not that he's even tried. He just stands there, looking into my window as I start my car and put it in reverse.

LOVE...IT'S WILD

I'm off his property before the sun sets. Yes, my exit is a little dramatic, even for me. Why exactly I bolted out of there like a bat out of hell is something I'm trying to figure out.

Seven

"WHAT DO YOU MEAN, you offered to live on a ranch with him?"

"Calm down, Melissa. Your eyes are like saucers. They make you look like a cartoon bat on caffeine." I swing open Melissa's refrigerator and grab a tomato and hand it to her. "It seemed like a good idea at the time."

She slices into the tomato. "Famous last words."

"Don't act like you haven't done impulsive things. Remember your junior prom dress?"

"We promised never to speak of such a thing."

"Your mother made you wear the most hideous dress. You looked like a Golden Girl."

"It was your genius idea to go all *Pretty in Pink* and start tearing off the sleeves and high neck in the restroom of the catering hall."

"I had no idea the entire dress would fall apart. I'm not a seamstress."

"Clearly! I had to tie the ends together behind my neck like a makeshift halter top." Her blonde ponytail sways as she gets animated.

I lean against the counter. "I mean … it was better without the hideous crinoline and shoulder pads."

She points a paring knife at me, accusing, "Enough of the detour, Tara. Tell me about your day at Rob's house."

"Who's Rob?" Jillian asks as she walks in with a bouquet of flowers and hands them to Melissa. "These are for you."

Melissa takes them, and her pale blue eyes well up with moisture. "They're beautiful."

I grab a tissue from the box and hand it to Jillian, who hands it to Melissa.

"Pregnancy hormones on a rampage today, huh?" Jillian remarks as Melissa dabs her eyes.

"I don't know what I was thinking, getting married while this pregnant. Did I look like a whale at the wedding?"

"Absolutely not!" I'm quick to respond as Jillian adds, "You looked gorgeous."

Melissa waves the air in front of her and smiles. "Let's shift the focus away from me. You guys know I tend to ramble when the spotlight's on me. Tara, spill about your day at Rob's."

Jillian has a perplexed look on her face, so I explain, "Will's brother needed help with the kids."

"Wait. Rob's the gruff older brother who barely says a word, right? The one who grunts at you and walks away?"

"Yes!" I exclaim. "He finally explained that at the wedding. A misunderstanding. He thought I was interested in him. Didn't want to give me the wrong impression, so he acted like an ogre and ran away."

"That's presumptuous." Jillian twists her face and crosses her arms. "Jerk."

Melissa takes the flowers out of the cellophane wrapping and sways her head. "Is it though? He is really good-looking. The entire Bronson clan is attractive, but Rob has that hunky, brawny, rugged, wide-shouldered thing going on. He's the kind of man you can swoon over as he throws you over his shoulder and carries you to bed."

Jillian gives me the side-eye and then looks back at Melissa. "Pregnancy's also making you a bit amorous, huh?"

"Oh my God, you wouldn't believe it," she states, to which we all laugh.

I open the cabinet above her refrigerator and grab a vase. "Rob is most definitely attractive. We all know that. And he's so gruff that he'd probably be really good at ... well, you know. However, that's not in any way a possibility. I'm too hopeful for him. He's too moody for me. We just ran into each other, and I heard he needed help, so I offered—end of story. I went there. I hung out with his kid for the day. I baked."

"You baked?" Jillian lowers her gaze. "You only bake when you're sexually frustrated—"

"Or dealing with emotional shit," Melissa adds, placing the flowers in a vase, now full of water. She gives me her full attention. "Which is it?"

I try to sound nonchalant, but the two inquisitive hens in the kitchen are staring at me like they're about to peck me to death if I don't spill the beans.

"I saw Patrick."

Jillian purses her lips with narrowed eyes as Melissa asks, as if the notion couldn't be possible, "Your ex-fiancé?"

"Yes. He was at the bakery on Main Street. With his wife. And his kids."

"Plural?!" Good thing she doesn't still have the vase in her hands because she would have dropped it with the dramatic flailing of her arms. "When did he have time to procreate?"

"Pretty quickly after we broke up. Clementine and Lemon."

Melissa twists her face as Jillian states, "Those are pretty names."

"Oh, just say what we're all thinking. It's weird to name both of your kids after citrus," Melissa gripes.

"It doesn't matter what he named them. He's a husband and father now. He has a gorgeous wife, and they moved to Newbury. Get ready to meet Victoria Murphy at the next PTA meeting."

"He's not even from Connecticut. What kind of jerk would move to his ex-fiancée's town?" Melissa asks.

"The kind who leaves a girl on her wedding day. I should have cut his balls off years ago."

"No, you did better," Melissa adds and then explains to Jillian, "She held an estate sale at his house and sold most of his prized possessions."

Jillian's eyes bulge. "You didn't?!"

I shrug. "I still had to pay for the reception. When a wedding is called off, people don't give you gifts. I should have sold those golf clubs for more money."

Jillian guides the conversation back on track with the snap of her fingers. "You saw him and what?"

"I got in my car and left."

"And ..." Melissa prods, sensing there's more to the story.

I lift my shoulder and look up at the ceiling. "I looked up his new address and might have ordered a new mailbox to be installed next week."

"What kind of mailbox?"

"It's a pig. A cute farmhouse one. I think they'll appreciate the housewarming gift."

"Tara, you are diabolical." Jillian grins while trying to maintain her composure.

"I've seen her do worse," Melissa adds. Her eyes look down as she places a hand on my arm, consoling me. "Seriously, Tara, that must have been really hard. You haven't seen Patrick in years, and now, he's going to be in our town with his new family. That has to sting."

"It does. Fuck, it does," I declare. "It's bad enough that I still think about him from time to time, but now, I have to walk around my own town on eggshells that I'll see him, or her, or their kids. I'll be fine. It's not like I still love him or anything. I'm just ... I'm just not in the mood to have to see him yet. I was blindsided. I'll be fine."

I run my hand through my curly, dark hair and then slap my hip. "Maybe it wouldn't bother me as much if I were with someone. He left me because I was quote-on-quote immature, called off the wedding, married someone else, had kids, and I'm still here, in the town I grew up in, *still* looking for love. I saw his face. I know his face. He was pitying me. I can't have that jerk pity me."

My life and the shenanigans I seem to get myself into have been group fodder for Melissa and Jillian. Now that they've settled down, my single status and the goings-on in my dating life keep them entertained. They are also pillars of strength when it comes to needing someone to lean on.

Tonight, however, isn't about me. It's about Melissa and the dinner she planned since we all haven't been able to get together since her wedding.

"Enough about me. How was your vacation?"

"Magical," she sighs. "I didn't feel sexy, prancing around with this belly, but Will made me feel so comfortable in my skin. He's amazing."

That is something no one can disagree with. While I managed to infiltrate the life of the grumpy Bronson brother, she got the cinnamon roll hero.

Her dreamy, swoony look is interrupted by the sound of a doorbell. I look into the den and count heads. Will is talking baseball with Luke—Jillian's fiancé—while Ainsley is playing with Hunter, and Izzy is on her phone.

"The gang's all here. Who are you expecting?" I ask.

"Oh. That's Rob," she explains. "He has the kids this weekend, so Will asked him to come over since they've been fighting. Apparently, Rob punched their cousin Kevin for no reason at the wedding. The mother was pissed. Will was annoyed. Rob won't say why."

My mouth opens to speak, and I'm temporarily at a   loss. "No. No way. That can't be right. Which one is Kevin?"

"The burly guy. Sweats a lot. He says he got kneed and then punched in the face at the wedding. I never thought of Rob as a *knee a guy in the balls* kind of man. Punching? Absolutely."

Jillian lifts a finger to her chin. "I saw some guy with ice on his face in the hotel lobby. Thought it was odd, but didn't care enough to ask. Why the hell would Rob assault his own cousin like that?"

I fiddle with one of the buttons on my shirt. "Maybe he was defending someone's honor."

"Maybe he just wanted to get some of that aggression out. When Tyler left me, I probably could've punched a cousin or two."

"Wouldn't have put it past you," I agree with Melissa.

Jillian grabs the knife and tomato that Melissa forgot about and starts cutting. "Families are weird. Glad I don't have a big one."

"I didn't finish the tomato salad." Melissa pouts, clearly plagued by her pregnancy brain.

With my hands on her shoulders, I usher her out of the kitchen. "Go play hostess to your family. Jillian and I have everything set in here." With another push, I get my friend out of the room.

While Jillian makes the tomato salad, I attempt to fix the bouquet of flowers. They are a thoughtful gesture and should be displayed proudly. I move a rose from the center to the side of the vase. It doesn't quite do what I need it to do, so I move it to a different spot.

Jillian raises a brow. "Someone's wasting time in the kitchen."

I give her a reproachful look. "These flowers you brought just won't sit right in the vase. I think there's another one in the cabinet somewhere."

"You keep searching, and while you do, you can explain why you're avoiding Rob."

I spin around at her accusation. "Avoiding Rob? Pfft. I barely know the guy. He's insignificant to me."

She hums, "You went from grunts to drinks to babysitting his kid. Quite the plot twist."

My aversion to Rob isn't what she thinks.

Actually, I'm not entirely sure what it is.

Thinking about it makes my head hurt.

"Just to prove how unaffected I am by his presence, I am going to walk this fine bouquet of flowers into the den."

"I thought you said they didn't look right."

"They're just flowers, Jillian. Stop overanalyzing everything."

She sticks her tongue out at me, so I hip-check her. I give my hair a fluff before walking into the den. Okay, I also stop by the foyer mirror at the opposite end of the house and check my appearance. Long curls are in check. Blue eyes are lined nicely in black liner. My lips are coated in gloss, and my boobs look spectacular in this blouse. Not that I'm trying to impress anyone, but feeling good outwardly is part of the self-confidence boost I need when waging a mental war on myself.

About what? Everything.

As soon as I enter the den, I hear a squeal.

"Madam Amazing!" Molly jumps up from where she's seated at the coffee table and rushes toward me, throwing her arms around my waist. "You left without saying good-bye the other day."

I return her hug, trying not to spill water from the vase. My gaze inadvertently moves toward the couch.

Rob is seated beside his brother. His jean-clad legs are spread wide as he leans forward, in conversation with the guys until he notices me standing here. His eyes are on mine—like embers ablaze, flickering in stoic intensity, which match his steel-like persona. There's a singe of something else there too. A palpable mix of appreciation for his daughter's affection and disdain for my mere presence.

I force my gaze away, focusing on Molly. "Sorry. I had to get back to Newbury."

"I went to that party and wore the outfit you'd made me. I got so many compliments!"

"That's because you looked hot!" I say, and Rob grunts in response, so I correct myself, "I mean, cool. Ten-year-olds are way too young to be considered hot." My words are more directed at Rob because Molly seems to completely understand what I'm saying.

Jesse is standing against the wall near the window. His head is buried in his phone.

I give him a wave. "Hi, Jesse."

He nods his head in return.

"Mind your manners. Tara said hello. Be a man and get your head out of that phone and say hi."

"It's okay—" I start, but Rob interrupts me.

"Jesse," he warns, and his son slides his phone into his pocket, crossing his arms and giving a reluctant hello.

Will puts his hand on his brother's shoulder and gives it a pat. "Man, you're worse than Dad was, and he was a hard-ass when we were kids."

"Jesse gets into enough trouble for the two of us and Cade included, trust me," Rob explains.

"I believe it." Will gives his nephew a pointed look. "Those idiots you hang out with were joyriding in Castleton last night. Sideswiped a car and almost crashed into the woods. They got away from the officer on the scene."

Jesse shrugs indifferently. "Then, how do you know it was them?"

"Everyone knows that crew," Will explains. "They're gonna end up in jail or dead. Good idea your old man has you under lockdown this summer."

"As his gopher. All he wants me to do is follow him around the worksite."

"A good day's work is what you need," Rob explains. "It's that or stay with your mom and your sister all summer. Your mom has a bunch of trips she plans on taking you on."

"And watch her and Mike make out all the time? Screw that," Jesse spits, and Rob makes a hollering sound toward his son.

LOVE...IT'S WILD

While Jesse gets reprimanded for using foul language, Melissa leans into me and explains, "Mike is the ex-wife's boyfriend. He and Rob were good friends for years. Their sons played baseball together, and the men coached their Little League team. Christine, Rob's ex, started dating Mike suspiciously fast after their divorce."

I nod my head in understanding. Rob doesn't just have an ex-wife. He has a dirtbag friend who snagged her as soon as the ink was dry on   the divorce papers. I thought seeing fruit in a bakery was bad. This guy has to watch his ex-wife move on with his friend. So do these kids.

Molly jumps out of my arm and walks over to Rob. "I don't want to spend the summer with Mom. I want to be at the ranch with you!"

Rob takes his daughter's hand. "I'm not happy about it either, but I just don't have another option. Jesse will stay with me and you will go with mom."

"Why does she have to go away with Christine?" Will asks his brother.

"Because Dad has issues," Jesse interrupts his dad before he can answer.

Molly throws her arms around Rob. "I want to be with you, Dad. I don't want to travel with Mom and Mike. I want to stay at the ranch."

Rob places an arm around his daughter's back. "I want you all summer, too, but I don't see how I can do that and keep you safe when I have no one to watch you."

"Sending Molly away with Mom and Mike isn't a good idea." Jesse takes his phone back out of his pocket and starts scrolling. "Mike's a jerk who tries to act like he's our father."

"Why didn't you tell us you needed help with the kids this summer? Melissa and I would have tried to work something out," Will offers.

"My house is an hour-and-a-half drive from here. You and Melissa have your lives in Newbury and the kids want to stay at the ranch. If I can't make that happen, then they have to go back to their mother. That was the deal I made with Christine."

"Mom said you were getting a nanny," Will states, but Rob waves him off. "I thought you had this taken care of."

"I'm not cut out for other people watching my kids. I had

someone try, but we had a difference in opinion on parenting style, so she stormed off like a child." His eyes glare at me.

"You said it wasn't going to work out!" I declare.

"Wait, you were the nanny?" Will looks at me, confused, and then turns to his wife, who puts her hands up as if she were being arrested for lying. "You knew about this and didn't tell me?"

"I just found out in the kitchen," Melissa states quickly. "She ran into her ex, Patrick, in the bakery in Newbury and found out he'd bought a house in town, so she needed a place to escape to for the summer so she didn't have to see him and his fruit."

My head falls into my hand as I mentally curse Melissa and her diarrhea of the mouth when she gets nervous.

Jillian and Luke are standing on the other end of the room, watching the interaction with interest. For people who don't have big families by any means, they must be horrified by the smattering of opinions and overtalkative dialogue.

"I should have known you were doing it for selfish reasons," Rob bites accusingly.

"Why did you think I was helping out? I never met your kids, except that one time Jesse tried to get a beer from me at the wedding. And I'm happy I did because Molly and I had a great day until you came in. And let me remind you, you said it wasn't going to work out."

"Dad, you told Tara it wasn't going to work out?" Molly looks at him like he's crazy. "She's, like, the only person who gets me."

"That's because she's a grown child. You need an adult."

I send him laser-beam daggers and imagine punching him in the balls right now. "Don't be such an asshole."

Rob stands up and declares, "See? This is the problem."

Jillian steps forward and interjects, "Perhaps this is a conversation you two should be having outside. Away from the children."

Rob gives her a curt nod. He steps toward me, takes me by the elbow with a rough pull, and escorts me out of the den, through the kitchen, and out the back door to the yard. I only allow him to because Jillian's right.

What I'm about to say to this Neanderthal is in no way appropriate for the ears of babes.

And boy, do I have an earful for him.

Eight

AS WE STEP INTO the cool evening air, the tension between us is palpable. I hastily brush off his touch, wanting to distance myself from his brutish presence. I walk briskly onto the deck, wrapping my arms around myself, a facade of annoyance covering the turmoil inside. I look back at him, my chin tilted defiantly, awaiting his words.

Who am I kidding? I'm not good at this *strong yet silent* thing.

"You're moodier than a cat in a room full of rocking chairs."

"What the hell does that even mean?" he retorts.

"I can't keep up with your mood swings. One moment, you're nice, and the next, you're a pompous ass," I snap, my patience wearing thin.

"I can't believe you lied," he accuses.

"I didn't lie. You are a pompous ass," I fire back, my temper flaring.

He takes a stern step forward. "Not about that."

"I had an awesome time with Molly. Why would I lie?"

His boots make a heavy thud as he approaches. "You lied about why you were helping me out."

"Sorry if my embarrassment isn't something I care to broadcast to everyone."

"Not wanting to see an ex-boyfriend is what teenagers do," he comments dismissively.

LOVE...IT'S WILD

Oh, for the love of ...

"Stop comparing me to a child! I have emotions. You should try having some instead of bottling them up into this cage of pent-up steel."

I grip the railing tightly and turn toward Rob, pouring my heart out with raw emotion in every word. "Patrick wasn't just an ex-boyfriend. I was supposed to marry him. The marriage license was filled out. I was in my wedding dress, for Pete's sake. My dad was ready to walk me down the aisle when I found out Patrick had gotten cold feet. Frozen feet that I wish I could wrap in concrete and push into the ocean."

I pace toward Rob. My head is swimming with ragged emotions, and my body is vibrating with nervous energy. I clench my jaw and will myself not to cry. I refuse to cry over Patrick.

"   Patrick's not just an ex. He's not some guy. He was going to be my husband, but he left me. Are you happy? Is that adult enough for you? You're not the only one who was left by someone. And please hold the judgmental comments. You were married for years and had kids. I didn't even get down the aisle, so there's no comparison. Doesn't matter what you think. It is fucking hurtful, and now, he's in my town with his family, and I just ... I need to get the fuck out of Newbury!"

My rant leaves me feeling both vulnerable and empowered. I swallow my emotions, narrowing my eyes at Rob, daring him to belittle me. There's no denying the pulsing knot that's formed in my stomach.

"I wasn't going to compare."

The ruggedness of his god-like face is softened by the flicker of empathy in his searing brown eyes. His look is so galvanizing that it sends tremors through my skin. It's a look of conviction, want, and white-knuckled anger, like he'd hurt someone for me.

"That's messed up—what he did."

I shake my head, not expecting his understanding. I'm sure it will be followed by another line. I've heard them all. The positive spins that people try to use to make me feel better in a situation.

I voice one of them out loud. "*You dodged a bullet, Tara. Imagine if you got married and he left you a year later. You were lucky it happened this way."* My bitterness is evident.

"You weren't lucky. You were screwed. It's fucked up."

I blink up at him, confused by his sudden change of tone. "Why are you being nice to me again?"

"A shitty thing happened to you. Sounds like I should cut you some slack."

"I bet you love this. Further proof happily ever after is bullshit."

A small smirk graces his face. "It is, but I won't try to change your mind. If you've been burned like that in the past and you still want another chance at love, then you might be as crazy as I thought you were." He slides his hands into his pockets and then adds, "And braver than I ever imagined."

His words hit me, challenging my defenses. There's tenderness beneath his hard exterior, a glimmer of hope that he's still capable of kindness. His physique and personality are so hard, yet there's vulnerability that wants to break through when he looks at me like this. Like maybe he still has a little hope left inside him. Maybe he isn't as mean as he wants me to think he is.

It's unnerving.

"Did you punch your cousin in the face because of me?"

"Does it matter?"

"To me, it does."

He purses his lips as he looks at me. There's a harsh, uneven rhythm to his breathing and heat in his gaze. With the way his skin colors, I can practically see the blood coursing through his veins, like an awakened river. I don't want to tear my attention away from him until he answers my question.

"Yes. Don't start looking at me like I'm some sort of hero for it."

"You're the last man I ever planned on coming to my rescue, nor do I need it. It's also time you quit being so condescending. There's no reason for it." I cross my arms and turn my back to him.

"I know."

I look at him over my shoulder. "You do?"

"I can't explain why I do it. I have a lot of stress, and I take it out on those around me." He lets out a deep, ragged breath. There's a clench to his jaw, like the words he's about to say are hard to utter. "My life is in shambles. Molly hates to be away from me, but I have no way of giving her my time, not with how strained I am at my job. Jesse hates me. I can't trust him for shit, and I want to. He wasn't always this moody teenager. He was a good kid."

"Divorce changed him?"

"Doesn't mean it's an excuse. He needs to get his act together."

"You could start by taking it   easier on him."

"The kid was caught shop   lifting, and that was after we found weed and used cans of spray paint in his bedroom."

"Oh," is all I mutter. Looks like Jesse is more of a troublemaker than I thought. "What's the deal with Molly? She's a good kid who just wants to be where her dad is. Why don't you trust anyone with her?"

His hand rubs his stubbled jaw as he shakes his head. His eyes level with mine. "The last woman who promised everything was going to be okay filed for divorce and started dating my friend three months later. Leaves a bitter taste in your mouth. You should understand that."

I do, so I nod. "I guess Molly will spend the summer with her mom then. That should be nice."

"Molly wants to be at the ranch, and I want to be with her."

"Then, find someone to watch her."

"She wants you."

I pause, taken aback by his sincerity. "It's better I can't. I have my own work to do in Newbury, and I can't run from Patrick forever."

"What if you didn't run from him, but rather walked in another direction for a while?" He closes the distance between us and plants his boots firmly in front of me. His chest heaves, as if the words he's about to say will be so powerful, so potent with meaning, that they will blow us both away. "I was wrong."

I let out a laugh like an exhale of relief. "That looked painful. The words out of your mouth were like splinters on your lips."

The sides of his mouth twitch. "I hated every second. I mean it though. I was harsh to you. Doesn't change my feelings on makeup, cutting up clothes, cursing—"

"You curse!"

"That's different."

"How so? Be careful how you answer because you're about to

sound like a misogynist."

"I can't go an entire summer without seeing my kids. I'm running out of time to find someone to help. Just the month of July. That's all I need. I'm gonna try to take time off in August. Take them on a real vacation. Until then, I need you. Do you think you can stand being around me for that long?"

"Depends. I like this Rob. Not the mean one."

"Can't promise I'll behave."

"Okay, fine. I kind of like your meanness. It's hot."

That low rumble I've become accustomed to grumbles in his chest. "Tara," he bites out as a warning.

"Man, you have some easy buttons to push." I flip my hair and jut out my hip. "If you want my help this summer, you have to beg."

"I am not begging you. And don't forget, you also need to get out of town for a while."

"I could go anywhere for the summer. There's this amazing invention called a laptop that allows you to work from all over the world and be productive."

He backs away. "Still not begging."

"On your knees, Bronson."

He turns his back to me. "You're crazy."

"You need new adjectives."

"I have plenty of them." He gives a little wave as he starts up the steps. "See you on Monday morning."

I roll my eyes and concede. "Fine. You don't have to beg so hard. I'll do it. Are you opposed to assless chaps?"

His feet stop for a moment, and he lowers his head. A small smirk is evident from his profile, and I pretend not to notice it.

"This is gonna be a long summer."

He's not wrong.

Nine

"DAMN, WOMAN. I said to pack for five days. Not five months," Rob grumbles as he carries my suitcases toward the house.

I hand Molly the grocery bags filled with snacks—I can't imagine going five days without a proper supply of junk food.

"I don't plan on lugging my things back and forth all summer, so this is my ranch attire, which will reside here," I explain.

He stops at the top of the porch steps, giving me an arched brow. "Your ranch attire?"

"There's an outfit for every occasion."

I open my arms to showcase the sweet floral dress I'm wearing, paired with a denim jacket and ankle boots. His eyes skim the short hemline of my dress, which stops even higher with the way I'm holding up my arms.

"That's an awfully short skirt, don't you think?"

"You're worse than a nun in a Catholic school." I pick up the skirt and show off what I have on underneath. "I have shorts on."

His eyes widen at the very tight booty shorts I have on that cling to my skin, but he doesn't say a word. I drop my skirt and snap my fingers, whisking his attention back to the house.

He stomps up the stairs, mumbling to himself, and I follow him in, hauling my tote bags and laptop.

Molly places the grocery bags on the kitchen counter, and I drop one of my totes on a chair when Rob nods toward the back of the house.

"Your room is this way."

Through a small corridor on the first floor, I'm surprised at the changes made to the room beside the first-floor bathroom. The once-stained couch that was here has been replaced with a double bed, brass headboard, and pale pink bedding with large white dahlia flowers. The walls are no longer mint green, but a soft rose, giving the room a feminine touch without being childish. On the wall is a piece of art—a painted picture of a woman dancing in a meadow, her dress, that matches the exact shade of the painted walls, is flowing in the breeze. The brushstrokes are soft yet detailed enough to show the curves of her body and the sway of her back and the tiny ringlets of hair that fall onto her neck.

I turn to Rob and look at him, leaning against the doorframe.

"This was very sweet of you. I didn't need a newly decorated room."

"You do. We haven't decided on compensation yet, and I plan to pay you fairly. A proper place to stay is the least I can do."

"I don't need to be paid. You're doing me a favor, too, remember? Trust me, I know I seem demanding, but this room is more than kind. I knew you had a soft spot in that cold heart of yours."

His eyes dart around the room as a hint of bashful blooms on his cheeks. "I'll pay you for your time. I don't take advantage, and I won't accept anything for free."

"I don't need the money."

"Doesn't matter what you need. It's about what you deserve. You're accepting payment, and that's final." His voice rises, and I startle slightly.

"Well, my price is steep, so you'd better be prepared to pay." I try to make light of the situation.

"The couch wasn't appropriate, so we bought this bed, and the desk is so you can still get your accounting work done."

It's a thoughtful gesture, one I'm not accustomed to. "The pink is pretty. Thank you."

"Molly picked out the bedding." Rob gives a curt nod and then walks out of the room.

Leaving my bags, I follow him out, stealing one last glance at the space put together just for me.

In the kitchen, I sort through the contents Molly has unpacked and grab a carton of muffins I brought from home. I wrap two banana nut muffins in parchment paper bags and hand one to Rob.

"What's this?" He stares at the pastry like I handed him a bomb.

"Breakfast." I extend another to Jesse as he strolls into the kitchen, looking like a sullen teenager. "Good morning, muffin. I got you a muffin."

Jesse looks at his dad, bewildered. "Did she just call me muffin or offer me a muffin?"

"Both, I believe," Rob answers his son, taking the parchment from my hands. "Did you make these yourself?"

"Yep!" I open one of my personal totes and grab two brown paper bags and hold them out to them. "I also packed you lunch. I didn't know what you liked, so I went with Italian subs for both. You each have chips, an apple, and a piece of chocolate because no meal should go by without something sweet. Don't get too excited. I bake and pack lunches, but I don't cook. I mean, I literally can when it's a necessity, but I don't make fancy dinners. That is going to have to be your department, although I do a spectacular job at ordering in. Do they deliver out here?"

Rob nods as he and his son stare at me, their muffins and lunch in each hand. "I can grill tonight."

I clap my hands together. "Love a man who can grill. Jesse, take notes from your old man because a guy who can cook is a total catch. You don't happen to do the dishes, too, do you?"

"He does," Molly chimes in. "And laundry."

I place my hand on my forehead like I'm about to faint. "The whole package. Maybe I need to expand my dating search to the countryside. It's an untapped resource."

"Dad, please make her stop talking," Jesse pleads, his eyes glued on me.

Rob playfully slaps him on the chest. "Get in the car."

"Good-bye, guys. Have a good day at work!" I walk them out and wave them off from the steps, making it a habit.

LOVE...IT'S WILD

The discomfort on their faces as I send them off with absolute fanfare only spurs me on.

As soon as they're gone, I take Molly's hand. "Let's grab some muffins and eat them on our walk. It's too nice of a day to stay inside."

Rob's house sits on a hundred fifty acres of land on the Connecticut border, neighboring Massachusetts. Molly and I walk farther into the fields, the mountains acting as a gorgeous backdrop to the cornfields around us. There's a tractor in the distance, so I hold my hand up to my face to see what is happening on the other side of the field.

"Dad rents the land out to a farmer because he can't do it himself. It's really cool though because we get lots of corn to eat." Molly picks a flower on our walk. We have a nice bouquet of various wildflowers coming along.

We stroll along a small stream weaving through the property. I hold her sneakers and the flowers in my hand as Molly dips her toes in the water when she gets too warm. She splashes and giggles as she runs through the stream. We stop to catch a frog and then let it go once our mission is complete.

"I can see why you love being here. It's beautiful."

"It's gonna be even better. Dad said we can get farm animals someday. Hopefully, when the shopping mall is done, he'll be able to take some time off and farm with us."

"Farming is a big job."

"I know. Dad says he can't do it alone since he works so much, but maybe he'll change his mind, and we can take over the crops too."

"What's the point in having all of this if you can't use it as intended?"

"That's what I said. First thing we're getting is a horse. There's a stable we can keep it in."

"Who is going to care for the horse when you are back home during the school year?"

Her dark ponytail sways as she jumps from one rock to another. "I plan on living here."

I play with the flower stems as we stroll. "I know you love it on the ranch, but why don't you want to be with your mom? Aren't your friends in Castleton? You could be at camp, playing games and hanging out with friends. Plus, most kids like being with their mom."

She stops in her tracks and speaks with downturned eyes. "Do you want me to go back to Castleton for the summer? You don't wanna hang out with me, do you?"

"Are you kidding? I adore hanging with you. Just trying to understand why a ten-year-old wants to walk along a stream and catch frogs instead of playing with other kids. Your aunt Melissa told me you're an awesome softball player."

"And an awesome basketball player. I guess I just don't want to be with my friends this summer. They're really fun, but it's exhausting—trying to be cool, worrying about what I'm going to wear, packing the snacks Nicole wants, or sitting around and talking about boys and gossiping about the girls and pretending to care. When you and I did my makeover, that was cool, and I liked going to that party and being seen. But that's not what I want all the time. I don't want to pretend to be something I'm not."

I waver, comprehending her understanding of the world. Molly is only ten yet she's far wiser than her years. Wiser than mine. "Sometimes, it's easier to pretend than let people know how you feel on the inside. People can judge all too easily. It's hard, being vulnerable."

"What do you mean by vulnerable?"

"It means being exposed emotionally or physically. It's when you let people know your true feelings in a way that they could hurt you deeply."

"You don't seem like that. I like that you act like yourself, no matter what Dad says about you. You're not embarrassed by the things you do and say because you're just being yourself. It's really cool. I hope to be more like you someday."

I smile at her flattery, but I level with her. "If that's how your friends make you feel, like you can't be yourself, then you're right to want some distance. Don't ever let anyone tell you to be someone you're not, but make   no mistake—I hide a lot of my emotions. I might not care what people think about me, but that doesn't mean I show them all my sides. I'm human, you know. There are some things that hurt me. I just don't let them overtake my life. My grandmother taught me this trick when I was a kid. Whenever I feel like I'm feeling less than my worth, I push my shoulders back, raise my chin, and walk into a room like I own it. If people see you as a success, they will treat you like one. If you act like a success, you will become one."

"I like that. I might try it."

"Not feeling comfortable in your skin around your friends is no reason to not stay with your mom. I bet she misses you."

"Doubt it. She and Mike are in Niagara Falls right now."

"You and Jesse don't like Mike very much, do you?"

She juggles a rock she picked up and tosses it far. "Not really."

"I get it. He's replacing your dad."

"No one can replace my dad. He's the best. You can't see it yet, but you will."

We're walking on the grass around the perimeter   of the property when I spot a wall of ivy about a hundred yards away with tall trees behind it. There seems to be something ivory in the background, peeking between the trees.

"What's that?" I ask, pointing toward what looks like a stucco tower.

"Dad says not to go back there."

"Is it not your property?"

She nods. "That's ours."

I lift a brow and start walking. "I want to see what's back there."

"I just told you, Dad says we aren't allowed."

"When are you going to learn that I am not good with being told not to do things?"

"He's right; you are a child," she says, holding her hands up and widening her eyes. "You're the one who's being defiant."

"And you're the one who just said you like that I'm me, no matter what anyone says about me."

I walk over to the ivy wall and run my hand along it. If I've learned anything from movies, there's always an opening in one of these walls. I'm searching through the streams of ivy when Molly loudly clears her throat.

"The entrance is right over here," she says. "And it's not hidden.

What do you think this is, a secret society or something?"

I stick my tongue out at her and walk to the large opening. Inside is an eight-foot-high wall enclosure is a structure that looks like the castle piece in a game of chess. There are wrought iron windows at the top and an arched wooden doorway at the bottom with a large, thick handle.

On the ground, is a maze of overgrown shrubs that we have to sidestep around as not to get poked by the branches. In the space before the doors, are two rectangular ponds full of algae and muck and various flower beds that have been neglected.

I walk along the cobblestone flooring and over to the filthy structure. Plant life has grown up around it, making it look like one of those abandoned castles in a Renaissance movie.

I pull on the handle of the wooden door. It's open. I walk inside the hollow stone structure with a small room and a spiral staircase in the corner. The stone makes it cool inside despite the warm summer air outside. The light peers in, bringing an ample amount of brightness.

"This place is awesome. Do you know what it is?" I ask Molly.

"Nope. It was here when we moved in. Dad drew up these plans to make it beautiful, but my mom said it was a waste of money. I thought it was gonna be a playhouse for me."

I place my hand on the stone and let the earthy feeling sear into my palm. It might have been forgotten, but this place is still sturdy, waiting for someone to come in and love it.

"This place could be anything. I'd make it a library and put a giant chair in the corner so I could sit and read all day."

Molly climbs the stairwell and looks down. "I'd paint it blue and cover the floor in Squishmallows and blankets."

"Blue? I thought you'd say pink. My room is very pretty, by the way. You picked a great color."

"I didn't pick it." Her voice is muffled, as she is now upstairs.

I look up at the banister, baffled. "You didn't pick pink for my bedroom?"

Her voice echoes as she says, "Dad said when he met you, you were wearing a dress that exact color and it looked very pretty on you."

LOVE...IT'S WILD

I think about the dress I wore to Melissa and Will's wedding. It was that exact shade of pink—a soft, feminine rose.

"Your dad said I was pretty?"

Molly pops her head over the banister. "I believe he said you looked pretty in the dress."

"Tomato, tomahto. I'll take a compliment when it's given. Now, what are we gonna do about this place?" I think of all the wonderful ways we can revitalize the castle in the grass.

Molly walks down the stairs. "Nothing. Dad was serious when he said that no one is allowed to come here."

I look up at the walls and wonder if Rob's concerns are because it's structurally unsafe. I mean, it looks old and could very well not be the soundest of structures. I can picture the walls crumbling down on us and a report in the newspaper about a woman and child who perished in the fall.

That visual quickly subsides. There's something about the way it feels, standing here. It feels solid. Like it was constructed in a time when people built things to withstand the elements, disaster. This feels like it has good bones.

It had a purpose, and I bet the story is absolutely beautiful. Like a film reel in a flashback setting, I can see it. A man who built this for his wife so she could have respite from harder times. Where she could garden and read and escape from the hurt that happened outside these walls. A place that was once deeply loved and then cast aside for one reason or another.

I can relate to this place. A stunningly beautiful tower, slowly growing vines to cover its vulnerabilities from the outside world.

Okay, so when I start comparing myself to buildings is when I begin to worry about my own sanity.

"Yeah, maybe we should get out of here."

"Let's make slime!" Molly hops off the staircase and heads out the door.

As we walk away from the structure and into the pasture, I still can't help but wonder what it once was and what it could be someday.

Ten

MY DAYS AND NIGHTS at the ranch go seamlessly over the next week. It can be a touch boring at times, yet the quiet is soothing for the soul. I get plenty of work done while Molly reads or has iPad time, and we fill the days with games and exploring the land surrounding the house.

It's an uncharacteristically cool night, so Molly and I open the windows and let a breeze from a recent rainstorm pass through the house as we play a card game. It's one of those picturesque nights out here on the ranch—that is, until the boys come home.

When Rob and Jesse return from work, it's with the sound of doors slamming and voices hollering. Molly and I exchange glances from across the living room coffee table, where we're playing gin rummy. Our brows rise with an equal look of *oh shit, wonder what happened now.*

Now being the keyword. Night after night, it's been the sound of father-son fighting. While the trigger to the fight of the day is always different, the underlying issue is always the same.

"I don't need to be on your damn leash!" Jesse storms into the house and throws his backpack on the floor. "I have my driver's permit. Why won't you let me drive? Every other dad lets their kid drive around. It's like some rite of passage you're supposed to want to do with me!"

"Maybe if you weren't so damn irresponsible, I'd trust you behind the wheel of my truck."

"I made one mistake."

"If shoplifting had been your first offense, I wouldn't be dragging you to my damn job to babysit you every day." Rob throws his car keys on the counter, his accusing voice stabbing the air. "The bad grades, the bad attitude, the spray paint, the pot—"

"It wasn't mine!"

"The flood in the bathroom when you were taking a shower."

"That was because the stupid plastic curtain isn't big enough," Jesse counters.

"You're sixteen! When are you gonna get your head out of your ass and pay attention to life? I can't trust you alone because you make bad decision after bad decision."

"I hate it here!" Jesse lashes out.

"Then, go live with your mother."

"She doesn't want me either, or did you forget that?" he battles back with contempt that forbids any other argument.

Rob punches the air as he sputters, unable to fight the words from his son. His jaw clenches, and he closes his eyes, gathering his thoughts.

"I never said I didn't want you. What I want is for you to wake up and live in the real world. What you did today was unacceptable." His tone still has a bite, yet it's calmer and pointed.

"How was I supposed to know the drill was on? You said to hand it to you. You didn't warn me it would start shooting nails out of it like a machine gun."

"You could have hurt someone." Rob brings the conversation back to an elevated level.

"I didn't."

"The point is, you could have, and then you had the nerve to ask to drive my car home. What did you think I'd say to that?"

Jesse's hands fly in the air, as if the answer were crystal clear. "I thought you'd say, *Yes, son, because you need to learn how to drive and I'd like to be the one to show you.*"

All week, the father-son duo have been at each other's throat. Molly is used to it, and I'll admit, it took me a few days to get into the normal that is the Bronson family. It usually ends with a dinner, where Molly and I ramble while the men say nothing, and then everyone departs to their respective rooms for the night.

I drop my cards on the table and rise. "Not to interrupt this powwow, but you two need to take a breather from one another right now. Looks like ten hours on the jobsite is a little too much of a good thing."

"Great idea." Jesse storms upstairs toward his room.

"Fan-fuckin'-tastic," Rob states as he heads toward the kitchen.

Molly and I leave the living room and follow Rob. He opens the fridge, grabs steaks, and slams the door, walking outside onto the back porch. We are left now standing in the quiet kitchen.

"That was exciting," I state.

"That was a typical Wednesday."

"I'm figuring that out." I give her a pat on the shoulder. "Why don't you watch some TV before dinner, and I'll check on your dad?"

"Good luck," she says with raised brows.

I grab two cold beers from the refrigerator, twist off the tops, and walk onto the back porch. Rob is on the lower landing, standing by the grill and staring at the grates as they warm up.

I head down the stairs and hand him a beer. He takes it appreciatively.

"Sorry about that in there," he says.

"You parent very well. Stern. Effective. I can see you're really getting through to him."

He gives me a deadpan stare.

"I get it. I don't have kids, so I don't know anything about raising one."

"I didn't say that, but"—he takes a swig of his beer—"you're right. You have no idea how hard it is to raise a teenage boy. There's no instruction guide on how to do this."

Leaning against the stair railing, I take a drink from my own bottle and stare at the sky. The moon is out tonight, covered slightly by clouds yet glowing and showing itself in any way it can. I sigh as I glance up at it.

"Do you ever feel like you're still growing up? One minute, you're fifteen, and the next, you're an adult with bills, responsibilities, and, in your case, kids. While we're aging, you can still remember clear as day what it felt like to be a kid."

"I wish I had the luxury of still feeling young. Men don't get to linger in their youth. We grow up, take on responsibilities. We provide, protect. When you have children, there's no time to play."

Rob and I have two very different mentalities. I can still feel and sense every moment of my youth like it was yesterday.

"When I was fifteen, I snuck out of the house," I say, and Rob snickers, as if that seems like an obvious thing for me to have done. "There was a keg party in the woods in Newbury, and I wasn't allowed to go. I told my parents I was sleeping at Melissa's house. I never went to her house. Instead, I went deep into the forest, drank my face off, and was left there at three o'clock in the morning with nowhere to go. It began to rain. I was wet, freezing, and starting to get sick to my stomach.

"I went to Melissa's house. She was a sweeter kid than me. She didn't lie to her parents, and she stayed home that night. Her neighbors had a tree house we hung out in. The ladder rungs were too slippery, and my head was spinning, so I couldn't climb up. I went to her window and threw these tiny rocks at the glass. Luckily, she woke up and let my drunk ass in. I wasn't quiet at all and woke her mom.

"Mrs. Jones was pissed at me for being such an idiot, but she brought me to the kitchen, gave me a cup of tea and some of Melissa's pajamas, and set me up on the couch with a pot next to me in case I got sick. The woman slept on the love seat all night to take care of me.

"When I got up the next morning, I was hungover and embarrassed. I was also nervous she was going to tell my mother. My parents were cool, but they wouldn't have dealt well with that level of betrayal. So, Mrs. Jones made me a deal. She wouldn't tell my parents what happened, as long as I promised that if anything like that ever happened again, I wouldn't throw rocks at the window. Instead, I'd go to the door and ring the doorbell because if Melissa hadn't heard the stones, I might have been left outside in the cold, and worse could have happened.

"I never had to ring the bell. I learned my lesson and never did that again, but it was good to know there was an adult out there who trusted me to make the right decision next time."

"Are you saying I should let him mess up, so long as he comes home at the end of the day?"

I boldly meet his gaze. "I'm saying to give him a chance."

His head drops, as if his defenses are subsiding. "I worry about him. I only have him for two more years before he either goes off to college or moves out and gets a job. He was a sweet kid. Loved Legos and comic books. One day, he started wearing all black and refused to wear anything but sweatpants. Forget about getting an actual jacket on the guy. Then, this attitude took over. He talks back, is moody, hangs out with the dredge of the earth, and his grades have been a disaster. I don't know how the kid passed sophomore year."

"He's just a kid, and kids make mistakes. Isn't it better if he makes them all while he's under your wing than you waiting to let him go and he makes even greater ones on his own? I'm not saying to give him total freedom, but a little personal responsibility could possibly do him good. I know you don't trust anyone, but if you're gonna start with someone, start with your own son."

"You don't know what kind of trouble he can get himself into."

"I can think of a few things," I say in a singsong voice in order to get a laugh. He doesn't react, so I give him a nudge. "Didn't you have a rebellious year?"

"No. I was the responsible one. I'm the oldest of six. Four boys, two girls. There wasn't time to act out. I was hauling my younger siblings around and keeping everyone on the straight and narrow. I did a pretty good job. Jack, Lori and Michelle are successful in their chosen professions and married with kids—lots of kids. Will is a hero cop and starting his own family. Cade is the only one who didn't follow in the Bronson family path. Honestly, I think my parents were so tired from raising the five older ones that they gave up on Cade around the time he was eight, and I was in college, so he practically raised himself."

"I met him at the wedding. Charming."

"He hit on you, didn't he?"

"Who doesn't?" I kid.

Then, I realize Rob is possibly the one man who hasn't hit on me, and I haven't tried to flirt with him either. Rob never gave me a chance to flirt because I know myself, and I most definitely would have given him the time of day. Heck, I would have given him the whole damn clock. But he was so repulsed by the thought of me wanting to flirt with him that he ran away from me. I file the unkind thoughts of myself away and wonder how I let my mind go from Jesse to Cade to my personal feelings toward Rob.

"Anyway, just food for thought. If you say Jesse was a good kid, then he is a good kid. Maybe he just needs a way to show it."

Rob looks back down at the grill. "Maybe. Who knows?"

I step onto the stairs. "I'll be inside, setting the table."

Inside, I call Molly down and show her how to turn the oven on, and we put in the loaf of bread we prepared earlier and let it rise. We make a large dinner salad and set the table. Molly shows me where her dad keeps the place mats, and we even set out some candles, deciding we need to change the aura in the house tonight and a fancy set table will do the trick.

When Rob comes inside with his finished beer and grilled steaks, he glances at the set dining table.

"Doesn't it look pretty?" Molly shows off the way the silverware is set properly. She pours iced tea into the glasses from the glass pitcher in the center of the table.

"Where did you get flowers?" Rob points to the arrangement of wildflowers in the center of the table.

"We've gone for a walk every day this week and gathered flowers. Have you not noticed them?"

Rob's face morphs from the serious, *lost in his head* expression he had when he walked inside into a calm grin. He looks at Molly. "The table looks beautiful. Get your brother. Tell him the steaks are ready."

Molly runs off to get her brother, and Rob puts the tray of steaks on the counter.

"The kid might hate my guts right now, but he loves steak. It's a surefire way to get him down here," Rob comments and then looks at the centerpiece. "Have you really collected flowers each day and I didn't even notice?"

"You've had a lot on your mind." I give him the excuse, which he doesn't seem to like.

I bring the salad bowl to the table while Rob slices the steaks and places it on a ceramic dish. I wonder if that's his usual style or if he's doing it because Molly and I made the table so nice tonight.

Jesse comes downstairs and takes a seat at the table. As Rob said, the kid loves steak, so he immediately starts plating slices for himself.

The air in the room is quite static, and I regret not putting music on. The four of us eat in silence, which is unusual for Molly and me, yet tonight, we don't have much to say. Plus, the steak is absolutely delicious. Rob is a great cook.

Rob looks across the table to where Jesse is sitting. "I was thinking … maybe you can take a break from coming to the jobsite with me tomorrow."

Jesse looks up at him like he's crazy.

"There's that driver's ed class in town. If there's room, I'll sign you up online. You can go to that. If that's okay with you, Tara. You'd have to take him."

"Of course," I answer. "As long as you trust me to do the job."

He lifts his fork. "Gotta start somewhere."

I have a big grin on my face, and I'm not entirely sure why Rob's change of heart is giving me a bolt of elation. "Molly and I can look in the shops. I've never been to town out here."

Her eyes widen. "We can check out the toy store. It has the coolest gadgets, and they let you try out everything there."

Rob pokes around his plate and looks up at his son. "Does that sound good to you, Jesse?"

Jesse nods, trying to appear like he's bothered by the idea, but says, "Yeah. That's what I really want to do. Thanks." He stabs at his steak and eats.

I look at Rob and give him a nod. He looks back at me. It's a calm and composed presence. There's no denying there's a depth of wisdom there. A window to the stories carried within. I'm glad I can impart some of mine his way as well.

For the first time since I met him, I don't think he's looking at me like I'm a grown child he asked to help him for the summer. This look is a little different. I can see it in the softness of his stare that burns hot with its length and hold.

I think Rob is starting to see me as something more than my reputation. More than an impression.

LOVE...IT'S WILD

In this moment, he sees … me. Perhaps it's time for me to show him more.

Eleven

AFTER DINNER, THE KIDS go upstairs to shower and get ready for bed while Rob and I clean up the table. While Rob loads the dishwasher and hand-cleans a few others, I grab a towel and start drying the large tray that is too big for the dishwasher.

"Thanks," Rob says, and I have a feeling he's not talking about my helping him with dishes.

"For what?"

"Getting my head out of my ass. Maybe Jesse does need a little space."

I place the platter back in the cabinet and turn to Rob. His back is now facing the sink, and he's leaning against the counter with his hands behind him. That broad chest is outstretched, and I can see the swells of muscle peeking through the cotton of his shirt.

"This could be good for you too," I offer. "Remember to enjoy your son and not feel the need to reprimand him every second. Let someone else do that."

"You mean, you? He'd walk all over you."

"Honey, I don't let anyone do anything to me that I don't allow willingly," I state. If I wasn't this close, I'd have missed the quick inhale he takes. I swallow. "You could use a little space of your own. Why don't you go out to the bar or something? Try meeting someone."

He opens his mouth to disagree, but I hush him.

"Don't say it. We already know I have love on the brain. The question is, why do you deny that you don't? I think one of the reasons you're so stressed is that you don't have any way to relieve it. You need to have fun. I know you want to. I saw you at Lone Tavern, remember?"

"That was not what you think."

"I think you went to have a drink because you were stressed about the kids' summer situation and you chose that bar because you were hoping to meet someone. When will you admit you might not need love but that you'd like some female companionship?"

I wait for him to answer, imploring him with my eyes as my heart hammers against my ribs.

He throws his head back and places his hands on his hips. "Fine. I'm not opposed to being with someone casually. I just haven't met a woman I'm interested in exploring that option with."

Triumph floods through me for being right, and then I wince at his words.

"Can I ask you a question?"

"I doubt anything I say would stop you from doing so."

My mind tells me to resist asking the question, but my mouth refuses to listen. "Why is the idea of me wanting to date you so repulsive?"

Rob's brows rise, and he stares back at me with a surprised intensity that burns into my soul and radiates down to my toes.

I keep going. "I just ... I realized something before, when we were talking outside. You've obviously never hit on me, and I suppose I never truly thought about the why of it until now. Yes, you ran away from me because you knew I was on the hunt for a man, but you never took advantage of that. There have been plenty of men who assume my wanting love means I merely want attention. And I was wondering, the fact that you were so opposed to me that you grunted and ran away ... well, am I that undesirable? I know I'm a catch in many ways. I don't need you to boost my ego. I guess what I'm asking is—"

"Tara." His deep baritone, mixed with the scorching heat radiating off his body, stops me from continuing.

He releases his hands from the counter and takes a step closer. A brief shiver ripples through me.

"My aversion to you has nothing to do with you being undesirable in any way. In fact, you're too desirable."

I can feel my pulse in my throat. "Too desirable?"

His eyes travel down to my cleavage, and he gives an appreciative lift of his brows, and then he looks down to my thighs that are showing from the hemline of my dress.

His eyes meet mine, and I catch my breath   .

His rugged features reflect a life lived with determination and purpose while his intense, piercing eyes convey a depth of experience and resilience. Those eyes—warm brown, reminiscent of earth—seem to hold a world of heartache within them. Yet, from the darkening of his pupils and the parting of his lips, I know he likes what he sees. I'm sure of it. I fight the urge to touch him because I know this is not what this moment is about.

This is Rob. Raw. Honest.

"Good night."

He stalks out of the kitchen, and I'm left alone with my thoughts.

Rob Bronson thinks I'm desirable.

Not gonna lie—that information gives me a little kick in my boots. I fling the towel into the air, catch it, and toss it onto the counter. My hips have an extra sway as I walk into my room and close the door.

"Too desirable," I mutter to myself and then repeat, "Too desirable."

Looking in the mirror, I take in my features. Dark blue eyes; curly, long, flowing black hair; and a complexion that even I know is crystal clear.

"What does that even mean?" I ask myself. "Am I a vixen? A temptress? Rob's not the type to say things just to be nice. He doesn't try to calm one's feelings. He's blunt, and he thinks you, Tara Parsons, are desirable. Obviously."

I laugh at my own antics of talking to myself in the mirror. That's another one of my grandmother's tactics of self-confidence. Always tell yourself how amazing you are. If you won't do it for yourself, why would others want to do it for you? I'm not ashamed to admit that I talk to myself in the mirror more than other adults do.

LOVE...IT'S WILD

As I slide off my dress, I catch a glimpse of myself again. I know I'm attractive. I might not be the most beautiful woman in the world, but I have many things going for me. Even naked, I like what I see.

I slide off my bra and pose for myself. It reminds me of a quote I heard on the show *Schitt's Creek*. Moira advises Stevie, the motel manager, to take all the nudes you can when you're young because, someday, you'll look back at them with kinder eyes and love what you see.

I've never taken a boudoir photo. I've sent sexy pictures of myself to men, but never in the flesh.

For myself, in this moment, with Rob's admission on my brain, I'm not opposed to it.

I take out my phone, hold it in front of me and to the side, and snap a picture. I look at the mirror selfie.

"Not bad," I say to myself.

Holding the phone up in the air, I spin the camera direction to face me, toss my hair to the side, lift my chest, and take a few more. I do a smile, a pout, and bite my lip. It's just silly. After I've taken a dozen, I erase them from my phone, but keep one for myself.

I've seen too many documentaries on how hackers can get into your text chains and emails, so I open my laptop and AirDrop the photo to my MacBook. It's just the one pic that I'll store somewhere safe and possibly look back on someday when I'm old and gray and say, *Damn, girl. You were hot.*

I wait a few moments for the photo to come through. My phone says it's sent, but the picture is not on my laptop. I go to AirDrop it again, and this time, there are two places I can drop the photo to. Two MacBooks. One is mine, and the other ...

Oh my God.

The realization that I just AirDropped a topless photo of myself to someone in the house other than me has me absolutely freaking the hell out.

"Please don't let it be Molly or Jesse," I beg into the open air.

Honestly, I don't know which one would be worse. Molly is impressionable and far too young to understand, and Jesse is a teenage boy, and the notion of him seeing me naked is just icky.

I toss on my pajamas and scurry out of my room and rush into the kitchen. Molly is in the snack cabinet. She looks at me with her hand inside a package of cookies and freezes like she was just caught red-handed, which she just was.

"Molly," I say to her, my breathing ragged, "do you have a computer?"

"Yep."

My eyes close in mortification. "What kind?"

"A Chromebook. They give it to us at school."

My heart settles a touch even though it's still racing a bazillion miles a minute. I clear my throat and try to act totally normal and not like some sort of perv who sends boob pics around the house.

"And Jesse?"

"Yeah, he has one."

"What kind?" The anticipation is going to burn a hole in my stomach.

"One of those gaming computers."

"A MacBook?"

"No. Dad has one of those."

My shoulders heave forward as a wave of relief pours over me. The kids don't have my picture. I must have sent it to Rob. He's the only other person in the house. This is so much better than sending it to the kids, but horrible nonetheless. I need to talk to him and explain the very clear misunderstanding that is me AirDropping a picture of my boobs to him.

It's possible he hasn't opened his laptop. If that's the case, I can swoop in and erase the photo, and all will be right in the world.

"Where might your father's laptop be right now?" I ask Molly, praying she says it's somewhere down here.

"It's in his room. He's on it right now." She takes a bite of her cookie and then waves. "Night!"

I give her a wave back and go into my room, falling against the wall behind me, totally shattered that I made such a colossal mistake.

Or did I?

Twelve

"MORNING! Would you like some cantaloupe?" I offer Rob the next morning, holding up the uncut round fruit for his breakfast before he heads to the jobsite.

He strolls into the kitchen and stops at the kitchen island, looking at my offering to him.

"I have watermelon, oranges, tomatoes, raisins. Produce comes in various shapes and sizes. What size do you prefer?"

"We need to talk."

Because the kids aren't downstairs yet, I decide to broach the subject out in the open.

"If it's about the fact that I accidentally sent you a photo of my boobs last night, please know that was misunderstanding. You saw my boobs. It's okay. No big deal. They're just breasts. Fine, they're full, attractive, voluptuous breasts that I happen to be very proud of. The fact that I AirDropped them to you was completely unintentional."

His eyes narrow as he crosses his arms, his thick forearms prominent as he aims his body toward me. "If you didn't mean to send it to me, who were you sending it to?"

"Myself," I answer easily, yet I'm unable to look him in the eye. "I understand this is awkward. I've been in your shoes. Worse actually. I've received unsolicited penis pics before, and it was a gross violation of my privacy and tender eyes that did not need to see half the things

LOVE...IT'S WILD

I'd seen. Word to the wise: if you're gonna send one, always hold the camera at a low angle, facing up. It makes it look bigger. Regardless, I meant to send the photo to myself as a little souvenir of sorts, and I hit the wrong button. Thankfully, it didn't go to the kids because that would have been tragic. You and I are adults though, and I'm sure we can handle this situation as such."

"Is that why you went from wearing a very revealing top yesterday to sporting a sweater today?"

"The weatherman called for a cold front."

"It's eighty degrees."

"Your house is old and drafty."

"It's been completely refurbished."

"Maybe I just didn't want to tempt you. My breasts are gorgeous, as you now know."

His gaze is riveted on my face, then moves over my body slowly. My heart jolts with the smoldering flame I see in his eyes. It startles me. It's as if he agrees with my statement.

"Is this because I said you were desirable last night?"

"No," I answer him like it's the most absurd thing I've ever heard. "It was a *Schitt's Creek* thing. You wouldn't understand."

"You and I can't happen."

I resist the urge to punch him in the balls. "Are we really at this again?"

He gives me a pointed glare. "Just checking."

"For the record, I wouldn't send you a naked pic if you were the last man on earth. You don't deserve to see these breasts. You wouldn't even know what to do with these gorgeous things."

"You sure about that?" he challenges.

By the cockiness in his tone, I'm not so sure I am. Like I said before, Rob can be nice, but he's also so damn mean at times that he probably knows all the right and the very wrong things to do with a woman's body.

I'm suddenly feeling very warm in my sweater.

"Enjoy your day," he croons with a wink as he takes the lunch I packed for him, pops a piece of cantaloupe into his mouth, and strolls out of the kitchen.

Molly walks into the kitchen soon after. "You're gonna want to change. Your face is bright red. Way too hot for a sweater."

I couldn't agree more.

Molly and I drop Jesse off at driver's ed and are told to come back for him in four hours. While he's learning how to man the road, us girls go shopping in the small-town shops that line this rural town. It's a short row of stores, yet it reminds me of my hometown of Newbury. There's something special about these villages. People are friendlier, neighbors look out for one another, and there are always the best ice cream shops.

I make Molly cross the street a few times on her own, watching as she sprints like a lunatic. I send her across and back to me until she's walking with her head looking both ways, yet not charging for the sidewalk like her pants are on fire. I also have her pay for our purchases because the child never has to use money for anything. Yes, she knows how to count currency from school, but the idea of handing a cashier a fifty and getting change back is foreign to her. As a reward, I tell her to keep the change.

Molly and I are sitting on a bench, enjoying chocolate cones, talking about ten-year-old happenings, when we see a car drive by with a familiar brunette boy with upside-down romaine lettuce hair in the passenger seat. The interesting thing about seeing Jesse in the car is that I'm pretty sure that is not a driver's ed vehicle.

"Come with me." I usher Molly and walk quickly toward my car that's parked on a side street.

She jogs behind me. "Where are we going?"

"I just saw your brother, and I don't think it was in a driver's ed car."

"How do you know?"

"One, he wasn't driving. Two, there wasn't signage on it. Usually, there's some sort of sticker or a license plate that lets you know a student driver is inside."

Molly gets into the passenger side. "Are you sure?"

"Nope, but I have a feeling I've been out-snaked by Jesse, who isn't at driver's ed, like he said he would be."

"Why do you think that?"

"Because that's what I would have done." I put the car in drive and then turn to her. "Don't judge."

I drive down the street toward the direction the car drove in. It was a beige Honda that had four teenagers inside, no adults. I look up the road and down some side streets, searching for the car. I spot it entering the drive-through line of a fast-food chain. While it sits in line, I park my car and get out.

"Stay here," I order Molly.

She hangs out the window and watches me march up to the Honda that is second in line.

The music coming from the car is loud, and the boys are yelling at each other while laughing. They toss some money at the driver, who counts it. I stand in the blind spot of the car and eavesdrop. They're too involved in their own world to know I'm standing outside their car.

"What the heck am I supposed to get for five dollars and fifteen cents?" the driver asks his friends.

"Order a bunch of stuff, get the bags of food, and then drive off. She should be happy she's getting five bucks," one of the kids says.

Jesse chimes in. "Yeah, it's not like they're losing money. It's owned by some huge corporation that makes bank off the little man. They won't even care."

"Plus, it's that fat chick working again. Porky probably eats all the food in there anyway. No one will know if some extra goes missing," the driver adds, and my blood boils at their ignorant bravado.

The car before them finally leaves, and they drive up to the speaker box. I step in front of it.

"Who the heck are you?" the driver asks.

"What can I get you?" the worker inside asks through the speaker.

I ignore her as I lean my hands on the window frame and stare into the car. When Jesse sees me, he practically jumps out of his seat.

"Holy smokes!" he exclaims.

"Hi there!" I state in the sweetest, cheeriest voice, paired with a scrunch of my nose.

Jesse's friends look panicked.

The one in the driver's seat drops his vape on the ground, startled and confused by the intruder at the window. "Do you work here?"

"I'm Jesse's babysitter."

"Bro, Jesse, your babysitter is hot," one in the backseat says.

"You have a babysitter? How old are you?" the other one in the back asks.

"She's not my babysitter," he explains, annoyed by his friends. "She watches my sister."

"And you. Today. When I agreed to drop you off at a four-hour driver's ed class. How's it going? Looks like you're learning a ton."

"Tara, this is … just what it looks like. We decided to, uh, grab some food."

"Hello? Can I take your order?" the intercom asks.

I lean my elbows on the frame and look at the driver. "You must be the driver's ed teacher."

"What the hell is happening right now?" the driver says out loud, picking his vape off the ground and putting it in his mouth.

"Nice vape. Do you know smoking marijuana can make you impotent? You do know what that means, right?"

"That's not true," one of the boys states while the other snickers.

"It decreases your testosterone levels and is known to lead to erectile dysfunction and decreased libido."

"You're lying," the kid in the driver's seat says.

"You sure about that? Only a guy with a small wiener would do something so lame as to shoplift and scam out a drive-through teller. I also heard you guys like to graffiti the neighborhood and race cars until you almost crash them. These are the lowlifes your uncle was warning you about, right, Jesse?" I stand up and motion toward him. "Let's go."

Jesse looks at his friends like he doesn't know if he should stay or go.

The driver shouts at him, "Get out, man! And take your babysitter with you. She's creepy as fuck."

Jesse storms out of the car and slams the door. The car skids around the drive-through, not ordering or taking any food with it.

Jesse glares at me. I glare right back.

"That was fucking embarrassing!" he declares.

"If that's the type of people you're trying to impress, then you've forgotten your worth," I assert, looking at Jesse with a raised eyebrow. "Is this how you spend your time? Mocking the system and stealing from workers? Do you have no respect for the value of hard-earned money?"

He nervously shifts his feet and mumbles, "It was just a joke. We were just messing around."

"Just a joke?" I reply sternly. "Do you realize that hardworking people depend on their wages to support themselves and their families? What you consider a joke can have real consequences for them. It's not something to be taken lightly."

"I thought you were cooler than this."

"Respect for others and their belongings starts with respecting yourself. It's about understanding the implications of our actions and treating everyone with the consideration and empathy they deserve." I storm toward my car, but stop as another thought pops into my head. "Porky? Is that really how you talk about women?"

Jesse starts to look genuinely remorseful. "That wasn't me. I'm not like that."

"What are you like? You lied to your father, took advantage of me, were going to steal food, and sat back while your friends belittled a woman who had done nothing wrong to you other than not be physically pleasing to your friends' eyes. If you're not that kind of guy, then please tell me who you are. I went to bat for you. I told your dad to trust you. To give you space. And you shit all over it. Did you even have driver's ed today?"

"It was over after an hour. My friends picked me up after. They were going to drive me back in time for you to get me."

"I can add liar to the charges then."

"Tara ..." He stalks behind me as I get to the car. "I'm sorry."

"You're better than this, Jesse. Your dad says you're a good kid, but you go out of your way to prove him wrong."

"My dad doesn't have anything nice to say about me."

"Then, you're not listening." I get in the car and close my door. Jesse follows to the passenger side. "You need to make amends for this, starting with cleaning up your mess."

The drive back to the house is silent. When we get back, I urge

Jesse and Molly to follow me into their dad's shed. I find three buckets. It's not enough for what I need, but they'll do for now. We fill them with water, and I have Molly grab dish soap and large sponges.

Together, we walk the supplies through the field. Jesse carries two water buckets while I have the other one, and Molly has the soap and sponges.

I guide them to the castle in the fields behind their property.

When we get there, I point through the ivy walls toward the filthy stone structure.

"You'll clean the walls of this castle," I instruct firmly. "It's going to take hard work and dedication to make this right."

"You're dishing out punishments now?"

"It's me or your dad, and honestly, I'd take my punishment over whatever he might plan for you."

"What does this stupid place have to do with anything?"

"It was important to your dad once, so you're gonna make it important to yourself now. The choice is yours—start hand-cleaning this entire tower or face your father's wrath and wait for the plethora of punishments he sends your way."

He grabs the sponge and then pauses. "You're really not gonna tell my dad?"

"No. Not because you don't deserve it. Because I don't have the heart to tell your father you failed after one day of freedom. I'll give you one strike. There's no three strikes and you're out though. This is it."

"This isn't just about me. You don't want him to know you messed up too."

"Get to cleaning," I order.

As Jesse starts scrubbing, I start walking.

"Where are you going?" he asks.

"I'm not the one who skipped class. I want this tower cleaned as high as you can reach. Next week, we'll get you a ladder."

"I heard Dad say you were crazy. I didn't believe him."

"Scrub, scrub." I turn to Molly. "And that's how you handle men."

"That's not how you handle my dad."

"Trust me, if I could lock him in this tower and have my way with him, I would." I stop suddenly, realizing my words sounded worse than I intended.

LOVE...IT'S WILD

Actually, it doesn't sound like a bad idea.

Molly doesn't even think twice about my statement. Her young mind isn't tarnished.

Mine, however, is.

And now, all I can think of is a tied-up Rob.

I need to meet a man. Fast. Because I'm starting to get some thoughts, and mounting Rob Bronson isn't a good one.

Thirteen

"LOOK WHO'S BACK ON this side of the state," Melissa sings as we walk into Beans and Leaves—a coffee shop near her business, Lavish Events, a wedding planning and design firm she co-owns with Jillian in Greenwood Village.

"I feel like I've been to every corner of Connecticut over the past week. From Newbury to Castleton and out to the country, I've certainly been racking up the miles."

"Have you been missing the luxuries of being in a real town?" she asks as we get in line.

"I'm actually liking being on the ranch. It's nice. Quiet. I get a lot of reading done. Walks are great. I had to come back though because I'm leading a kickboxing class tonight and my mailbox is overflowing both at work and at home."

I sift through my bag and take out the stack of mail I collected this afternoon. I toss the junk mail and keep anything that looks important.

Melissa takes a step forward in line. "I bet it's great because Rob is at work all day. Nights must be miserable."

"Not really. Rob is so ornery at times; it's fun to push his buttons."

"Hold up. Does this mean you're enjoying playing house with him?"

"Don't make it sound sexier than it is. Although … I did send him a risqué picture of my tatas."

"You sent him a boob pic?" Melissa states loudly, just in time for us to step up to the register.

The barista looks positively frightened.

I ignore my friend's outburst and place my order. "Brown sugar espresso, iced, shaken."

"Decaf vanilla macchiato with oat milk, please. And a decaf caramel Frappuccino," Melissa orders.

We pay for our coffees and step toward the pickup line.

"Okay, so please explain why you sent him a topless photo."

"Total accident. Death by AirDrop."

"You know what Sigmund Freud says—there's no such thing as an accident."

"Freud didn't have access to a touch screen device and a self-facing camera."

The door to Beans and Leaves opens with a ding. Jillian comes in, looking ravishing, as always. Her red hair is up in a bun, and she's wearing a silk dress and blazer, paired with designer heels. Our orders are announced, so I grab mine while Melissa takes the other two, handing the Frappuccino to Jillian.

"Hey, Jillian. Surprised you went with decaf."

"Thanks. I am swamped upstairs with work, but I don't need the added caffeine. I'd be up all night. Hey, Tara. How's playing sexy ranch hand with the broody brother?"

We walk our coffees to a table in the back.

"Good. He saw my nipples."

Jillian gives a blank stare to Melissa. "Do I want to know why?"

Melissa shakes her head. "It's everything you imagine it is. A typical Tara moment. The question you do want to know is, how did he react to seeing them? Which is information I haven't gotten yet."

I sit down at the table and continue to sift through my mail. "Obviously, he loved them. They're spectacular. But, no, he didn't get the wrong impression or anything. Like he always says, nothing can happen between us."

Melissa settles her very pregnant self down at the table and grips her back. "Good. Sex is overrated, especially when you're carrying around a bowling ball. I forgot how uncomfortable the last few weeks of pregnancy are."

Jillian is eyeing Melissa's growing stomach with a look of concern. "You're right. You do forget how awful the end of pregnancy is."

I open up one of my envelopes. "Good thing I don't ever plan on going through that. The change in your body, the spit-up, and changing diapers—"

"Someday, she'll stop lying to herself and realize she's full of shit," Melissa states to Jillian. "Tara would be an awesome mother, and she knows it."

I take the letter out of the envelope. "I'd be the best. Do I really have to explain to you why my ability at mothering   has nothing to do with not needing to be a mother?"

The two friends give each other a look like they're in on a secret that I'm not. I ignore them and read the letter I just pulled out of the envelope.

"Oh my God!" I yelp as I look at the gold emblem at the top and read the exquisitely typed letter.

"What?" Jillian asks.

"I'm getting an award for distinction in the accounting profession."

Melissa smiles big for me. "They have awards for that?"

"They have awards for everything. I was nominated by my boss. I had no idea. It says I'm getting a leadership award from the county for my notable professionalism and distinguished accomplishments within the accounting industry as a whole. The governor will be there."

Jillian boasts, "I always knew you were amazing at your job, and this just confirms it."

"It's a gala at the Wolfson Manor. Perfect. Close to home, and I know exactly what I'm going to wear." I grin as I look at Jillian. "Your V-neck rose-gold gown that gives off the Jessica Rabbit silhouette."

"Might as well. I can't fit into it anymore," she says with a sly wink.

I put the paper down and stare at her with narrowed eyes and a tilt to my head. "Okay, you are definitely keeping something. Decaf coffee. Not fitting into dresses. Passing on wine at dinner at Melissa's house. I know I'm not supposed to ask because it's rude, but screw it.

LOVE...IT'S WILD

We're friends, and I don't care if you think I'm crass. Jillian, are you pregnant?"

Melissa twists her body to her business partner and stretches her fingers out in excitement. "Oh my God. Tara's right. You've been extra tired and complaining about your bra feeling too tight, and you almost vomited when the vanilla-scented candles arrived. You are so pregnant. Say you are. We can have our babies together. Please tell me you're pregnant."

A blush creeps up Jillian's face. "We just hit the ten-week mark, so it's early, but yes!"

Melissa throws her arms around Jillian, and I stand as well, rushing to her side of the table and hugging my friend. I'm surprised to find I'm actually crying with how excited I am for Jillian. It wasn't even a year ago when she was commiserating with me on how horrible the dating scene was. Unlike me, she wasn't looking for anything and truly believed it would never happen again. Here she is, beautiful, glowing, getting married to the love of her life, and having her second baby with him.

Rob could say happily ever after is bullshit, but I have a front row seat to it right here. It isn't a fallacy, and these two women are living proof.

Now, if only the universe would behave and give me my turn.

The ding of the coffee shop door has me turning my head toward the entrance again. This time, instead of being happy for the patron who walked in, I drop to my knees and hide my face between the table and the wall, using Melissa to block me from view.

"What are you doing?" she asks, concerned, as I accidentally kick her in the shin as I crawl away.

I point toward the door. "Patrick just walked in."

"No way!" She spins quickly and looks toward the entrance. "Why are you hiding?"

"Because I'm not wearing something spectacular. Everyone knows the cardinal rule of seeing an ex is, you must look fantastic."

"I see him," Melissa says, and Jillian looks with her.

I start to beg them not to gawk because Patrick would recognize Melissa when I hear, "Melissa Jones? Is that you? I was wondering when I'd run into you."

She shifts her body toward him. "I can't believe you bought a house in Newbury. What kind of psychopath are you?"

Patrick was going in for a hug, but he steps back, now seeming to think twice about it. "Um … oh, you're joking. I think? Um, well, my wife loves the schools there."

"They're good. They're also good in pretty much every other town. If you bought a house in Newbury, why are you in Greenwood Village today?"

"My law practice opened an office here."

Melissa doesn't know how to pretend as well as I do. "You are just infiltrating everyone's world now, aren't you?"

I would high-five my best friend for giving Patrick some flack, but I'm currently crouched on the floor, hiding from him. Ugh, I can't believe I'm hiding. Why exactly am I hiding when I've done nothing wrong?

"Found it!" I declare as I pop up from the floor.

Patrick's eyes widen as he watches me shimmy from behind Melissa's seat and over to my own.

"What were you doing on the floor?" Patrick asks me.

"My contact," I answer easily as I flip my curls behind my shoulder, take my seat, and sip my shaken espresso.

"You don't wear contacts or even glasses. Or do you? I suppose a lot can happen in seven years. Look at me. I'm married with kids," he says, pointing out the obvious.

I glare at him. "So I've noticed."

Patrick looks at me with a shift in his stance. He looks at Melissa and Jillian and then back to me. His hands open and close, like they're sweaty. "Actually, Tara, I'm glad I ran into you. I stopped by your office the other day, but they said you were out of town."

"Why were you at her office?" Melissa asks defensively.

"Just hoped to chat in private. Maybe we could get together sometime. Talk. When we saw each other at the bakery, you seemed off. I just wanted to make sure you were okay," he starts.

His eyes trail down to my ring finger again. There it is. The pity eyes. I hate that look. It's sad and downturned, like my single status is a terrible thing. I'm not happy about it either, but at least I haven't broken my own heart. He's the one who has to walk around with that guilt. While I want him to be miserable with that knowledge, I refuse to let him look down at me the way he is.

I'm no one's victim.

"I am only in town for the afternoon. I'm spending the summer on a ranch," I tell him and see his eyes widen in surprise. "My boyfriend's ranch," I add, and Jillian nearly chokes on her coffee.

"You're living with someone," he states, as if clarifying this information.

"We're very happy. No plans to get married. We don't believe in the arbitrary binding of it all. So barbaric and takes away the romance."

Jillian groans at my words while Melissa seems enthralled with them.

"They're married in the eyes of God," Melissa adds. "That's all that matters."

"Oh dear," Jillian says to herself.

"Tara is killing it at the game of life right now. She's even getting an award for being an awesome accountant," she adds.

I lift the letter I just received. "That's right. The governor is giving me this incredible award at the end of the month. I'll have to pick out a gown and get my boyfriend a tuxedo. He looks so good in a suit."

"He does," Melissa sighs. "Definitely going to look good out of it, too, if you get my drift."

We giggle as Jillian places her head in her hand, and Patrick stares at us, wide-eyed.

"I look forward to meeting him," he says, and Melissa and I stop giggling. "The gala at the Wolfson Manor, right? My office just bought a table. Figured I'd go so I could meet some of the fine people in this county. It'll be good to see you there. I would like you to get to know Victoria, especially since we'll be neighbors of sorts. Speaking of being neighbors, you wouldn't happen to know who I talk to about having a mailbox removed, would you? It seems the previous owners planned on having a giant pig mailbox installed on the property, and now, it's cemented in, and I can't remove it myself."

Melissa laughs out loud while I take a deep breath and shake my head, holding in my own fit of giggles.

"Nope. Sorry."

"All right then. It was good to see you today, and I'll see you again in a few weeks at the gala."

Patrick leaves our table, and I bang my head on it.

"You two are idiots," Jillian states.

I agree and then look up to Melissa. "I feel like you could have been a better friend and bailed me out before I said something stupid."

She's still laughing from the pig mailbox comment. "Girl, if that were the case, I'd have put a muzzle on you when we were twelve."

Jillian leans back and takes a drink. "Now to explain to Rob that he's your live-in lover and he has to escort you to a gala. Oh, and that you're deeply in love. This should be fun."

Fourteen

I'M SURPRISED TO FIND myself driving back to the ranch on Sunday afternoon. I told Rob I'd arrive on Monday morning, yet after the weekend I had, I just wanted to get out of town.

First, it started with the run-in with Patrick at the coffee shop. After that, I went home and tried to get work done, but I was distracted. I had my kickboxing class, which drove up my endorphins and made me feel like I had control of my life again. I went out for happy hour to a pub near the train station. The financial guys head there to unwind after a long week, and I've had success over the years, meeting men. Problem is, I've been on that scene a while now, and I've tapped out most of the resources, and I was not interested in double-dipping.

"Are you a time traveler? Because I can see you in my future," one particularly saucy gentleman asked as he sat on the counter-height seat beside me.

My response was the same as when he'd delivered that pickup line to me two years ago. "You also saw me in your past. We went out to dinner. You ordered the lasagna and drank an entire bottle of wine. I had to drive you home."

He looked at me with a smooshed face. "A bottle of wine's not that much."

LOVE...IT'S WILD

"On a first date, it is, especially when you picked me up. I wasn't planning on going back to your house that night."

"Did we ..."

"The fact that you can't remember the answer to that makes me thankful I took an Uber home."

"I remember that. Yes, we did go out. We had a nice time. That's why I drank so much. I was nervous. Let's pick up where we left off."

I gave him a closed-mouth smile. "We should. Let's start with me going home solo because you were too drunk to continue the night."

I grabbed my purse and walked out of the bar before eight o'clock.

On Saturday, I ran errands around town and found myself constantly looking over my shoulder. The last two times I had run into Patrick, I had been caught off guard. Luckily, I didn't see him, his wife, or their fruit, but I was uncomfortable all day. On edge. I hated it.

At night, I went on a date with a man I'd connected with on a dating app. We met at a French bistro I love and had a great meal, and it was going well until another woman walked in and sat at a table on the other side of the restaurant.

He couldn't take his eyes off of her. I thought it was odd at first, and then it became obvious. After some prodding, I learned she was someone he had gone out with before and liked very much. We spent the next hour discussing all the ways he might be able to get her to notice him again. At the end of the night, the two were at the bar in an intimate conversation while I ate my chocolate soufflé, alone.

I hope they name one of their future children after me.

Sunday morning, I went for a run in the park with my running group. I've connected with some amazing new people and met some great men, but today was not that kind of day. I just wanted to be in my own world, listen to music and get my workout in.

After I showered, I looked around my apartment and felt bored. There was nothing for me to do, and I suddenly felt very cooped up in my sacred space. I packed a bag, hopped in the car, and drove out to the ranch.

I pull up next to Rob's truck and am surprised when he comes out the front door before the kids. He's wearing his jeans that hug his thighs just right and a cotton T-shirt.

"Surprised you're back early." Rob leans against the railing at the top of the stairs.

"Miss me?" I ask with a flirty pop of my hip.

He just looks down and smiles.

Molly comes bolting out the door and calls from the top of the stairs, "Madam Amazing, you're back!"

"I thought we said you wouldn't call her that," Rob admonishes.

Molly laughs. "I agree with Tara. It's fun to push your buttons."

His brows curve inward. "I don't have buttons."

"Yeah, you do, Dad. They're big, grumpy buttons. I love you anyway." She gives him a hug and then runs back inside.

I climb the stairs and meet him at the top. My bags dangle from my shoulder. His fingertips brush my skin as he slides the bags down and takes them in his hand.

"What are you teaching my daughter?"

"To never kneel to old men."

"Who are you calling old?"

"You." I tap him on the nose and brush down his sideburns. "I see some gray. It's very debonaire."

He lets out one of those low grunts I haven't heard in a while. "I can think of one reason why I might be going gray."

"If I'm affecting you after a week in your house, I can't wait to see how the rest of the month goes." I open the door and head inside.

"You and me both," he drawls, following me in.

Jesse comes down the stairs with his sneakers in his hand. He looks shocked to see me here. "Oh. Hey, Tara. Why are you here?"

I give him a reassuring look, letting him know I'm not going to spill his secret. I just hope he keeps up his end of the bargain and stays on the straight and narrow.

I notice that the three of them are all dressed, hair combed, and they look like they're about to go out somewhere. "Are you heading out?"

"There's a carnival in Castleton. Wanna come?" Molly slides her sandals on.

Rob holds his hand out to stop his daughter. "Tara just drove out here. She doesn't want to get in the car again."

The hour-and-a-half drive was long, but I came here because I didn't want to be alone in my apartment. This house is much bigger, and there is plenty of land to roam, but I didn't plan on being here without them.

"Actually, if you don't mind, I'd like to join you. I love carnival rides!"

Molly grabs my hand. "They have the Gravitron, the Zipper that spins you around, and the Beast. Jesse said he'll go on them with me. I'm too scared to go alone."

"I said I like rides, but not to get sick to my stomach," I joke and then look up at Rob. "Unless you mind me crashing your party? You don't get to spend a lot of time with the kids alone. I shouldn't have offered without asking first—"

"We'd love to have you," he croons.

I lift my eyes to the ceiling and grin. "I know. I just wanted to hear you say it."

I make a quick trip to my room to switch out my shoes for canvas sneakers and change my shorts and blouse for a spaghetti-strap floral dress. It's a warm day, and it should be the same well into the evening. I pin my hair up and transfer my things to a crossbody bag.

"Ready!" I state as I meet them back in the foyer.

Rob eyes my sneakers and gazes up my legs. "Do you have an outfit planned for every occasion?"

"By now, you should know I love a good costume change."

I swish past him and head down to his truck. The four of us head to the carnival, which is a forty-minute drive from the house. The kids want to go since their school friends and local community will be in attendance. We get there, and the first thing we do is get funnel cake because it is my absolute favorite fried food ever. The air is ripe with the smell of cotton candy and the sounds of children screaming from laughter.

I go on a few rides with Molly while Jesse talks to his friends with Rob keeping a watchful eye on him. They aren't the same guys from the drive-through, but another set that Molly says are nice kids. I smack Rob in the stomach playfully, pulling his attention away from his son, and usher him to have a little fun. He groans when I take his hand and physically move him toward the carnival games because the man is boorish with the way he's trying to control his son's behavior.

We walk up to the water gun game. Molly and I take seats, and Rob hands the vendor money while Molly and I wait for the other eight seats to be filled. The game begins, and I think I'm going to win until the bell is rung and another station is lighting up.

"Bummer," Molly says as she looks at the kid at the other end of the trailer pick out his stuffed animal.

"You have to have perfect aim before the game begins. You were both off-center and had to correct yourselves because these guns are built to lose."

"You think you can do better? Have at it," I challenge him.

"Come on, Dad! I want to win the stuffed bear. If there're eight players, they give out a prize on the high shelf."

Rob reluctantly takes the seat and hands money over to the vendor. "You do realize I could buy you that bear for cheaper than it's costing us to play?"

I put my hands on his broad shoulders and give them a rub. "Where's the fun in that? Every girl wants a guy to win her a stuffed animal."

His back rises as I press the tips of my fingers into his muscles. This man works hard every day. I wonder if he ever takes care of himself the way he should. Probably not.

Rob leans forward and lines up his shot. I move my hands so as not to mess with the stone-like posture he has as he aims his gun at the bull's-eye.

The game begins.

It's no surprise that the man wins by a landslide. The light above his station dances in a circle, declaring him the winner.

Molly jumps up and points to the shelf. "Can I get the pink bear?" she asks the vendor, and he hands her the stuffed teddy bear.

Molly takes it and hugs it tight to her body. "Thank you, Dad!" she gushes up at him.

Rob's cheeks tinge   as Molly skips away, and we follow her.

I rest my shoulder into his side. "That was the best fifteen dollars you ever spent."

"Worth every penny."

We walk down the row until I see the goldfish game.

"I love this game," I tell Rob. "Before you explain you can buy a fish for fifty cents, I'd like to remind you that it's the excitement of winning the fish that's the best part."

"And then you're stuck carrying the little guy in a plastic bag around the carnival."

"But he'll be happy because he's going home with us."

"What goldfish doesn't want to hang out in a sandwich bag while you stuff your face with cotton candy?"

My jaw drops. "Was that sarcasm I heard? I didn't know you were capable."

"Which fish do you want?" he asks as he takes a step toward the half-wall separating us from the tables of glass fishbowls.

"You're gonna win me a fish?"

He hands the vendor money, and she gives him three ping-pong balls.

He holds up a ball as he tells me, "I thought every girl wanted a guy to win her a prize."

"Glad to know you're listening."

Rob throws a ping-pong ball toward the bowl I pointed to and misses, but then he gets it on the second try.

Molly and I cheer for Rob as he's handed a goldfish in a clear plastic bag.

"What are you gonna name him?" Molly asks me.

I look at the little guy with his downturned mouth and pissed off face. Rob's right. He doesn't look happy to be in the bag.

"I'm gonna call him Bob."

Molly loves the name while Rob looks at me with a less-than-pleased reaction.

I talk to Bob the fish. "You are coming home with us! It's a big, beautiful ranch, but not the kind of ranch you might think. There are no animals or tractors, but there is a cowboy."

I give Rob a wink, to which he just shakes his head with the slightest tilt of his mouth.

Rob, Molly, and I walk through the game vendors. Jesse finds us, and I give Rob an *I told you so* look that I knew Jesse having some freedom would be a good thing. He hung out with friends and then came back to us when he was done.

"Can we go on the Zipper?" Molly asks her dad. "Jesse promised."

"I did," he agrees, and the two hold their hands out to Rob for tickets.

Rob gives them more than they need. "Have fun. Stay together and meet Tara and me back here when you're finished with those."

"Really?" Molly asks in disbelief that they've been handed a roll of tickets and freedom.

"Go before I change my mind."

Molly hands Rob her bear, and the two run off toward a section of rides at the far end of the park. Rob and I start walking in that direction.

I gesture toward the fish and bear in our hands. "Who knew you were a master at carnival games?"

"My brother Jack and I came to this carnival when we were kids. It came to town once a year, and we practically lived here. When we were in high school, we got jobs as game vendors and learned some were rigged."

"Do share your secrets, good sir."

"If I did, I'd have to kill you."

I want to snicker at Rob's cheesy line, but I hold it in. I like this side of him.

He points to the balloon dart game to our left. "The balloons are underinflated, and the darts are dull. You have to throw the dart as hard as you can to break the balloon." He points to another game next to it. One where you throw a ball at jugs. "You have to aim between the jugs at the bottom of the pyramid. They're weighed down extra heavy."

I nod toward the basketball hoop game.

"Damn near impossible. The hoop is oval-shaped, and the backboard is padded."

"I can't picture you as a carny."

"Hardly consider a teenager working at a carnival for two weeks in the summer a carny," he says with a glint in his eyes. "But I know what you're saying. I don't present myself as a fun guy."

I rub the soft fur of the bear in his arm. "You have your moments. It would be nice to see you smile more. You have a great smile."

"Isn't that something I'm supposed to say to you?"

"A compliment now and then would be appreciated."

"I like your smile too."

"You're just saying that because I complimented you."

"No. It's cute with the way it's lopsided. You raise the right side of your mouth a lot. Makes you look like you're up to no good, which I suspect you usually are. You're doing it right now. It's usually followed by a bigger smile, and you look up at the ceiling, like we're all idiots but you enjoy us anyway."

I can't control the way I do exactly what he just said.

The sun begins to set, painting the sky with hues of orange and pink, casting a warm glow over the carnival. The neon lights on the various rides and game stalls start to come to life, creating a vibrant and magical atmosphere. The air is filled with laughter, screams of delight, and the distant jingles of carousel music.

And our eyes are locked, as we walk and talk, like we're the only people in the park.

"Rob? What are you doing here?" a woman says, breaking the spell between us. She has short brown hair and dark eyes, and she's holding hands with a man who is fit, balding, and looking very uncomfortable with seeing Rob here at the fair.

"I'm with the kids," Rob tells her, stiffly. "I thought you were in Niagara Falls."

She motions toward the man she's with. "Mike and I got back this afternoon. You should have told us you were coming. Where're Molly and Jesse?"

Rob nods toward the direction the kids went. "On rides. They'll be surprised you're here."

The tension pouring out of Rob's body is palpable from where I'm standing. I look at him and then to her, wondering what kind of awkward standstill is happening.

I cut in and introduce myself. "I'm Tara." I extend a hand.

The woman takes it awkwardly, and then I shake the man's hand too.

Then, I hold up my fish. "This is Bob."

The woman looks curiously at my fish and then back at me. "I'm Christine, and this is Mike."

I know these names and have heard them quite a bit over the past week. "Are you Molly and Jesse's mom?" I ask like I just met a rock star.

"I am. And you are?"

"Tara's helping me with the kids this summer."

Christine looks surprised. "You're the babysitter. I was expecting a teenager."

"She's an accountant. And a friend. Who's spending the summer with us."

"I pictured someone else altogether. By spending the summer, I assume that means you're sleeping at the house." Christine shifts as she drops Mike's hand and looks at the teddy bear. "Did you win that for Tara?"

"The bear is for Molly," Rob replies.

"Cute." She turns to me. "He was always good at carnival games. I used to leave here with an armful of stuffies."

"Too bad you're stuffie-less tonight," I comment and then see Jesse and Molly jogging toward us.

"Mom!" Molly exclaims as she throws her arms around her mother.

Jesse looks just as confused to see Christine as Rob did a moment ago.

"You're supposed to be away," Jesse comments as he hugs his mom and refuses Mike's handshake.

Christine explains her change in travel plans. Rob just stands here, silent and observing her talking to their kids. The divorce must have been a contentious one because Rob, while civil, has that steel persona of his up.

"Do you guys want to hang with us for a little bit?" Christine asks the kids, and Rob's entire body tenses beside me.

"Actually, we were just about to go on a ride," I state.

"Mike is afraid of heights, so as long as it's not something high up, we'll join you," Christine offers.

"Drats," I say. "We're going to the Ferris wheel. You ready, kids?"

"That's a shame. We were just going to head out anyway. It was a long drive back from the falls today." Christine holds out her arms to Molly. "I'll see you next weekend."

"Later." Jesse storms off toward the Ferris wheel.

Molly gives her mom a hug and then chases after Jesse to join him. "Wait for me!" That girl will not let a ride be ridden without her presence. Rob and I exchange awkward pleasantries with Christine and Mike and then follow the kids.

The Ferris wheel itself stands tall against the backdrop of the darkening sky, adorned with colorful lights that shimmer and dance. The faint sound of creaking metal as the wheel turns has me laying a hand on my stomach and taking a deep breath.

Jesse and Molly get in the first available carriage. Rob and I step into our designated one, and I feel a mix of anticipation and a touch of nervousness as we ascend slowly into the twilight while the ride allows for more passengers to get on and off the ride.

"Thank you for not letting the kids go with Christine and Mike," he says as we lift higher and stop.

"She didn't even have the audacity to tell her own kids she was in town. Don't worry. I got your back."

The gentle breeze carries a hint of coolness, causing a delightful shiver to run down my spine. I glance over at Rob, and our eyes meet, exchanging a silent understanding.

"He was my friend. You don't make friends as an adult, but we became close. Mike used to come over every Sunday to watch the game."

"Did they have an affair?"

"She says they didn't."

"Do you believe her?"

"Does it matter?"

"Yeah. If she left you, it's nice to know there's a reason."

Rob snakes his arm on the cart behind my head. His other resting on the bar in front of us. He lets out a deep groan. "She left because of me."

We sit for a moment, the carriage moving to a higher level every minute. I don't try to fill the silence. Rob's forehead creases, like he's working through something in his head.

"You said something the night of the wedding. Take a chance. Do something spontaneous. Christine used to tell me that was our problem. I wasn't spontaneous enough."

"Trust me, you do enough to keep a woman on her toes."

"I'm all the things you accuse me of being. Grumpy, too on top of my kids. I forgot how to be fun. I didn't try hard enough. I didn't fight for her when I felt her slipping away. It killed my marriage."

"That's bullshit," I declare. "I don't know who you were back then, but I can tell you that whatever it was, it wasn't solely your fault. You're a great father, Rob."

As we reach the peak of the wheel, we're greeted with a breathtaking view of the moon. I look at it with a sense of appreciation—until I look down at the carnival below. The vibrant lights create a mesmerizing mosaic of colors, illuminating the surrounding area. The distant sounds of laughter and music fade into the background, and for a heartbeat, I forget that we're high up in a death trap that has a grave possibility of plummeting to the ground.

I lean back in my seat and close my eyes, feeling the cool metal against my fingertips. The soft hum of the wheel's mechanics reverberates through the structure, causing my nerves to be at an all-time high.

Rob's voice breaks my internal dialogue of the many ways this piece of metal could break. "Are you okay?"

"Not the biggest fan of this ride, especially when I can't vouch for the engineering of it. It's like being in a plane. I know it physically moves people from one place to the other, but I can't understand how."

"The girl who I caught when she fell out of a tree is afraid of heights," he states as if he's baffled.

"I don't like things I can't control."

He puts his hand on my shoulder and pulls me closer to him. His other hand lies over my fingers that are gripping the handlebar.

"Look at me, Tara. Don't close your eyes because you'll expect the worst. Just look at me. Breathe."

I turn to him, and it takes me a minute to ignore the fact that we're at the highest peak of the ride. I concentrate on the chestnut eyes before me and the way the moonlight reflects in the caramel accents.

"Breathe," he reminds me, moving his lips to do just what he told me to do.

I follow his actions and take long, deep breaths. I can feel his breath against my mouth, and I watch as he drinks mine in. I look at his lips and wonder what they taste like. I could kiss him right now.

I want to kiss him so damn badly that my body aches. I swallow and look back up to his eyes, which are trained on mine.

"This helps," I breathe. "How does this thing even stay upright? It feels unnatural."

"It's all about force. The push and pull. The key lies in centripetal force, which acts on a rotating object, pushing it toward the center of the rotation."

"Push and pull, huh? Kind of sounds like our relationship."

"It certainly does."

We share a smile, a connection strengthened by the beauty of this fleeting moment. Perhaps because we're sitting so close or because he's being so personal, I opt to ask him a question I don't know if he'll answer willingly. Still, I ask it anyway.

"Do you miss her?" I start, and he looks at me for clarification. "Christine. Do you miss her?"

"No," he answers easily. "I miss the family we had. I wasn't a good husband, and she left because of that. I'm just not cut out to be someone's forever."

As we descend back to solid ground, he asks me his own question. "Do you miss Patrick?"

"I miss the girl I was before he left."

There's a startle in his eyes, like what I said was the wrong thing. Something unfathomable yet completely relatable. He looks back at me and opens his mouth. Nothing comes out at first. I wait. It kills me to wait, but I feel like what Rob is about to say is important, and I don't want to miss it.

As he stares at his hand on mine, I hold my breath. My heart starts to thump in my chest as we rise back to the top. When his eyes meet mine again, he looks like he's changed his mind on what he was about to say.

"Thank you."

His words might not be what I thought he'd say, but I'm taken aback nonetheless.

A lock of my hair falls across my face. Rob lifts his hand and moves it across my cheek and tucks it behind my ear. His hand doesn't leave the soft skin though. Instead, he rests his knuckles against my jaw. He stares at his hand on my skin. If he regrets touching me, he doesn't make a move to change.

I like the way I feel in his arms. There's something about the way he's holding me, protectively, that feels… right.

Our eyes lock, and while the ride is moving faster now, time seems to slow as we move closer to each other.

A surge of electricity courses through me. Perhaps it's the chill that comes from the breeze caused by our movements, but I feel exhilarated. No, it's not the breeze. It's him.

His hold.

His stare.

The way he only speaks his truth and if he's thanking me, it's for good reason.

Now, it's my turn to look startled by a comment. "For what?"

"Not backing down from me when I was so hard on you."

"How could I when you think I'm so desirable?"

He sighs and drops his hand. A smile graces his face, and it's beautiful. "Why do I tell you things?"

"Because you love me," I answer with the perfect hint of sarcasm. "I'm very easy to love."

"I bet." He sounds like he means it.

The ride comes to an end. Jesse and Molly are waiting for us. I take Molly's hand, and Rob puts his arm around Jesse. My heart is quivering over the moment spent with Rob. It feels as if there's something intense brewing, and yet his past words reverberate through my core and echo in my ears.

"You and I can't happen."

Those words are powerful, and there's strength behind them. Desirable I might be, but I'm not the kind of woman Robert Bronson wants. He's not what I want either.

He's not romantic. He's not meant for forever. He's not mine.

Even after a moment like we just had, where I imagined, for just a second, he could be.

"Let's go get some real dinner," I say to my summer family. "Funnel cake was good and fun, but we need something real."

Suddenly, I wonder if I'm talking about something other than what we need to eat.

Fifteen

"HOW MUCH LONGER ARE you going to make me do manual labor?" Jesse asks at the top of the ladder, where he's cleaning the castle walls.

We've resorted to officially calling it *the castle* while we fix it up. Jesse is working on the outside, doing a spectacular job with the supplies we have. Molly is cleaning the inside while I've been elbow deep in weeding.

I found the keys to a four-wheeler Rob keeps in the shed, so we've been driving pails of water back and forth to the site. Jesse is more than happy to make the trips since driving a four-wheeler is hella fun.

"Don't act like you're not enjoying this. It's nice out here, and it beats going to work with your dad—or better yet, having me tell him you lied about driver's ed."

Jesse grunts at me, and I laugh.

"Besides, Molly and I are out here too. You hear us complaining?"

"That's because you're both equally weird."

The long ponds in the front of the castle are nearly cleared out. I've been throwing the weeds into the nearby woods. My hands are hot and sweaty under the rubber gloves I'm wearing, but it's better than ruining my manicure, and I have no idea if what I'm pulling out is poison ivy.

"It looks good in here!" Molly sings from inside the upstairs room.

She's been sweeping for the last hour. Before that, we gave her the leaf blower and let her go to town with dusting out the place, removing cobwebs, scaring off a few mice, and getting rid of the general muck that had accumulated over the years of neglect. She loved the task, and the inside rooms were cleaned up quickly.

There's still some charge left in the leaf blower, so I use it to remove excess foliage around the paths leading up to the wooden door. The machine eventually dies, so I go back to weeding.

The overgrown shrubs are something that will wait another day. I may need a chain saw.

It's only been a few days of making improvements, and the transformation is already incredible.

"Dad is going to love it!" Molly beams as she sweeps debris to the outside of the castle.

"No, he's not," Jesse scoffs, and the two of us look up at him. "He never comes out here. When we first bought the house, he was over here all the time with his sketch pad, but since he and Mom broke up, he doesn't even look in this direction."

I pause my weeding and think about what he said. "Did he plan to reimagine the castle for your mom?"

"Mom hates this place. I don't mean the castle. I mean the entire ranch. I think …" He pauses and then shakes his head, as if what he was going to say was inappropriate. He looks over at Molly and then shrugs. "Never mind."

Molly rolls her eyes. "I'm ten, but I'm not an idiot. I know what you're gonna say, Jesse." She looks over at me and explains, "He thinks Mom convinced Dad to buy the ranch, so when she left him, Dad would have a place to go."

My head snaps to Jesse. "Seriously?"

His eyes widen at Molly. "How do you know that?"

"I heard you say it to Mom once. You're not exactly quiet when you're arguing. I know a lot of your theories."

"They're not theories. You were too young to hear the fights and see the events as they unfolded," he bites back.

"I heard more than you think, Jesse."

"Then, you know Mom didn't like it here when Dad said he wanted to buy it. She told him no, and then suddenly, she changed her mind. Even after they bought it, she came once. Dad took us here alone. He fixed up this house while watching us. Mom was never here. A few months later they separated. Do you get what I'm saying?"

I blow out a loud breath. Watching your parents go through a tumultuous divorce must be horrible. It's no wonder Jesse's so damn moody. It's a surprise Molly isn't. These kids have been privy to too many of their parents' secrets.

"You two know that just because your parents couldn't be a good husband and wife to each other doesn't mean they're not amazing parents to you, right?" I tell them.

Molly nods. "I love my mom and dad. I wish they were still together, but I'm okay with the way things are. They fought a lot. Maybe they don't talk now, but it's better than the arguing. I was young, but I remember that."

Jesse dips his sponge in the bucket, drenching it in the water and then squeezing it. He repeats the motion a few times. The six-year age difference between them is evident in the way they process their new lifestyle and memories of the past.

"What exactly is this place going to be?" Jesse asks.

I shrug. "I don't know. What I do know is, it's gonna be spectacular."

Jesse nods his head while Molly scrunches her nose.

"I thought it was gonna be a playhouse?"

"It could be, but you're going to outgrow that soon. We'll think of something awesome. Maybe we'll even see what your dad planned for it to be. In the meantime, this will be our little secret."

The days pass quickly as we spend the better part of our week working on the castle. While Jesse's at driver's ed, Molly and I head to the garden center and pick out new plants for the garden and learn the ponds are going to take a lot more work to make them habitable for fish. By Thursday night, the three of us are bone-tired.

"You guys are sunburned," Rob comments at dinner.

Tonight, he made a meatloaf when he came home, and I enjoyed helping, as the recipe reminded me of baking, except instead of flour, it's chopped meat.

"We were out in the fields all day. Found the keys to your four-wheeler and had some fun with it," I explain.

Rob twists his mouth. "Be careful on that thing. It's not a toy."

"I know ... *Dad*," I state sarcastically. "Be happy we were busy and not inside, playing on iPads."

"You're gonna run out of gas. I only have two canisters in the shed."

"We know," Molly answers him. "We went to the gas station, and I refilled them."

Rob lifts a brow at his daughter. "You learned how to pour gas?"

"Tara showed us both. I did the car, and Molly did the canisters."

Rob looks at Jesse, impressed. "How is driver's ed going?"

"Good. Tara took me driving after class today. She said I'm a natural."

"You let Jesse drive your convertible?" Rob's surprise is evident.

I swallow my meatloaf and explain, "Yeah. His class was only an hour, so I let him drive us home. It's all back roads anyway."

His fork waves in the air. "With Molly in the car?"

"She was buckled up." I push my fork against his and lower it. "When Jesse gets his license, he's gonna drive her around eventually."

"I'd prefer it's after he has a few hundred hours in."

Jesse drops his fork on the table in annoyance. I give him a staredown.

"Pick that back up. Your dad made this meal for you. Just because he's worried about Molly getting hurt doesn't mean he's a horrible person."

Jesse picks his fork up and starts eating again.

Rob glowers at me. "What else did you guys do today?"

I shrug. "Just driver's ed, a lesson, and hung out outside."

Rob shifts his gaze from me to Molly and Jesse as we sit and eat like the tired beings we are. "Jesse, I'd like you to come with me tomorrow. There's no driver's ed, and I have something I want you to do on the jobsite."

"Be the coffee errand boy?" he responds as if that were the worst job in the world.

"There's some pipe being laid. Thought you might like to learn how to use the equipment."

"I can solder?" His eyes light up.

"You can try, and we'll see how good you are."

"That's awesome!" He beams, and Rob looks pleased that he made his son so happy.

Molly and I wink at each other. Looks like some distance from one other is doing these two some good.

After dinner, I'm sitting in my room, looking over some spreadsheets, and watching Bob the fish swim around his new bowl, when there's a knock on my opened door. Rob is standing there with a crystal glass in one hand and a glass of wine in the other.

I slide my glasses off my face and look up at him. "Double fisting it tonight?"

"I was going out to the deck to have a drink and thought some company might be nice. You wear glasses?"

I look down at the frames in my hand. "They're blue light lenses to protect my eyes when I'm working. I stare at a computer a lot."

"You should wear them more often. You look nice in glasses." His comment makes me blush. He holds up the glass for me. "Care to join me?"

Rising from the chair, I hold up a finger. "Just give me a minute."

"There's no need to change." His comment gives me pause at the fact that he knew what I was about to do. "You're planning on changing out of your comfortable clothes, and there's no need." He lifts the glass of wine in the air and offers it to me. "It's just a drink. Not a marriage proposal."

With a smile, I slide on a pair of flip-flops. "Pinot grigio?" I ask. When he nods, I take the glass out of his hand and have a sip. "Like heaven in a glass."

He chuckles as we walk through the downstairs hallway and out the front door. The late evening sun is on the last stages of setting. The mountains in the foreground are majestic in the distance. I stand by the railing and breathe in the sweet summer air. I like the country. It's agreeing with me in more ways than I thought possible. It almost feels like I breathe better out here.

Turning around, I see Rob has taken a seat in one of the white chairs. His bourbon is resting on the arm of the chair. He leans back and looks completely content on his porch, looking over his land. I look at his jeans, all snug and masculine, then down to my terry-cloth shorts that are barely peeking out from my oversize sweatshirt.

"Do you ever put on shorts?" I ask him. "I bet you have great legs."

His eyes dart down to my calves before he answers, "No. Don't start buying me shorts just so you can make me wear them in some sort of sick fashion show you have in your head to get me to dress more comfortably. I like jeans. They're easy, reliable. I can't get them too dirty, and there's no task I can't do in them."

"I bet I could think of a few," I tease and listen to him grunt quietly. "What's the craziest thing you've ever done?" I ask him.

"Bought this house."

"You know what I mean."

Rob grins as he takes a sip, then licks his lips, his tongue sliding slowly across them. He angles his head back and tilts it mischievously. "I can't tell you."

"Why not?"

"You're gonna get all excited and do that clapping thing and jump up and down."

I look down at my hands and grimace. "I don't do a clapping thing."

"Tara, there're a lot of things I bet you don't even realize about yourself."

I place my wineglass on the floor and then shove my hands behind my back and lean against them. "Promise I won't react with a round of applause. Now, tell me the big secret. It'd better be good because the lead-up is too much."

He groans as he rolls his head and looks back at me. "I arranged a flash mob for my high school girlfriend."

My hands fly out from behind me, and I clap my hands, then squeal, jumping up and down. "That's the cutest thing I've ever heard."

"You're doing that thing with your hands," he observes.

"Who cares? You made a flash mob. Please tell me all about it." I get my glass off the floor and lean against the rail as I wait for him to tell me this story.

His shoulders square off, and his chest puffs out. A gleam of pride sparkles in his eyes. "It was pretty cool, if I do say so myself."

"What song?" I motion my hand in a circle for him to continue, desperately needing more information.

" 'Everybody (Backstreet's Back)' by the Backstreet Boys. Please don't squeal again."

Smashing my lips together, I do a spin at this news and stomp my foot on the painted porch. "You have to show me the video."

"There is none."

"Bullshit. Someone filmed it. I'll find it. If there is one thing I will do before I leave this ranch, it is getting my hands on that tape. And to think, you're a BSB fan. I never would have taken you for one."

"It wasn't the whole song. Just a small snippet of it. My girlfriend at the time wanted a proposal, and that was way before they became a thing. I asked her best friend to come up with some choreography, and she did better—she had her dance troupe help out."

"Robert Bronson, you are a romantic."

"I was also a horny teenager who wanted to make his girlfriend happy. Trust me, it wasn't as big of a deal as you're making it out to be. I shouldn't have told you."

I bite my lower lip and look at Rob—a man with a strong jawline and thick, dark hair with his intense, piercing eyes convey a depth of experience and resilience. Those eyes seem to hold a world of stories within them. Surprisingly, not all of them are filled with disappointment.

"I bet she was a puddle of goo for you."

He looks down and smiles. "She was happy. It was kind of fun too. Never did anything like that again."

"Why not?"

"You get older, and you lose your ability to make a fool out of yourself without caring."

LOVE...IT'S WILD

"Looks like you do know how to be unpredictable, so don't ever let someone tell you otherwise. Once a romantic, always a romantic."

My comment causes the lightness in his aura to dissolve and his steel to creep back up his face. I see it in the way his fists open and close, and then one hand moves up to his mouth as he starts to become lost in thoughts. I refuse to let him morph into the version of himself that becomes closed off.

"I'm happy to know you're not a serial killer," I add and take a drink.

His eyes flicker up to mine. "Was that a possibility?"

"You do have a room in your basement under lock and key, and even your kids don't know what's inside of it."

His brows rise with a questionable stare. "You tried to get into my workshop?"

"Of course I did. There's no way in, so I wasn't successful. What's behind the door of mystery, Rob?"

"None of your business."

A deep V forms on my forehead. I can feel it digging into my skin. "Now, I'm starting to wonder if you are hiding something criminal down there."

"I'm not ..." He pauses with annoyance and then leans forward. "It's my personal space. A man is allowed one off-limits area in his own home."

My hand flies to my mouth, and I gasp. "You have a sex chamber. Oh my God, that's your red room of pain down there, you kinky son of a gun."

"My red room of—" He stands up and tries to wrap his head around my presumption. "I don't have a sex dungeon, Tara."

My excitement dies, and my shoulders fall. "That's unfortunate. I was picturing leather walls and velvet curtains. Maybe a crop and a belt or two."

"Seriously, woman, you're mad."

"Then, what's down there?"

He points at me. "Let it go."

"Never. If you don't tell me, I'm gonna assume the worst."

"Tara—"

"Taxidermy station for the animals you kill when you're bored."

"It's not—"

"You have every McDonald's Happy Meal toy ever given to you since you were a kid, and you play with them in a pink padded room."

"You think I'm the crazy one—"

"You keep wax figures of your favorite celebrities and have tea with them each night."

"You're quite possibly the most—"

"Torture chamber," I state, and he stops from trying to speak. "If it's not for pleasure, it's for pain."

He halts all movement and blinks at me as if I'm positively insane. His momentary silence has me wondering if I finally hit the nail on the head and Rob is indeed a psychopath with a torture chamber in his basement.

Wait. No. Rob's not crazy. I'm the one with the overactive imagination, and I warned him I'd assume the worst. I don't know what it is, but the truth is, he does have something downstairs he wants to be kept a secret.

"I don't have a torture chamber in my basement." His words are ripe with conviction.

"Prove it," I challenge.

His eyes dance across my face, cautious and scrutinizing, as he tries to decipher if my intentions behind wanting to know his secret are well intentioned. There's a discernible wariness in his expression, a hesitation that hangs in the air.

He exhales a breath as he concedes. "Come with me."

Sixteen

I PRACTICALLY SKIP BEHIND him as he heads down the stairs to the basement. The lights in the game room remain off, yet some light from the Pac-Man game and the neon sign that sits on the far wall illuminates the space.

We walk to the back of the basement. Rob stops by the door of mystery and produces a key ring from his pocket.

My palms are sweaty as I wait to see what lies behind the door. I rub my hands together and look at him as he slides the key into the lock and turns.

When he opens the door, he lets me walk in first. The lights are off, so I have to wait until he flips the switch to see what is in here.

Art.

The room is a private art studio with walls adorned in a kaleidoscope of colors from various canvases of work. Easels stand like silent sentinels, each displaying a canvas in different states of transformation. Some are mere sketches, awaiting an artist's touch. Others, like the piece closest to me, is of a woman. Her back is in view, and she's surrounded by a field of flowers.

The air carries a faint scent of paint and freshly dyed pigments. Brushes, palette knives, and other tools are meticulously organized on a sturdy wooden table. Jars of water and cleaning solvents cover the space.

Shelves and drawers house an array of art supplies—pencils, pastels, charcoals, and a multitude of paints in every shade imaginable. Against the wall, more half-finished canvases are stacked like soldiers, forming a vibrant tapestry of potential masterpieces.

This studio is more than a physical space.

It's a creative realm where an artist's imagination can breathe.

Where Rob's imagination can exist.

I walk over to a painting leaning up against the wall and look down at it. It's a landscape photo. A gorgeous sun sets over the field as a child runs through the grass. She has messy, dark hair and wears overalls with a daisy in her hand.

"That's Molly," I state. "She looks so young."

Rob stands beside me and looks down at her gorgeous smile in the photo as she laughs in the field. "She was six when I painted that one. We'd just bought the property, and I had this image from the first weekend we were here. This was how she looked when she first played outside. When she knew this land was her home."

It's a gorgeous portrait with precise brushstrokes, making her look almost lifelike. It reminds me of the one in my room.

"You made all of these?" I ask, walking to where a painting of the house is hanging on the wall.

He nods. "This is my studio. Are you upset it's not a torture chamber?"

"I'm impressed. But I don't understand. Why keep it under lock and key?"

"It's my private space. I don't like people in here. My hobby hasn't always been well received. It's not a cool thing to do when you're a young man. As a husband, it ate up my personal time, and it took up too much space in our home. I have way too many half-finished pieces. Not everyone appreciates what I do down here."

"The kids should see this. They'd be so proud."

"They've seen my art."

"Like the one hanging in my room?" I add. "It's stunning. I noticed it when I moved in. You have talent, Rob. True talent. Don't hide it behind a closed door."

"It's just landscapes and some people. The human form is mesmerizing. The way people move. The whisk of wind moving through hair or the pain that can be seen through a line on your forehead."

I temporarily forget where I am as I become enraptured in him. For a man who seems very closed off, he sees a lot more than he lets on.

"Have you done any nudes?"

"Why is that where your mind goes?"

"Because all artists work on nudes." I traipse around the room, letting my finger linger on the wood of an easel. "Where did you train?"

"I took some classes as a kid, but I'm mostly self-taught."

"Even more impressive."

In the corner, there's a seating area. A small sofa with large cushions.

I drape my body across it, resting the back of my hand against my forehead. "Paint me."

He slides his hands in his pockets. "I'm not the royal portrait painter. You can't commission me."

My hands find the hem of my sweatshirt. I lift it over my head and discard it onto the floor.

"What are you doing?" he asks, a picture of confusion.

His eyes widen as I reach around my back and unhook my bra. I take that off, too, and fling it toward an easel, where it lands on the edge of it. It makes me giggle.

"Don't be shy. You already saw these beauties in the selfie I sent you."

My hair is up in a bun, so I pull the hair tie out and let my curls spill down my shoulders and stop at the top of my exposed breasts. My nipples harden in the cool air of the room.

"*Paint me like one of your French girls*," I say in a breathy voice.

"This is not *Titanic*, and I'm not Jack."

"I love how you understand all of my pop culture references. Come on. Paint me. Please."

Rob stares at my clavicle, and then his eyes roam down my chest and stop on my breasts. His pupils dilate, and I suddenly feel more naked than I am. It's as if he's undressing my soul with his gaze, and I'm completely vulnerable. I didn't truly think this through—another one of my spur-of-the-moment bad decisions—but now that I'm bare, I want nothing more than for him to stare at me and paint me just as I am.

With the clearing of his throat, he pulls a chair over to the space between an easel and the sofa. Grabbing a sketch pad and a few pieces of charcoal, he moves a small table over as well and takes a seat.

Rob takes one look at my chin and shoulder and starts sketching.

I stay still as I watch him work.

Brawny fingers grip the charcoal and rub fast on the page as he looks up at me, brow furrowing and a haze of concentration and adulation. His eyebrows lift slightly, revealing a sense of intrigue and eagerness. His shoulders square off, and his chest pushes forward as he looks at me and back down at the page, over and over, his hand viciously tracing and sketching, moving the black along the white to bring me to life on the page.

There's a natural magnetism to his movements. A fluidity that seems to pull my soul in his direction. He might be looking at me like I am the artwork, but watching him in action is the true masterpiece. His actions become more purposeful, his gestures powerful and expressive as his hand dances along the paper.

There's a darkening to his gaze when he stares at my breasts, and my nipples harden under his stare. His legs widen as he shifts his hips and takes a deep inhale. His teeth grip his lower lip, and those nostrils flare. His eyes are on my body, and it's quite possibly the sexiest I've ever felt in my life, and I'm still completely covered from the waist down.

"I have a favor to ask you," I start.

His eyes remain fixed on the art while he simultaneously pays attention to my words.

"Thought that's what I was doing right now. First, you asked to see my secret space, and then you asked me to paint you."

"I need a date," I state and watch his hand slow down considerably from the rush of drawing.

He's now listening more than he's working.

"Not a real date per se. You see, I'm getting an award for my job, and I need to bring a guest. I know I could find someone to go with me, but I made a big mistake. I ran into my ex and might have told him that I was living with my lover because it was easier than telling him I was still a spinster who hadn't found anyone to love me back."

He stops what he's doing and looks up at me. "Might have told him you lived with your lover or you *did* tell him?"

"I did. And I said his name was Rob. So, pretty much, I told him you were my boyfriend. You don't have to go. I just thought that maybe if you did, it would save me from having to find me a man to swoop in and come to this thing with me. And pretend his name was Rob because the odds of me finding someone is slim, so he'd have to fake it. I can't even find a decent guy to take me to dinner, much less magically find someone to play my *in love with me* boyfriend."

"I have to pretend to be in love with you?"

"Just for the night. For my dignity. I know you think it's me playing games, but I assure you—"

"I'll do it."

"You will?"

"I know what it's like to have your ex look at you with pity in their eyes. I'd much rather have a woman look at me the way you are right now."

"How am I looking at you?" I breathe.

"Like I've finally done something right."

I smile bigly. "Thank you. I'll behave."

"If you did that, you wouldn't be you," he says with a grin, and if I could melt off the chair, I would. "Just promise me one thing. Don't call yourself a spinster ever again. You're gorgeous, brave, smart, and you have the wildest sense of humor of anyone I've ever met."

"You forgot desirable."

"Very desirable."

The magnetic pull he has on me is heightened with the way those warm eyes hold mine in a silent conversation. We've found our common ground. I'm not entirely sure what it's made of, but we're standing on it—together.

"You moved."

I blink at him, confused by his comment. "Huh?"

"You moved your body."

"I did?"

I try to correct myself, but he shakes his head.

LOVE...IT'S WILD

"To the right. Down. Just shift slightly to the right—no, not that much."

He tries to give me direction. I follow, but he doesn't seem to be happy with what I'm doing.

"Here," he says, getting up from his seat and walking over to me.

Rob kneels in front of me and places his hands on my shoulders. The calluses are coarse against my skin as he angles me just right. I look up at him and am startled by the intensity in his eyes. My chest rises, forcing my nipples to brush against the cotton of his shirt. His hands squeeze my shoulders, and I shiver.

That hedonistic, daring mouth that spews the meanest and sweetest things is so close to mine. I smell the musk of his masculine scent and revel in the way his body makes my skin feel. Warm, empowered.

I imagine him kissing me. I can almost taste the mint of his tongue and harsh feel his hands tugging at my hair. If I were seated anywhere else, I'd adjust my hips because the pressure mounting between them is palpable.

Rob leans forward just a touch. His eyes darken as he stares at my mouth. I let my tongue peek out and dart across my lower lip, and my teeth bite down, causing him to let out a deep, low, gravelly sound.

It's not a grunt of annoyance.

It's a prayer.

His hand dances up the side of my neck, and I shiver at the contact. His thumb traces a tender line up my vein. Its featherlight touch is overpowered by the roughness on his palm, touching me with tenderness.

My breath hitches. A subtle gasp escapes my mouth, betraying the fluttering excitement within my body. The proximity between us is too close for a clothed man, and a woman radiating with sexual energy. He must sense my desire. It's ripe in the air and pouring off of my body.

He dips his head ever so slightly, closing the gap. Our breaths mingle, the teasing praise of a kiss scorching the air and setting fire to the moment.

It's now or never.

We have to decide whether we jump into it or douse the flames before we scorch the earth.

"Dad!" Molly calls, and we jump up.

"Shit," he says, and I know he's not worried about her seeing his art room. He's concerned about the half-naked woman he was sketching.

"Go. I'll get dressed and lock the door."

He sprints out of the room, and I'm left alone. My bra and shirt are put on quickly, but I take a moment to see what he was drawing. It's not nearly done, and yet it's gorgeous.

My breasts are defined with great detail. He is beyond talented.

I look down at the table beside where he was sitting. Torn sketch papers peek out of a pile. There's a familiar stone structure on it that has me pulling the paper out of the pile. It's a rendering of the castle, the same building we've been restoring. Behind it is another and yet another, all of Rob's plans to re-create the tower into a private space.

Now, I have his plan. If I put enough effort into it, I might just be able to make it happen.

Seventeen

I'M IN MY ROOM in my apartment. Usually, I'd be asleep, but I've been tossing and turning tonight. My body has become accustomed to the quiet of the ranch through the week, and now, my apartment in Newbury feels too loud.

My body is also becoming used to being around Rob. Wanting him in more ways than I should. Yes, he's attractive, and I'd love to jump into bed with him. He's shown signs he's interested too. And yet he has a way of putting up that steel curtain.

If I could solder it down, I would.

Unfortunately, I don't have the tools to do so.

Yesterday was a prime example. After our near kiss in the art room, I would have sworn the electricity between us would be sizzling. It was the complete opposite. Business as usual and a bite to his voice. It's as if nothing ever happened.

Maybe it didn't. Maybe my flight-of-fancy mind is conjuring up romantic scenarios.

My cell phone rings, and I nearly bolt out of bed at the sound. I roll over and look at the clock. It's after one o'clock in the morning. No one calls me at this hour. They know I'm either out at the bar or asleep, and if I'm asleep, I'm dead to the world.

I pick my cell phone up off the nightstand and see Jesse's calling me.

"Everything okay?" I ask with urgency.

"Tara," he starts, and I can hear the plight in his tone. The sixteen-year-old, who has quite the bravado when it comes to his own teenage angst, sounds like a young boy as he pleads on the other end of the phone, "I need your help."

"Emotionally or physically?"

"Please, come get me."

My feet hit the carpeted floor in seconds. "I'm on my way."

Jesse has called my cell phone before. Molly and I were late to pick him up from his driver's ed class, so he called to see why we were running late. I've even received a text or two from him while we were working on the castle, confirming what supplies were needed before driving the four-wheeler back from the shed.

We've had many conversations in person over the past week especially. I've learned he's actually a funny kid, smarter than I assumed, and he really likes to talk about history and world politics.

What I've never heard was him sounding so desperate.

I keep him on the line while I get dressed quickly, slide on a pair of shoes, and head out the door.

My engine revs as I hightail it out of my driveway and head toward him.

"It's gonna take me a while. I'm in Newbury, but I'm on my way. Where exactly are you?"

He drops me a location pin, and I enter the information into my navigation. It says I'll be there in forty minutes. He doesn't want to talk, but agrees to stay on the line. Sometimes, I hear voices around him, but mostly, it's just silence and his breathing coming through the receiver. I hope his cell phone doesn't die.

My foot hits the gas, and I drive faster than normal as I speed on the highway toward him. This would not be an ideal night to get pulled over. I'd be let go with a speeding ticket, but there is no time to waste.

I need to get to Jesse.

The address he sent is a house on the outskirts of Castleton. While the town Jesse and Molly live in with their mom is a beautiful suburb, it is bordered by a less-than-ideal section of row houses that aren't quite abandoned yet riddled with neglect as people continue to occupy them fail to upkeep. Will has stated that he gets called to this section of town quite often as a police officer and was once shot in a nearby store.

"Jesse, what the hell are you doing on this side of town?" I ask him as I turn my shiny red convertible down the street.

He doesn't reply.

My car sticks out like a sore thumb. I'm not worried about being carjacked. I just really don't want to draw attention to myself, especially since Jesse has been silent on the other end of the phone, as if he doesn't want those he's with to know he's being picked up.

"I'm here," I state as I park on the curb and turn my headlights off.

To my surprise, Jesse doesn't come out of a building. He emerges from behind a dumpster and jogs toward my car. As soon as he's in the passenger seat, we drive away.

He's wearing jeans and a T-shirt that has a stain down the front. His backpack is tossed onto the floor between his legs, which are vibrating with nervous energy. He looks pale despite his sun-kissed skin. Flushed, like he's about to vomit or just did.

It's a hot summer evening, yet he's shaking beside me. I grab his hand and hold on to it. He squeezes it back.

"Are you high?"

He shakes his head. "I didn't take anything."

When I look at his knee that's bouncing and his face that's clenched tight with the downturn of his eyes, my heart sinks. "You're frightened."

"I didn't know what to do."

I head onto the highway and drive toward the nicer side of town. "Did someone hurt you?"

He swallows. "No. They were just doing some scary shit, and I didn't want to be a part of it. I left and hid outside because I didn't know what they'd do if they found me."

"You're worrying me, Jesse. What were they doing exactly?"

"Playing with a gun."

"A gun!" I cry, horrified that teenagers would have a weapon. "When I was sixteen, we were dancing in clubs and having fun. We weren't in quasi-abandoned houses, waving around assault weapons."

"My friend, the one who was driving that day at the drive-through, he brought us out here. Said his cousin likes to party in that house. I don't know who it belongs to, but they were smoking some funny shit, and it wasn't weed."

"If you did any of the drugs, you have to tell me. I won't be upset. I need to know what you put in your body."

"Nothing, I swear. I drank a little. I sat in the corner and figured I'd wait it out. Then, the gun made an appearance. He was waving it around like an idiot. Some guy showed him how to load it, and they were laughing while pointing it at our heads. I didn't like what was going on. I told them I had to go home, but he knew I'd lied to my parents, said that I was sleeping out. He knew no one cared where I was."

"Don't your parents have one of those apps on your phone where they track your every move?"

He lets go of my hand and places it on his lap. "I disabled it. My mom doesn't care. Dad can't say anything when I'm with my mom because I'm her responsibility."

I nod as I realize Rob never would have allowed Jesse to sleep out. This was definitely Christine allowing her son to sleep out because she didn't want to fight with him, and it appears to have backfired.

"You know better than to hang out with those losers, Jesse. What didn't you learn when they helped you lie to me? Your uncle even told you they were no good."

"I know they're messed up, okay? They're the only friends I have."

"You were talking to some decent kids at the carnival."

"These guys, they're what I know. My friend has a car, and that's unlimited freedom. We can go anywhere we want. Do anything we want."

"Be as dangerous as you want," I add. "You were scared tonight. So much so that you hid behind a dumpster. When are you finally going to learn that crew is bad news? You're a great kid, Jesse. You've forgotten your worth, and trust me, it's more than what those guys are. Ditch them now. They offer you nothing but trouble when you have so much to give to this world."

"That's not true."

His defeatist attitude is disheartening.

"You're handsome and smart. You know more about current events than any teenager I've ever met. You're a hard worker and a great brother. Your sense of humor is awesome, and you're so very good, Jesse. Inside and out. If you would just get over this horrible teenage angst that you carry, you'd get out of your own way and see just how amazing you are."

He twists his fingers around each other, looking down at his lap, and gives a small nod. "I think it's time I find new friends."

My shoulders fall as I sigh in relief.

"Where am I taking you?" I ask him as we drive through Castleton.

"Can you take me back to your place?"

"Mine?"

"I can't go home. It's two o'clock in the morning. Mom will be pissed I woke her up and then know something is up. Mike will pretend to be the authoritarian and grill me for hours. He's always comparing me to his own perfect son. I'm the loser of the family, and Mike lets me know every day. I can't go back there."

"What about your dad's house?"

"Absolutely not. Are you serious?"

"I have to tell him what happened tonight. I can't lie to him."

"What was the point of me calling you? I should have just called him or my uncle, and they would have been here faster. I called you because I needed a friend."

Damn, this kid knows where to hit me with the emotions.

I nod my head. I know he's right. Rob will lose his mind if we show up at his house this late. Jesse will be in a world of trouble, and while I know Rob will eventually see Jesse did the right thing in calling me, Jesse will never trust me again.

That's a huge part of the equation.

Jesse made the right decision tonight, but he has two more years of high school, and beyond that, there are plenty of years where he might need an adult he can rely on. Someone he can ask for help, no questions asked. If I bring him to his mother's or father's house, he'll never trust me again.

I can't fathom a night where Jesse never leaves the spot behind the dumpster—or worse, never leaves the dangerous party.

"I'll take you back to my house," I agree. "I'm not your friend though."

LOVE...IT'S WILD

My comment punches him in the face.

I explain, "I'm your Tara. An adult who you can disappoint with your lies to your parents yet respects your decision when you call when you're in trouble. I'd rather be disappointed in you and have you safe than you risk harm to yourself because you're worried about getting punished. I promise you, Jesse, I will always pick you up when you need me, and I won't tell anyone what happened. What you did tonight was stupid. It was also very brave. I'm glad you called me, and I'm proud."

Despite the dark, I see his eyes are glassy, as the dashboard lights illuminate his face. He nods and sniffs back his emotions.

I start the drive back to Newbury. I'm not entirely sure it's the right thing to do, but it's the middle of the night, and this child needs a place to sleep. In fact, he passes out in the passenger seat beside me halfway into the drive, his heavy breathing a melody to the evening.

I nudge him awake when I park in my driveway, and he walks into my house like a zombie. Inside my house, he looks around with bloodshot eyes.

"You baked," he remarks, looking at my messy kitchen.

"Yeah, I was"—*thinking about your father*—"bored."

I lead him into my living room, and he falls onto the couch, completely dressed. His sneakers stink something rotten as I pull them off, and I almost gag when I remove his socks. Teenage feet are disgusting.

My favorite blanket lies on top of him, and he snuggles against one of my furry, oversize throw pillows. I plug his cell phone into a charger and turn the living room light off.

With Jesse in slumber, I head into my room and set the alarm for eight in the morning. He and I need to sleep, and I'm sure no one is expecting him home until nine at the earliest. I leave the bedroom door wide open in case he needs me, and it affords me a direct view of the couch so I know he's safe.

A half hour later, I still can't sleep. I take a pillow and throw blanket and walk into the living room. I lie down on the love seat, curl into it, and feel more comfortable, sleeping near him in the same room.

Thank goodness he called me tonight.

I just pray I did the right thing.

Eighteen

A FEW DAYS LATER, I'm back on the ranch. Jesse and I haven't
spoken since I dropped him off a block away from his mom's house.
He wore clothes he had in his backpack and marched through his
front door like the night before never happened.

I have a little guilt about not telling Rob, yet I've made up my
mind. If it happens again, I'll call in the big guns. I gave Jesse my
word, and I will keep it.

"What did you do to my son that he's being so respectful tonight?"
Rob asks, walking into the kitchen as I load the dishwasher. "Look at
you, cleaning the kitchen alone. I feel like I'm in the twilight zone."

"Anytime someone exceeds your smallest expectations, you're
amazed. You don't put a lot of faith in people."

He laughs a deep, hearty chuckle. "You're right."

I scour the bottom of the only pan left in the sink. It has severe
burn stains on it, so I put some elbow grease into it.

Rob bends down under the sink and takes out a silver canister.
"Here. Sprinkle this on and let it soak a little."

Leaning back, I sway my head to move hair away from my face
and rest my wet hands on the edge of the sink.

"What's that?" I ask.

"Bar Keepers Friend. Gets any stain out of stainless steel." Rob
does as he directed me and creates a paste of sorts with the powder

and water. He takes the scouring pad from my hand, and the pan is spotlessly shiny in minutes.

I admire his handiwork. "And I thought I was the Mary Poppins around here."

"You're doing just fine in that department," he jokes. "I'll be outside. Need to get some work in before the sun sets."

"Outside?" I ask as he walks toward the front door.

"I'm going to cut firewood."

"Shut up. Legit?"

I dry off my hands and follow him out the front door and down the porch steps.

"It's what you do in the summer so it has time to dry by the time you need it in the winter."

"Finally!" I cheer. "I get to witness an actual ranch activity."

"You know anyone can cut firewood."

I catch up and walk beside him. "That might be the case, but I've never seen it."

We get to the shed, which is an old barn, and I look down at the mountainous pile of wood that is placed just outside.

"Where did all this wood come from?"

"The farmer I lease the land to, he cleared some area high up on the hill and brought this down to me."

The wood is cut down into logs the width of the trees that were taken down.

"Could have cut it for you."

"Where's the fun in that?" His smile glistens in the early evening sun as he grabs an axe from the side of the shed. He places a log on a nearby tree trunk and lines the blade up with the center of the log.

His shoulders, broad and defined, move in harmony with the swing, the muscles rippling with each effortless motion. With every strike of the axe, there's a controlled power, a raw masculinity.

His eyes are focused, a stormy intensity set against the backdrop of the serene wilderness. There's a determined furrow in his brow. The way his jaw clenches, strong and resolute, like a man who's in command of the job at hand.

"This would be even sexier if you took your shirt off."

He smirks with the shake of his head. "They only do that in the movies."

I take a seat on the four-wheeler that's parked nearby. My sundress lifts as I cross my legs. His eyes move to the sliver of thigh that is accidentally exposed. I cover it up.

Rob clears his throat and goes back to his task. "Go on any dates lately?"

A deep sigh rumbles from my throat. "Not this weekend. I'm taking a hiatus. I've done it before. It's been more common lately than not. I'm just over the dating scene."

That and every man I meet, I compare to Rob. Externally, I feign interest. Internally, I keep thinking of how their eyes aren't quite so chestnut, shoulders not as broad, voice not as deep, or expressions not mean enough. Yes, Rob has been sincere lately, but he still bears that overbearing, masculine hold about the world. Call it my toxic trait, but I can't *not* think about Rob even if he's not the man for me.

"What I'm looking for isn't out there."

"I forgot about your long list of what makes the perfect man."

"The list changes, you know. I'm changing."

"That much has changed in a few weeks?"

"I think so."

"Care to share?"

"No."

Our eyes meet, and it's like a subtle connection, an unspoken question. I've never hid an answer from him. I've been vocal in my convictions, and yet here I am, too shy to speak for what I want.

"When I'm done with my revised list, you'll be the first to know." I give him a hand-pistol salute with a wink and a click of my tongue.

Rob narrows his eyes at me. He goes back to chopping wood. I sit back and watch. Beads of sweat glisten and trail down the nape of his neck, leaving a tantalizing path along the defined ridges of his chest. He's like a portrait I'd love to hang above my bed and stare at as I go to sleep.

"You never showed me your painting of me," I call out between his swings.

"You've seen it."

"I think I'd remember a portrait of my half-naked body."

He halts his work and looks up at me. "Oh. That one. It's not done."

"Can I see it?"

"I let you in my studio once. I don't plan on making it a regular thing."

"Why do you hide your talent like that?"

"It's not about hiding. It's about keeping something for myself."

"So, you want to keep a picture of my breasts. I'd be creeped out, but instead, I'm quite flattered. They are amazing."

"On second thought, you can have the painting."

"You don't want a souvenir of my breasts?" I ask, mock offended, and look down at my hands twisting in the flowery silk of my dress because I'm lying. I am offended. Just when I think I have a bond with this man, he throws ice-cold water on the fuse, and it dies.

"I like the souvenir I already have," he states.

My head jolts up. Our gazes are locked in a magnetic embrace, and the moment is charged. His eyes caress me with an intensity that travels down to my soul. I feel vulnerable, a sense of being seen and desired in a way that's both exhilarating and intimidating. It's a silent negotiation, an understanding that the connection between us is tangible.

There's a story between us, a story that's yet to be written, a tale of desire that hangs in the balance, awaiting the courage to be set free. I just wish he'd pick up the damn pen and start writing it.

He's the first to look away. My heart drops to my stomach.

"Would it really kill you to take that shirt off and just let me live out one teeny-tiny fantasy?" I say with a flip of my hair and a shimmy of my shoulders.

He rolls his eyes. To my surprise, he does exactly as I asked.

My jaw falls, and I clench my invisible pearls at the sight before me.

If there ever was a perfect piece of art, this man is it in the flesh.

Broad and powerful? Check.

Rippling biceps, contoured to showcase his sinewy muscles? Double check.

Abdominals that flex subtly, revealing his core's strength that extends down to his hips, emphasizing the V-shaped taper of his waist and accentuates his masculine form? Triple check.

His eyes are trained on mine as he lifts a brow. "Happy?"

"Very." My eyes are still focused on his gorgeous skin.

His pectorals rise and fall with each heavy breath he takes.

"Tara," he warns, and I blink up at him, a hum coming off my lips to let him know he has my attention. "You can't look at me like that."

"Sorry. I wasn't prepared for all of this." I wave my hand at his perfect frame, attempting to be witty when, in reality, I'm gobsmacked with attraction.

"All of what?" His tone is serious.

It snaps me out of my haze, and I look up at him, to his chestnut eyes and searing good looks that render me helpless.

The words are barely audible, yet I breathe them out. "You're beautiful."

"Fuck." His hiss is low and grumbly.

"Are you mad?"

"Pissed."

"Why?"

"I like the way you look at me."

I swallow hard. "That's a bad thing?"

"Terrible."

He drops his axe.

I stand up.

Rob closes the distance between us. The air in my lungs halts in my chest, and I gasp as he inches over to me.

He's right here, close enough that I can feel the warmth of his breath against my skin. The atmosphere is thick with anticipation, a palpable tension that crackles between us.

My head is down.

His chest heaves, heavy with his panting breaths.

"Tara." He breathes my name.

I look up.

Our eyes lock, and time seems to hold its breath.

His gaze dips to my lips, a fleeting yet electrifying touch. Rob's chest is now flush with breasts, his forehead bowing down to meet mine, and I lose all air from my lungs. My heart is thundering, a cacophony of nervous excitement. We've been here before. Had these intense moments where the universe urged us forward, nudging us to bridge the gap, to take that leap.

His eyes flicker back to mine. The unspoken question hangs in the air.

Fuck it.

It's now or never. I lean in, drawn by an irresistible force, feeling the electric charge between us intensify.

I kiss him.

I skim my fingers through his hair and draw him to me. His breath is hot. His lips taste like wildfire as I suck on them, begging entry to take what I've been craving. His mouth parts, and when his tongue slides against mine, the warmth entering me is like heaven.

Fingers and hands are gripping and pulling as he claims me with a visceral groan. His hands rise to hold my face, and his kiss sinks deeper. The pads of his fingers press firmly into my hair, possessive.

I close my eyes and give in to his kiss, so mesmerized by the moment that I can't even think coherently enough to ask questions.

Rob grabs me by the waist and lifts me off the ground. His kiss is intoxicating. I'm overwhelmed by the sensation of his hands on my ass, his mouth on my neck, and the steel of his physique pushing against me as he walks us inside the shed.

My back hits the side wall, and the full weight of his body pushes up against me as I'm settled on my feet. He entwines his hands with mine and raises them above my head. Instinctually, I lift my leg and wrap it around his, digging my heel into his ass, willing his forward.

I can feel every inch of him—hard, so very hard. The granite planes of his chest against my pebbling skin, his strong thigh pushing mine apart, and the rock-solid mass between his legs making me hot and warm and ready for him to take me.

Our kisses are hard and fast, like we're making up for lost time, yet there's no time lost at all. His hands run up under my skirt and grip my hips, opening my legs so he can bury himself against the apex of my thighs.

The feel of him is glorious.

There's no baking in the world that could quench the impenetrable desire I have for this man. I haven't even truly had him, yet just his kisses, lush and intoxicating, paired with his gruff hands on my skin and his commanding hold of my body, let me know I'll be ruined forever.

Ruined in the very best way.

He sucks on my bottom lip and then moves to my neck, licking and sucking along the tender skin. I moan and let my hands roam against his shirtless torso, feeling every hard plane dip under the tips of my fingers. The straps of my dress fall down my arms, exposing the lace of my strapless bra.

A low growl vibrates against my neck, and I shiver.

"You're even better than in my dreams," I breathe as his lips graze the side of my neck.

His mouth stops moving. His lips are still on my neck, yet his hips are inching away from me.

My brow furrows as I sense the heat from our bodies dissipating at a rapid descent.

Rob pushes off the wall behind me. His jaw is tight, and he seems angry.

"I fucked up," he says.

I lift my spaghetti strap onto my shoulder and glare back at him. "Not exactly what a woman wants to hear after she was just kissed by a man."

"You want the fairy tale, and I can't give that to you. You live in a dream world."

"You're not serious—"

"This can't happen, Tara."

Rob backs away and leaves the shed in a huff. I'm left to gather my thoughts. Brushing my hair off my forehead, I look around. I don't go outside immediately. I'm too confused. Too angry.

Walking outside, I see his shirt on the ground, the one he took off to chop wood. I pick it up. It smells like him, musky and laced with testosterone. I hate the smell of this shirt. I hate it because it reminds me of him. The man who has me so damn wrapped around his finger that I can't even breathe.

My thoughts are running rampant in my head. We haven't known each other long, and yet it feels like I've been at war with him for an eternity. What kind of battle are we even in? I'm so frustrated that I could scream.

This man has brought me to the brink before, but this time is far too different.

This time, I'm not letting him off the hook that easily.

Nineteen

I STOMP INTO THE house. The sun has set, casting a cascade of darkness over the property. The downstairs rooms are vacant. No one is in here, so I storm over to the basement. All the lights are off, including the back room.

I walk upstairs and onto the second floor.

Jesse and Molly are in their rooms. I pass their doors and hear their televisions on inside.

Rob's bedroom door is closed, but it doesn't stop me from barging in and closing it behind me.

He's standing beside his bed, his boots and socks off, yet he's still in jeans and no shirt.

I throw his shirt at him. He doesn't move to catch it, his eyes are wide and allured by the fact I'm standing here, in his room.

"I've had enough," I declare. My cheeks flush, and I know it because I can feel the heat radiating through my body.

"You shouldn't be up here."

"Shut up," I tell him. "Shut the hell up, Robert Bronson, because I am about to unleash fury upon you, and you will listen. Starting with the fact that I'm sick and tired of you telling me what can and cannot happen."

I take a step toward him, my hand out as I tick off all the idiotic responses he's said to me. "*You can't look at me like that. You and I can't happen. You want the fairy tale. I can't give that to you. You live in a dream world."*

"I've told you before, I like living in this damn head of mine. It's fun and free and far better than your stupid brain of resentment.

"The reason I'm here, the reason I'm barging into your room and demanding an answer, is because I know you felt it. I know you've felt these moments simmering between us. The near kisses and almost touches. I know you felt how powerful what just happened between us was in the shed. It's real, and it's tangible.

"What I don't get, what I can't wrap my mind around, is why you run away from me. I'm desirable, yet I'm revolting in a way that makes you run from me every chance you get. This time, it's worse than grunts. This time, I know what your lips taste like. I know what that skin feels like beneath my fingers. I know that whatever it is about me that you find so abhorrent is what keeps you running in the other direction. What is it, Rob? Why do you find me so repulsive?"

His hand rises to his hair and he pulls at the strands. "You think that's why I push you away? Keeping away from you is the hardest thing I've ever had to do in my entire life."

"Then, why do you do it?"

"I can't think of anything else other than kissing you," he explains, stretching out his hand and holding it in a tight fist. His heavy steps closing the distance between us. "I'm so damn attracted to you. That's why I ran away all those times before we even met. You've been an addiction to me since I first saw you. I've wanted to kiss you. I've wanted to touch you. Fuck, I've wanted to bury myself between your thighs so damn deep that I'll never be able to return."

"What the fuck are you waiting for then?"

"I'm not waiting any longer."

He takes my mouth in his. Our kiss is a fury as he backs me against the bedroom door. His hand sneaks to my hip, but he doesn't grab me. Instead, he locks the door.

He hoists me up, and my legs grip his hips as he carries me not to his bed, but into his master bathroom. I'm settled on the sink, and it's confusing, yet I don't want to stop his movements.

He turns the shower on.

"You have to be quiet. My kids can't hear a thing."

"I can be a good girl."

"Finally."

He kisses me again. His tongue glides along mine and dances back and forth with our lips entwined.

Our bodies are pressed together as he snakes his hand around my back and unzips my dress. The straps fall down my arms as he unhooks my strapless bra. Once the undergarment is removed, my dress falls down to my waist and my breasts fall free, seeking the heat of his bare skin.

I sigh as he breathes heavily against my lips. I can taste our shared breaths, feel the thud of our combined heartbeats as we fumble to find who can place their hands on the other person faster, who can grip harder and utterly possess the other.

His mouth is on my neck, my chest. My breast.

My nipple is in his mouth, and it sends shock waves straight to my core. The pounding steam of water muffles my gasps as I claw at his back and bang the back of my head against the glass.

He slides my panties off my legs, and they're discarded onto the tiled floor.

Rob drops to his knees, his hands push my thighs apart, and he buries his mouth right against my swollen clit.

I cry out, and it's audible and loud. I cover my mouth with my hand and grip his head with the other as I revel in the pleasure of him licking and sucking on my pussy.

"I knew you'd taste good, but I had no idea it would be fucking heaven."

Stars career across my line of vision as he slides a finger up and down the folds, never entering, yet teasing me in a vicious torment of need.

I lift my hand off his head, and release my mouth, calling out in silent cries as I play with my nipples. They're so sensitive and swollen, begging to be touched as he sucks hard on my clit, sending me into a tailspin of pleasure.

Rob looks up. His eyes feast on my hands squeezing and tweaking my breasts as I writhe in enjoyment from his mouth.

He grins. It's sexy and intoxicating.

It's enough for me to come.

"Don't stop," I beg.

"Fuck me, you're gorgeous."

My head falls against the mirror as I drink in his words, eyes closed, and then I fight the scream as he drinks in my arousal pouring down from me as I climb the edge of orgasm.

The room is foggy from the hot shower continuously cascading down the drain. The water a backdrop to my stifled moans and pants of erotic proportions.

Rob nips and sucks, laps and licks every inch of my core. His fingers continue their teasing dance, and I start to convulse. My legs shake, my back arches, my core tightens, and my eyes bolt open.

I climax. Waves of desire rush through my body as I gyrate on the vanity, half-moving away from his mouth against the ultra-sensitive bud and half-moving closer to him because I need more.

My thighs grip his head. I'm unable to control my body's raging desire to scream with satisfaction and jump off this vanity and mount him against any surface I can handle.

He rises to his feet and kisses me. The tang of my arousal coats his lips.

My hands find his belt buckle, and I free him. His cock is thick and hard; he's clearly turned on from the pleasure he derived with his very mouth.

I stroke the long length of him in my hand, and he hisses against my tongue.

"You don't have to return the favor."

"I've been dreaming about having this cock in my mouth."

"Fuck, you can't say shit like that."

"It's true. I want to drink your pleasure and suck the meanness out of you."

"When you have me like this, I'm putty in your hands."

I fall to my knees and look up at him. My mouth is so close to the head of his cock as I open and close it, teasing him with the darting of my tongue.

"Tara," he warns, and I smile as my commanding man is back.

With my eyes trained on his, I take him into my mouth. My tongue wide against the base, I curve up the tip and flick the pleasure vein before dipping back down.

He grips the edge of the vanity as I feel his hips flex.

I grip his balls and take one in my mouth, sucking on it fully before going to the next. As I go down on him, I hold his balls in my hand and grip his ass with the other, fully encasing him.

"Baby, I'm about to come."

I grip his ass harder, letting him know he isn't going anywhere.

He comes, and it's hot and more than a mouthful. I drink him in.

When I'm done, he pulls me up by the shoulders and kisses my neck, my nipples, my clavicle, and then my lips.

"We can't do this again," he sighs against my neck.

I push him away, but he pulls me flush against his chest.

"Not with the kids in the house. This was risky."

I relax into the scent of him. "I haven't had to sneak around like this in decades."

He takes a step back and brushes my hair off my face with the palm of his hand. "I can't give you what you want, Tara."

My heart drops at his words. I lift my chin and smile anyway. "I'm a grown woman. I know how to handle a casual relationship." I bite his shoulder and then shimmy away.

Rob takes my underwear off the floor and holds them out to me.

"Keep them. A souvenir to remember me by when I'm all alone downstairs with only the memories of what that mouth just did to my body."

He lets out a visceral growl. "You're gonna be the death of me, aren't you?"

"That's the plan."

Twenty

"GOOD MORNING," I sing as Jesse walks into the kitchen. "I made waffles. Take a plate and get to eating before you head to work with your dad."

Jesse walks over to the cabinet and gives me a quizzical look. "You okay?"

"Yeah. Why?"

"You're extra happy this morning."

I spray the waffle iron and pour a cupful of my handmade mixture over the heated skillet. "Just felt like making a hot breakfast this morning. Something wrong with that?"

"Not at all." He plates himself a waffle from the stack on the counter while I pour syrup into a bowl and slide it over to him.

The thud-like steps of the man of the house cause a beating in my heart and a nervous wave of energy to course through me. Rob walks into the kitchen, and I hold my breath. He looks incredible this morning in a navy T-shirt and jeans. There's still dew on his skin from his shower, and the scent of soap wafts through the air—a fierce competitor against the smell of my waffles.

"Morning," I state as nonchalantly as possible.

My eyes flicker up to his. He catches them for a beat and then looks down.

"Waffles." Rob takes in the kitchen island, filled with eggshells, milk, mixing bowls, and remnants of flour.

"Stop eyeing the mess. I'm going to clean up after Molly wakes up and has her breakfast."

The timer on the waffle maker sounds, and I open it, lifting a fresh waffle off the iron. I plate it for Rob, and he eyes it warily, as if I were offering him cyanide.

"You usually send us off with a pastry in a bag. Why did you decide to change things up?"

"It's just breakfast, Dad," Jesse states with a mouthful. "Grab a fork and enjoy them."

"They're just waffles. Not a marriage proposal," I say, playing off a line Rob said to me before.

He grunts as he takes the plate from me. He doesn't bother taking a seat. He stands in the middle of the kitchen, cuts his food with the side of his fork, and begins scarfing it down.

He looks at Jesse. "Eat quickly. We have to be on the site early."

"Why?" Jesse remarks with a shrug. "It's nice to actually sit down and have breakfast for once. These are delicious, Tara."

"Thank you." I lean my hip against the counter and fold my arms, giving Rob an intense staredown, willing him to look at me.

He doesn't.

His focus remains on anything but me. In fact, the syrup-less waffle on his plate appears to fascinate him, to the point that he can't do anything but eat. His plate is in the sink before Jesse is finished with his own.

"We gotta go," he says to his son, and he gives me a curt nod.

Jesse rolls his eyes and starts shoving the last bits of his breakfast into his mouth. He throws his backpack over his shoulder and heads out of the room behind his father. He stops at the edge of the doorway, turns around, and gives a grin. "Breakfast was delicious. Thank you for making it."

I return his grin. "You're very welcome. Now, get out of here before the big grump yells at you."

"What's his problem anyway?"

"I have an idea," I sigh as I wave him off. "I'll take you driving when you get home."

"Awesome!" The kid is smiling as he walks out to his dad's truck.

I watch them walk to the vehicle and continue my staredown at Rob. For a man who knows how to be verbally gruff when he's annoyed, he certainly is the master of avoidance when the time suits him.

Too bad for him, I'm not.

"One minute, we were arguing, and the next—"

"He had you spread eagle on the marble vanity."

Melissa is on the other line as I take a few minutes to give her an update on my life while Molly is inside on her iPad, playing Roblox with her friend.

"Melissa, it was hands down the greatest sexual experience of my life, and we didn't even have sex."

"Will you?" she prods, needing to know what will happen next. "Will you do the deed?"

"I don't know. I'm open to it, but Rob got all weird on me this morning. I made him waffles."

"You cooked?"

"Yeah. You would have thought I was professing my undying love. He's so different from other men. He's assertive, yet there's this vulnerability to him. When I first met him, he had this wall up, and slowly, I've been chipping away at it to uncover this very sweet man behind it. He's also frightened as shit to start something serious."

Melissa hums, and then there's a silence.

"What?" I ask, stone-cold and serious.

She gives a reluctant sigh. "It sounds like you're over-fantasizing him."

"Trust me when I say, Rob is the last person I would have chosen to have a fling with. Yes, he has this soft side to him, and the fooling around is top-notch, but I know where he and I stand."

"Do you?"

"He doesn't want anything serious. He's still reeling from his failed marriage. I don't need that kind of baggage. The man I want has to believe in love and happily ever after. Case closed."

"If you don't think this relationship will go anywhere, then why are you even considering going to bed with him?"

"Have you seen the way the man looks? I can't keep my eyes off of him. All brawny and tanned skin with the muscley definition of a god. Excuse me, waitress, I'll have some of that!"

Melissa laughs lightly. "You know, Tara, this doesn't sound like it's going to end well."

"I called you so we could overanalyze my amazing experience with Rob and why he shut down over waffles. I'm supposed to pretend like I'm not going to fool around with him again, and you're supposed to convince me it's a good idea, so my conscience remains clear when this ends badly."

She lets out a groan, and I can picture her swiveling in her desk chair at her office. "Fine. Go. Be naughty and wreck this man's days. You only live once. I'm such a bad influence. You should have called Jillian."

"I probably should have. She's way more levelheaded than us."

"Just be careful," she adds.

I roll my eyes. "Don't worry. I won't get my heart broken."

"I wasn't talking about yours."

I laugh as we hang up, and I try to imagine a world where I could break Rob's heart. As if.

I spend the day with Molly. The fishponds make each of us gag as we empty and clean them. The smell that pours out of the basins is nothing short of rancid.

I take the longest, hottest shower before Rob gets home. I put on light makeup and spray myself with a vanilla scent. The sundress that always has Rob staring at my thighs is a perfect outfit for dinner.

He's not home for five minutes when I catch him gawking at the hemline, his gaze even lingering a beat at the sweetheart neckline that's demure yet sexy as hell. It also doesn't help that when he and I are the only two in the kitchen, I decide I need a cup that's on a high shelf in the kitchen cabinet. The cotton of my dress glides up my legs, inching toward my satin panties. Yes, today I went sans booty shorts.

Rob walks over and helps me get the glass, his body flush with mine and that scruff brushing up against my hair as he effortlessly gets me what I need. I press my butt into his groin as I lean over and grab the pitcher of lemonade, pouring myself a glass.

I know Rob won't make a move on me again with the kids in the house. He has a ten-year-old girl who could pop up at any time. It doesn't stop me from rolling my body over his so we're chest to chest. I jut my hip out and lift my breasts as I take a long drink.

My eyes are on Rob's as I politely ask him, "How was your day?"

"I know what you're doing."

With a long, lingering swipe of my tongue, I clear the moisture off my lips. "I don't know what you're talking about."

"You're trying to tempt me with that dress."

I drop my jaw, acting wildly insulted. "As if. Have some decorum, Bronson. There are children in the house. Including one I told I'd take out driving before it gets dark, so if you'll excuse me, I have somewhere to be."

I hand him my glass and walk out of the room with an extra sway because I don't have to turn around to see he's looking at me.

After taking Jesse out driving, I'm working in my room when Rob brings me wine in a stemless glass that he places on top of a coaster. I think he wants me to join him for a cocktail. Instead, he slides his hands in his pockets and appears almost bashful.

"The kids and I are going to rent a movie tonight. If you want to watch it, too, we'll be in the living room."

I slide off my glasses, lean back, and run my teeth over my lower lip, assessing the way he shifts from one foot to the other. "Mr. Bronson, are you asking the nanny if she'd like to join you for a movie date so we can play footsie under the blanket?"

"The kids will be there," he warns.

"When are you going to realize when I'm joking and when I'm not?"

LOVE…IT'S WILD

My question catches him off guard, and he furrows his brow and looks deep into my eyes, to the point that I inhale a shallow breath.

"You scare me," he breathes. His tone is deep and serious, and it has me releasing my breath and nodding.

"How so?"

"I'm not ready to explain."

My shoulders fall as I look up at him. I rise from the chair and stand before him. "Until then, stop looking at me like I'm a ticking time bomb or like I'm asking you for more than you're willing to give. I know the ground rules."

"Only one we ever set was no swearing and you've broken that ten-fold."

"When it comes to us there was only one rule. *We can't happen.*"

"Broke that one, too. Nice to know you listen, though."

"I'm a smart cookie. You should consider hiring me."

"Shit. I haven't paid you."

I pat him on the chest. "Too late for that, buddy. First of all, if you start paying me now, I'll feel like a prostitute. Second, I make a whole lot of money, doing what I do. And believe it or not, I've been having a really great summer with you and the kids."

His eyes soften. "We like having you here."

I want to say something witty or sarcastic or weird. Instead, I just smile.

I take my glass and head into the living room with Rob. Jesse and Molly are arguing about what film to watch. Since I'm the guest of the house, they let me choose. I select the film *Housesitter*, featuring Goldie Hawn and Steve Martin. The four of us settle on the sofas. Jesse spreads out on the love seat. Rob, Molly, and I take the sofa with Molly sandwiched between us. Our feet are on the ottoman, and blankets are over us.

As the movie plays, the kids chuckle at a few lines, and I only have to cover Molly's eyes for one scene that feels a little inappropriate. I slide my hand on the back of the couch and use my other to shield her view.

We're laughing at Steve Martin's antics when I feel Rob's hand on mine on top of the sofa. The tender gesture catches my off guard. I lace my fingers with his and bask in the heat of them. We stay like this for a fair amount of the film.

I've dated men with kids before, but I've never shared a moment like this with one before. One where we're snuggled on the couches, watching a movie at home and feeling like a family.

I like being part of Rob's family. When I'm here, it feels … right.

The movie ends. Jesse walks himself up to his room with his phone in his hand. Molly has fallen asleep, so Rob gently removes her from the sofa and sends her up to bed. She starts walking up in a zombie-like state with Rob trailing behind her to make sure she doesn't fall.

I fold the blankets and straighten up the living room. With everything nice and tidy, I head toward my room. I'm near my door when I'm pulled back. Rob is behind me, taking my hand, and he swings me around until I'm face-to-face with him. My hand lands on his chest, and I stare at his Adam's apple.

I look up. He has no words. Instead, he brands me with a kiss. His lips are warm and soft, his needy tongue begging entrance, and my lips part slowly. Our bodies press together heatedly against the wall. I can taste our shared breaths, feel the thud of our combined heartbeat as we fall deeper into the kiss.

Rob's hand is on my face. His thumb rubs my cheek as his fingers claim my neck. He pulls back. His chestnut eyes are filled with promise as he kisses me yet again.

"I just couldn't let you go without a kiss." As he speaks between kisses, I feel his words against my lips.

"What happened to *we can't do this again with the kids in the house*?"

"I was a fool to think I could stay away." He kisses my jaw, my cheek, and then my forehead. He takes a step back, giving us distance, yet his eyes make me feel like we're inches apart. "I wish I could stay with you tonight."

"The fact that you won't because your children are in the house makes me want you even more. Apparently, hot single dad is catnip for me."

He blushes. The man actually has the nerve to stand here and blush, making him look so damn cute that I could mount him.

"Good night, Tara."

I bite my lip, let out a groan, and then let myself into my room, closing the door. My heart is beating rapidly, and my hands are vibrating with the feel of his body still lingering on my skin.

If I'm not careful, I could fall hard for Robert Bronson. In fact, I might have already.

<h1 style="text-align:center">Twenty-One</h1>

OVER THE NEXT FEW days, life moves in an easy flow. Rob comes home earlier than usual from work. Jesse is shocked when Rob says he's going to take him out for a drive on the highway. We spend the evenings with the kids, playing basketball and board games, and making smores in a firepit in the yard.

At night, Rob and I sit on the front porch and talk. We don't share more than a few kisses, which is frustrating as hell, yet it's … nice.

After the bathroom experience, I know he doesn't have a fear of physical intimacy with me. Although I could definitely go for another countertop rendezvous right about now. Especially when he's sitting here, looking sexy as hell after his evening shower. His legs are dressed in jeans because the man wears nothing else, apparently. It's one of the things I like about him.

I've never allowed myself this amount of time to get to know someone. Then again, I've never lived with someone I hooked up with. Not since Patrick, and we all know how that ended.

Under the soft glow of the moonlight, I'm laughing as Rob recounts tales of his siblings.

"My mother pulled the duvet down, and there was a toad in her bed."

"That's awful." I giggle as I imagine Rob's mother, a woman I know well because she's Melissa's mother-in-law—and kind of a pain in the ass in my opinion—gawking down at her sheets and seeing a slimy toad. "Your brothers were little devils."

"Brothers? That was the handiwork of my sisters. Never underestimate how evil they can be. I brought a girl home once for dinner. She was very sweet and already nervous to meet my mom. I don't know if you've met my mom, but she can be a bit … opinionated."

"I have. She seems lovely."

If I know one thing from being on the dating scene since I'm seventeen, it's that you never insult a man's mother even if he is forty years old. At the heart of every man is a mama's boy who won't let go.

"The visit was going well until we sat down for dinner, and my girlfriend looked like she was going to gag. My mother asked if she was unhappy with the meal. One look around the table, you could see the eight of us Bronson eating with gusto. This girl just smiled and raved about the cooking, but as she took her next bite, her eyes widened. She kept saying it was good but chased each bite with a huge gulp of water. I thought she was acting weird, and then I saw my sisters turning pink and about to burst out of their skins with laughter. Turned out, they'd kept adding salt to my date's food until it was inedible."

The kids are asleep upstairs, so I cover my mouth to control my laughter.

"Please tell me they're still up to no good. I bet I'd love them."

"Believe it or not, they're both super uptight now and pretend they weren't half as rotten as kids." He sits back in his seat and looks up at the stars, a sense of wonder in his eyes. "Do you have any siblings?"

"A brother. He's much older than me. Lives in New York with his wife and kids. He was already in high school when I was born, so we weren't close. That's probably why I've always been so close with friends. I never had the kind of sibling I could get into trouble with or confide in."

"I get that. How about your parents?"

"They're the best. I don't have anything to complain about. I think that surprises people. Usually, a woman who is still single at my age is thought to have daddy issues. I'm the opposite. My parents are amazing. They moved to Florida a few years ago, so I don't see them as often as I'd like, but I make my way down there a few times a year."

"You love to travel." He pushes away a tendril of hair from my face so casually that it's like he's done it a million times before.

"Very much so. I've been to every continent and many of the most famous cities more than once. Paris, London, Dublin, LA, Dallas, New Orleans—"

"What is your favorite place you've been?"

I sigh and look up at the moon, white lit and waning. Choosing my favorite place in this great, big world is difficult.

"It's not so much a question of which city is my favorite, but the experience I had there. Bathing an elephant at a rehabilitation sanctuary in Thailand is up there. This beautiful animal was abused and mistreated, and now, he is at a sanctuary where he feels safe and loved."

"You traveled halfway across the world to stand in mud."

"In Paris, there's this small bistro hidden in a little alley. The menu is preset, and that particular evening, soup was the first course. The waiter handed us a piece of dark chocolate and instructed us to let it sit on our tongues, but not to eat it. We then drank this lobster bisque, and while it passed the chocolate, it infused the soup. It was delicious, like nothing I'd ever tasted."

"Maybe it was because you hadn't tried it before that it became so unique. I wonder if you ate it at my kitchen table every night and not at a quaint little bistro in Paris if it would lose its appeal."

"You're a real buzzkill—you know that?"

"I do."

With a slow smile and a pinch to my eyes, I ignore his comment.

"In Vegas, I went on a helicopter ride to the Grand Canyon that landed next to the Colorado River. You've never seen anyplace as majestic as the red rocks of the canyon. It's so beautiful and vibrant, but it's also scary as hell because I was convinced one of the helicopter blades was gonna hit the canyon. Your depth perception is way off in there."

"Do you travel alone?"

"I do. My mother likes to travel, and I have some friends who are looking for a getaway. My friend Jillian has gone on a cruise with me. Melissa's done spa weekends, and I went with her and the kids to Disney. For the big trips, the long flights, if no one's around, I have no problem with going by myself. Why sit at home, waiting for someone to do things with, when I have this perfectly awesome built-in travel companion who loves to try new foods, never complains about walking too much, and will go on any tour even if it's boring?"

"You."

"Yes, me. I'm quite a lovely travel companion, I might add. Highly recommend."

His throaty chuckle croons in the air. "Good to know. I've never left the East Coast."

"Shut up. Never?"

His shoulders rise with indifference. "I got married at twenty-three. Had my son the following year and was working fifty-hour weeks. After Molly was born, I started my own business. There was either no money or no time off. Next thing you know, you realize you worked your way through life and missed out on a lot of the important things."

I nod, yet there's this fleeting feeling radiating in the air that he's talking about more than vacations. Rob has said he doesn't miss his wife, yet I wonder if she wanted to return to him, to rebuild the life they'd had, would he take her back?

"I can see how time slips away from you."

He looks at me with a curious eye, and then his attention turns up to the night sky. "You look at the stars a lot when you speak."

"Not the stars. The moon. It reminds me that no matter how wildly things change, there is at least one thing that is reliable."

Rob smiles. "It's pretty amazing how we're all connected, even under a vast sky. I like your theory on the moon. Something you can always trust to be there."

There's a comfortable silence between us. He reaches over and entwines his fingers with mine, the warmth of the connection palpable. He gives a gentle tug, and I stand, walking myself over to his seat and gently falling onto his lap. My legs curve up and over the armrest as I sit sideways across him.

His lips touch mine in a feathery kiss.

"I like the taste of bourbon on your lips," I tell him.

"You hate bourbon."

"On you, it's far more tolerable."

I grip his stubbled face and pull it closer to mine, diving my tongue into his mouth, eliciting a deafening moan from him. Thank goodness for his self-restraint because before I can get too handsy, he settles my head against the crook of his neck. I'm buried against his skin, safe and comfortable. It's almost as nice as kissing him, yet not nearly as much as having him buried between my legs, but beggars can't be choosers. Still, it's nice.

"I'm really enjoying having you here." I feel the rumble in his throat as he speaks.

"If you want, I can start making inappropriate comments and being extra sarcastic just enough to piss you off so you'll be happy when I have to leave this place next week."

"Wow. Next week already?"

"You said just for the month of July. I can't avoid Patrick forever, although I will have to see him this weekend."

"Your gala."

"Yeah. Are you still coming?"

"If you want me there, I'll go."

"Right now, you're my only option, so you have to come. I'd be really annoyed if I had to head out to the bar tonight to find myself a cowboy to take."

Rob grunts, and I laugh against his chest.

Yes, I'm enjoying getting to know him. Enjoying it too much.

"ARE WE EXPECTING COMPANY?" Molly asks, looking out the window.

"No. Why?" I ask from the living room, where I'm setting up the board game that she selected for us to play.

"There's a car outside." She's pulling the curtain back and craning her neck, bending forward. I get up to see what she sees when she pops straight up and shouts, "It's Uncle Cade!"

I stand behind her and watch as the black Porsche parks where

Rob's truck usually is. The door opens, and out comes Cade, dressed in black pants and a matching button-down. His hair is brushed back and styled like a Ralph Lauren ad. He's a handsome devil, that Cade. Add in the mischievous smile he has as he slides on a pair of sunglasses and struts up the stairs with a bouquet of roses, and he's downright swoon worthy.

Molly bounds through the front door. Her arms are up as she shouts for her uncle and runs toward him. Cade catches her with one arm and gives her a huge hug, tugging her along with him as they walk into the house and he sets her down.

"How's my favorite girl?" He hands Molly the bouquet of flowers. "These are for you."

She takes the flowers and holds them close to her chest. "Uncle Cade always brings me flowers when he visits."

"You certainly know how to charm a woman."

He looks at me with a sideways grin. "I have to somehow make up for being an absentee uncle."

"What better way to train your niece how to forgive a man who doesn't give her attention than with flowers?" I say, and he throws his head back and lets out a great peal of laughter.

"When I heard you were staying here, I was hoping you'd put some of that sass to good use with my brother. What time is he getting home?"

"Not for a few hours."

"Good. That means we get to spend some quality time together without his saying no to everything."

Molly looks up at her uncle with her brows curled together. "What kind of things would he say no to?"

He winks with a nod toward his car. "Go look in my trunk."

She runs down to the car as he pops the trunk from the key fob. Cade and I watch from the porch as she looks inside. As she lifts her face up to us, the pure elation on her expression shows she likes what's inside.

"Water guns!" she declares.

He shouts down to her, "Better. They're paintball guns."

She takes one out and holds it up in the air. "These are so cool!"

"I bought three. Figured Jesse could join us, but since he's not here, maybe Tara wants to join. The two of you against me."

Cade eyes me with that twinkle in his eye. I roll my eyes at him.

"What? Too scared you'll mess up your hair?" he chides.

I flippantly reply, "I just think it's funny you find yourself to be so good that you can take us both on."

"You think you two will beat me?"

"I know we'll beat you. You have underestimated my competitiveness and desire to be the best at everything."

I jog down the steps and over to the trunk, where Cade has the three guns and a box of paintballs.

This activity is right up my alley. *Game on!*

The three of us go inside to change our clothes into things we don't mind ruining with paint. I make the added suggestion of wearing long sleeves despite the heat because gun pellets hurt when they hit your skin.

The three of us follow the instructions and get the guns filled with paint. We place our masks over our faces and go to war. The nearby woods are the perfect spot for our battle. We enter the wooded battlefield, and the scent of damp earth mingles with the faint smell of paint, setting the scene around us. Molly and I go on a covert operation, ensuring Cade has to hide from us as we zero in on his territory. We navigate the trees and natural obstacles, seeking the perfect vantage point. We find him hiding behind an oak. Paintballs fly through the air, creating vibrant bursts of color against the backdrop of greenery.

Molly gets hit first, but we made a five-shot rule so the game wouldn't end too fast. We run from tree to tree and hide behind some brush. I shoot Cade in the ass after he gets Molly for a third time.

"Aren't you supposed to let her win?" I ask him as I hide behind a tree.

"Would you?" he calls out in question as I jump out and try to shoot him.

I squeal when I get him in the leg.

"Never. If the kid wants to play a game, she has to play to win."

"Great minds think alike." He spins around and shoots Molly, who was trying to sneak up on him. "Next time, don't make so much noise, squirt."

She shoots him in the chest in retaliation.

I'm laughing like a fool, so Cade shoots me in the boob.

"Ow. That freaking hurts."

He aims the gun again, so I aim my gun at his groin.

"You'd never."

"You sure about that?" I tease.

Cade runs through the woods, and I chase after him. He's laughing as he jumps over logs and sprints from side to side. There isn't a ton of paint in these guns, so I don't want to waste it unless I know I have a good shot. I hit him in the back twice.

He spins around and gets me in the arm, so I duck, running to the left.

Now, it's his turn to chase me.

I'm not very graceful, so when I reach the edge of the woods, I fall on my face. Cade barrels out after me, shoots me in the back, and then falls to his knees, hysterical with how unladylike I just went down.

"That's five. You're out," he says, his breathing rapid as he comes down from the physical exertion of the game.

"You killed me!" I mock cry.

He rolls me over. Kneeling over me, he takes off his mask and grins down at me. I remove my own mask.

"Even covered in paint, you're pretty," I tell him. "It's unfair."

"You don't look so bad yourself," he says and then is interrupted by a very loud, very annoyed grunt.

I look behind me and see Rob standing on the grass. His legs are spread wide, as if in a fighter's stance, and his fists are clenched. That strong jaw is practically granite as he bites down, looking at the scene before him.

"What are you two doing?" he bites out.

Cade and I both lift up our guns.

"Paintball," we say in unison.

Rob raises an inquisitive brow. "Just the two of you?"

Suddenly, a rush of noise comes from the woods, and with a loud pop, Molly shoots Cade in the back.

"I win!" She jumps up and down as Cade and I start laughing with how sneaky the little bugger just was.

Jesse comes jogging over from the truck. "Paintball! Cool. Did you bring these, Uncle Cade?"

"I did. And now, I'm dead. I could go for round two if you're up for it. I need payback from this little twerp." Cade takes Molly's hand and pulls her toward him so he can give her a noogie on the head.

"Yes! I'll go change." Jesse heads into the house.

I stand and slide my mask completely off my head. I feel something in my hair so I glide my palm down to get it out.

Cade appears behind me, picks something out of the strands, and then holds it up to me. "You have leaves in your hair. Wouldn't have happened if you hadn't chased me and eventually tumbled to the ground."

I take it from him and roll my eyes. "Because you shot me in the boob!"

Rob grunts again, eyeing Molly.

Cade and I stop and maintain adult decorum.

"You're home early," I state.

"Not really. You must have been having such a good time that you didn't notice how late it was." He turns to Cade. "What brought on the surprise visit?"

"I was in town to see Mom and thought I'd drive on out here to see the kids. Heard Tara was staying with you. It is all the family wants to talk about. Apparently, there's quite the family drama with everyone sharing their thoughts. Mom would like you to return her calls, by the way. She said she's been calling you."

I blink up at Rob, finding it interesting that he's been dodging his mom's calls.

"Why doesn't she just come out here?" I ask.

"I saw her last weekend when I took the kids to her house. Tell her to stop acting like the martyr. I'll call her when I have time." Rob states to Cade and then asks, "You staying for dinner?"

"If it's not too much trouble. I'd like to spend time with my girl," Cade says and Rob furrows his brows until his eyes look to Molly and he nods.

"I'm making ribs." Rob turns around and walks toward his truck. He takes out a large box of tools and then walks it down toward the shed.

Jesse returns from the house, wearing a long-sleeved shirt but still has his shorts on, paired with old sneakers. "Whose gun am I taking?"

"Take Tara's," Cade offers. "I want a chance to kick your ass. This time, we're making it ten shots to the kill. You got that?"

Jesse and Molly nod while I slide my gun off my body and hand it to Jesse.

The kids are reloading their guns with paint as Cade whispers in my ear.

"Go follow the big lug. I'll keep the kids busy."

I curve my brows. "Why would I do that?"

"My brother gets jealous over nothing, especially women. That encounter just confirmed what I and half of the Bronsons believe—that there's something going on between you and Rob out here. Now, go follow the brute. I'll even get the kids in the shower."

I eye Cade skeptically. "I can't tell if you're more of a cad and a troublemaker than I thought or if you're my new best friend."

"Just a guy who likes to see good things happen to good people."

Cade puts his mask back on and shouts over to the kids, "Who's ready for round two?"

With Cade now with the kids, I walk to the truck, spying a canvas duffel bag in the back. I take it out and bring it to the shed.

Twenty-Two

ROB IS IN THE back of the shed, putting his tools away in meticulous order. I lean against the door and stare at him. His jeans accentuate his long, sturdy legs, and that fitted T-shirt hints at the sculpted physique beneath. The fabric stretches across his shoulders and chest as he focuses on the shelves.

Like a magnetic pull dragging him my way, he turns his head and sees me standing here.

"I thought you were playing games with my brother," he says, a serious look on his face.

"He's fun. We get along well."

"Why are you in here and not out there with him then?"

I hold up the duffel bag I took from his truck. "Just thought I'd come out here and see if you needed a hand. You left this in the truck."

"That goes in the house."

"I know. I've seen you bring it in every day."

"Then, why did you walk it all the way out here?"

I lift my shoulders in a playful way. "Mistake, I guess. Do you want me to walk it back to the house? I could, but then that would ruin my excuse to come out here and see you. Maybe be alone for a little while."

His eyes are like wildfire as he tilts his head and watches me take two steps forward. "You looked awfully cozy out there with him.

What would have happened if I hadn't arrived?"

"We'd have played another round because that was all we were doing. Playing a game. Are you jealous, Bronson?"

"No."

"Are you sure? Because your jaw looked like it was gonna crack from how tight you were biting down. And you have this deep line that forms on your forehead when you're angry. It's cute."

"Cute?"

"Yeah," I tease. "Sexy and masculine and commanding too. But I know you hate it when I say how hot I think you are when you're mean."

I close the distance between us and stand before him. Our bodies are practically touching and yet not at all. I lift my chin defiantly as I look into his eyes. I see the steel barrier start to waver. There's a discernible wariness in his expression. Skepticism flickers in his eyes, indicating a desire to trust, but a reluctance based on past experiences.

The look makes me swallow. "Do you think I'd go after your brother?"

His lips part with uncertainty of what he's about to say. "It's hard for me to trust people."

I nod my head and take in his cautious yet guarded state. Curiosity gets the better of me. "Is it everyone you distrust or just me?"

There's a flicker in his dark eyes as my words strike him. This close, I can feel his heart beating rapidly and the heat of his anger pouring off of him. Instead of waiting for him to answer the question, I do it for him.

"I don't want Cade. Sure, he's charming as all hell, but I'm staring at the man I want. A man who has been keeping his distance from me for a good reason and doesn't have to anymore."

Rob's brows crease, like he's trying to understand.

"Cade has the kids for as long as we need him to. No one is coming out to this shed, so we can stand here and wait for you to get over your tantrum, or you can remove my clothes to do very wicked, very dirty things to me."

He hisses through his gritted teeth, "Fuck, Tara. What are you doing to me?"

"Is it because I'm sweaty and not wearing one of your sundresses?

Or perhaps it's the paint? I know I'm a mess."

He grips my hip and pulls me so close, I didn't even know there was room between us to close. "You know you're so fucking sexy that you'd look gorgeous in a goddamn tarp."

I smile, still not touching him.

"I walked all the way out here, so if you need help with anything, I'm happy to assist. Do you need anything from me?" I ask in a barely there whisper.

"I do," he states, his stance wide and strong as he remains in the center of the room. "Kiss me," he dares.

"You didn't say please."

"It wasn't a request." He grips me by the other hip, and I gasp at the feel of his body, hard as marble against my soft curves. "I've been thinking about you all damn day."

His fingers dig into my ass as he lowers his face to mine.

I kiss his stubble. It tickles my skin, yet I want more of his sinful mouth. I lift up onto my toes and link my mouth to his. Languidly, I kiss him, taking the lead on this one task, not using tongue at first, but teasing him with my lips. His hands are still at my hips and ass, digging and pressing, yearning to rip my clothes off based on the way his fists clench at the fabric.

His mouth becomes desperate as he parts my lips with his tongue and lavishes me with the sweet, erotic swipes of an impenetrable kiss. Unlike our previous kisses, he controls this one. Demanding in a way that's possessive with his movements.

I like this side of Rob. I like when he takes charge of me, controls me. Manhandles me. Perhaps it's because I've been handling myself for so long, taking care of myself, loving myself, that I want this kind of action. I don't want to think. I want to just be handled in every way.

From the power in his hands, the slickness of his mouth, and the thick bulge that presses into me, there's no way I can keep my hands at my sides anymore.

My hand glides down the front of his T-shirt, taking in the delicious contours that I had the pleasure of viewing days ago and crave to see again. I let them slide lower and rub the front of his jeans and feel the thickness of his arousal pressing against the fabric.

The action is enough to elicit a visceral reaction from Rob in the form of a kiss. He turns his head, grips my head, and lands the most soul-shattering, heat-seeping kiss on my lips. My mouth parts on instinct, and we become a tangle of lips and tongues, lashing at each other in desperation.

"What are we doing?" he husks against my ear.

"Trusting each other."

"Is that all?"

"That and the fact that all I've been thinking about today was how good it felt to have your cock in my mouth."

"You have a filthy mind," he groans as he releases my mouth and then bites down on my neck.

"You love it."

His eyes close, and his fingers move to the skin between my pants and the sweatshirt. I'm so damn hot from the summer heat to the way this man sends passionate waves of fire my way. I need to cool down. I lift my hands so he can rid me of the sweatshirt and tee beneath it. He follows my order and discards my tops, leaving me in just a bra.

He travels past my collarbone and then straight to my breasts, which he frees with the skill of a man who knows how to remove a woman's clothing. I kick off my shoes and feel his body flex as he does the same. We kiss and move in a skillful dance toward the back of the room. The sunlight doesn't reach the space where Rob keeps his tools, so I have to open my eyes slightly to see where we're going.

There's a ladder in the back. He ushers me toward it.

"Secret hideaway?" I look up toward the rectangular opening in the ceiling.

"Something like that," he says as he follows me up the ladder.

When he bites my ass, I yelp and then fall onto the plywood at the top.

I can't stand so I crawl on my knees toward the center of the space. It's hot and dark with little light shining through the crevices in the wood.

"Just when I thought we couldn't get more creative than the bathroom."

"Shit. This was a bad idea—"

"Shut the fuck up." I lean forward and take his mouth in mine again.

He might be the one in control, but I'll be damned if he puts the brakes on us. My body is humming with a fierce desire for this man.

I need to have him.

I need him now.

Rob leans down and makes love to my breasts. Licking, sucking, and biting. He's ravenous as he swirls his tongue around one nipple and then sucks it hard. I play with the other because my insides are about to combust with how full my breasts are with arousal.

He takes turns, giving attention to each, nipping and placing his full lips around the areola and looking up at me with a heated gaze.

I open my jeans and slide them down to play with myself. Over the cotton of my panties, I rub circles over my clit.

"Jesus," he moans. "Baby, you are going to make this end sooner than it needs to."

"No way. I know a man who likes a challenge, and you, Robert Bronson, are not going to stop until I am coming all over your cock."

"No woman of mine is leaving unsatisfied."

I gasp as he replaces my hand with his own, this time pushing my jeans further down to make room for his massive hand as he cups my pussy and rubs his finger over my swollen clit.

How could he have thought I'd possibly want any other man when he makes me feel this way with just his touch? My head is spinning, my eyes see stars, and I'm already on the brink of collapse, and we haven't even gotten started.

I use a free hand to undo his belt, zipper, and button—a task that's not easy when I'm writhing in pleasure and having my neck devoured with filthy, open-mouthed kisses, sending shivers through my body. I free his cock and run my hand along the length and glide my fingertips across the head and back down. His cock twitches under my touch. With a tight fist, I pump up and down the length until his lips release my neck because he's basking in his own pleasure and in need of a breath.

He takes my head with both hands and holds it as he kisses me. I get lost in the passionate kiss. His wet lips and magnetic pull have me melting and boiling up in a wild frenzy at the same time.

I remove my jeans and underwear, leaving them to the side. Together, we discard his jeans and boxers. Before he can lean back down and kiss me again, I crawl onto all fours and take his cock in my mouth.

A deep growl comes from his throat as I go fast, sucking him off at a rapid pace. Knowing we don't want this to end early, I release him with a pop and then give one more long swipe of my tongue from base to tip.

"Your cock is so damn big. And so damn delicious."

I take him in my mouth one more time, and he surprises me with a slam to the back of my throat, burying himself to the hilt. I gag lightly as he pulls out, and then I rise. If he does anything like that to my pussy, I'm going to be climbing down from this loft with a soreness between my thighs and a grin on my face.

Rob lies down on the ground, and I start to mount him when he grips my hips and flips me around, lining my pussy up with his face and my mouth with his cock.

I cry out as he spreads my legs, places his hands on my ass, and pulls me down to his eager mouth. He flicks his tongue over my clit and then glides down over my lower lips, dipping his tongue in and out and then back up to my throbbing core, and he sucks with the most meticulously perfect amount of pressure.

"I missed this," he says.

I can't even respond to the fact that he's missed eating me out when he's only been down there one other time.

He flicks his tongue in short, brief strokes, building up the base of my orgasm.

I fall forward and thank him for the pleasure. He feels different in my mouth from this angle. The hard back of his member against the roof of my mouth is like a metal rod. He's swollen and engorged. I can't imagine him being any more aroused. I have to stop every once in a while to moan or cry out shouts of expletives into the dark, cavernous space. His mouth is doing wicked things to my body. The crescendo of pleasure builds within me.

"I'm gonna come," I pant.

Rob moves his head and pushes up on my hips.

I yelp in aggravation, my body tight with an orgasm that's on the brink of explosion.

I don't have time to think or the proper sight to see what is happening. Rob sits up, grabs me by the waist, and guides me to the floor. My legs are spread wide as he climbs on top of me. He has one hand at the back of my head and another at my lower back, holding me tight.

"Are you comfortable? This floor is hard as a rock."

"I don't care about the damn floor. I need you, Rob. I'm dying for you."

"Good. Because I'm about to fuck you so hard that you won't be able to feel a thing. I'm gonna fuck you as desperately as I've dreamed since the night you fell out of that tree."

I grab his dick and line him up with my entrance, which isn't difficult since he's already pointed toward me like a heat-seeking missile, ready to explode.

He pushes into me with force, and I temporarily lose my vision as he pumps in and out.

My hips move in synch with his, feeling every nerve in my body shiver as I hump and rub, letting his long strokes in and out of my body build me to pleasuring heights.

The senses inside of my body vibrate and shake as my orgasm draws near. My neck arches, my breasts rise, and when he leans down and sears me with a powerful kiss, I come undone.

I claw at his back and then move to his butt, which is clenching with every possessive flex of his hips. This orgasm is his, and he is owning every piece of it.

My arousal spills through me, and I gasp and scream and writhe with undulling pleasure. I'm lost in the moment when he pulls out from me, rises, and then comes on my stomach, moaning and calling out my name as he releases himself onto my skin in hot spurts. His moans are light as he comes out of his own haze and then rolls onto his back, leaning on the dusty, hard flooring.

"That was …" I can't finish my sentence.

He leans up and then grabs his shirt, using it to clean off my stomach and then himself.

I finally find the word. "Unexpected."

He places a kiss on my forehead. "With you, everything is unexpected. And, yes, it's a good thing."

Twenty-Three

YOU KNOW WHEN THEY say all good things come to an end? This good thing does with a simple text.

Where are you?

Rob's text arrives at a rather inopportune time. Molly and I are in the midst of pumping water into the fishponds. Discovering a hidden spigot on the edge of a stone wall, long covered by shrubbery overgrowth, elicited jumps of joy from both of us. The arduous task of shuffling buckets of water back and forth from the house had left us exhausted. Throughout the morning, we had diligently filled the ponds to their brims.

We're just nearing the edge when the second text comes in.

Get back to the house now.

I glance at Molly, confused. "I think your father's home. He wants us back."

She quickly jumps to her feet. "Dad's never home this early. Something must be wrong."

"I hope not." I wipe my hands on the sides of my shorts and turn the spigot off. "We'll finish this tomorrow."

The two of us hop onto the four-wheeler and zoom back to the house, the machine revving so fast through the fields that the air whips through our hair.

Whatever has brought Rob back from the jobsite early must be important. I hope everyone's okay. Jesse must be fine since Rob's here and not at a hospital somewhere with his son. Unless it's someone else.

Maybe Melissa …

I rev the engine faster.

I haven't seen Rob since he left for work this morning. He looked refreshed after our romp in the shed, after which we had a great dinner with his brother. Cade tells the best stories yet struggles to keep them kid friendly. Earmuffs in the form of my hands over Molly's ears were worn a few times.

When Rob went up to his room, it was with a long kiss that almost turned into more, but we kept our minds in the right place even though our bodies were raging. That man lit me on fire yesterday, and I'm still trying to cool off. I even splashed myself with water a time or two this afternoon, and it had nothing to do with the late July swelter.

My heart is racing into my throat as we park the four-wheeler and jog back to the house. Rob's truck is parked next to my car. We head through the screen door and inside the living room just as Rob walks in from the kitchen. Jesse is seated on the couch. His hair is a mess, like he's been pulling at it for hours. His eyes are red-rimmed.

"Molly, outside. Jesse, take your sister for a walk. Now!" Rob's command is met by a cautious ten-year-old who knows better than to argue with her father.

She heads outside, followed by Jesse, who looks at me with an apologetic and downtrodden look.

The door closes behind them, and Rob walks up to it, slamming the main door closed too. It's just us in the vacant house with silence filling the air, like a screaming inferno that's about to blow.

Rob glares down at me.

His typical visage is contorted with a storm of emotion, transforming his attractive features into a portrait of anger. My racing heart drops to my stomach, and I have a wave of butterflies in anticipation of what he's about to say.

"Why did my son send you a pin at one o'clock in the morning from the slums of Castleton?"

I gasp at his question. I was bracing for something horrible. An injury or a death. Thoughts of Melissa and the baby in trouble crossed my mind. I wasn't prepared for the urgency to be about Jesse.

"You're not asking a question. You're insinuating."

His usual warm eyes—which, hours ago, sparkled with allure—are now narrowed and ablaze with intensity. The smooth lines of his face are drawn taut, accentuating a furrowed brow and tightened jawline.

"Goddamn it, Tara. Just answer the question."

"He needed me to know that location."

"Why?"

He steps toward me, feet heavy, making the wood creak. I press my lips into a long, thin line. After the week we've shared—heck, the month we've lived—I'd have thought he'd at least talk to me like an adult, be rational, knowing I would never do anything to harm his kids. I can understand why he's upset and, more so, worried as a parent.

His accusatory tone and condemnation, instead of him first learning the facts, are crippling.

"Damn it, Tara, stop lying to me and tell me the fucking truth!"

"Stop yelling and just talk to me about what you figured out instead of making me grovel in the form of a story you already know the ending to."

"Why does life always have to be a game with you?"

"It's no more of a game than you're playing with your vague, shouty texts, ushering me back here like I'm one of your kids and not a woman you just fucked yesterday in a dirty shed."

The words pain me as they come out. The moment we shared yesterday didn't feel dirty at the time. Now, it feels downright filthy and in the worst way.

His steps draw closer. I can practically feel the testosterone on his skin with how wild his body is raging.

"I'll ask again, why did my son drop you a pin after calling you on Friday night?"

His tone is so condescending that I go on the defensive. "How do you know he called me?"

"I went through his phone."

"Your trust issues know no bounds."

"I'm his father."

"Did he hand you his phone to go through, or did you just pick it up because you have serious issues?"

"I pay the bill; therefore, it's my phone. If I want to look through it, I will."

"Great. You looked and saw he called at one o'clock in the morning and then sent me a pin. You're a real detective, Rob. Congratulations."

I storm past him and head into the kitchen, stopping at the far end of the island and turning around to face him as he takes his stance on the opposite end. The eight feet of granite is a large barrier between us, yet the way he's looking at me with fierce disappointment is so powerful that he might as well be standing right next to me.

"I should have known you'd keep secrets. I told you this was my concern on that first day in the game room. This was a bad idea. You knew what my kid was up to last weekend, and you hid it from me. Just like you hid what he did at driver's ed."

I blink up at him with a slack jaw, my hands gripping the cold stone of the granite to ground the adrenaline coursing through me. "How do you know about that?"

"His text messages. His friends think you're some super-hot nanny who's crazy as shit, and they're not wrong." He walks to the side of the island and puts his hands up in prayer as he dramatically moves toward me with a red face, iced jaw, and a tone that elevates with every word. "Now, please, stop fucking lying to me, act like an adult for once, and tell me what the hell is going on."

"Fine, Rob! Just stop it," I shout, my words echoing through the house. "Stop it with the rage. Stop it with the accusations."

I push back off the cold granite and place my hands on my hips. "Your son called me because he'd found himself in a bad situation and needed a friend. Someone who wasn't going to read him the riot act. You can be angry as hell at him for being in that horrible place, but you should be proud that he was brave enough to remove himself and ask for help. I picked him up, and I took him back to my place because I knew he'd be safe. He didn't need someone to scold him for just trying to grow up."

"Damn it, Tara. This is serious. You can't take a sixteen-year-old boy home with you."

"Be careful with what you say next because you're sounding very accusatory."

"He's a child, and you have to bring him home. You can't play the role of cool aunt with every kid you meet."

"Where was I going to bring him? To his mother, who clearly didn't care enough to make sure that her son didn't turn off his cell phone tracking so she knew where he was or the fact that he was sleeping out when he was already grounded for the summer. She had him for one weekend and couldn't be bothered to parent him. I sure as shit wasn't bringing him back here," I declare. "You see this." I motion a large circle around the space between Rob and me that's bubbling with a toxic, angry energy. "The way you're behaving would have been ten times worse."

"He's my son. Not yours. Mine. If anyone should be getting him out of a shithole and taking him home, it's me!"

His words are like a blast to my chest. Their power leaving a wound in my skin.

"You're not mad because I helped. You're pissed because he didn't call you. You're so damn controlling and lost in your own pissed off universe that you don't even see what's happening around you."

"Don't act like I don't know my own son. I know who he hangs out with. I know they're trouble, and I have asked him time and time again why he runs with those dirtbags. That's why I've been keeping him with me."

"Maybe instead of asking him why he hangs out with them, you should ask yourself why an awesome kid who was so close to you suddenly spends his days with the dredge of the earth. He's hurting, Rob. He's heard too much. Knows too much. Yet he's a good kid. And smart. You spend more days screaming at him for his faults than looking at him through the lens of a father and being proud of the small successes."

"You come in for one month and think you magically know what it's like to raise children. You don't even want kids. You have no idea what it's like and no idea what we've been through."

"You're right. I don't. It still gives you zero license to scream at me like I'm a child!"

"Only a child would hide this from another adult. It's all lies with you. First, it was why you wanted to come here. Now, it's my son. I bet there are more, like where the hell you and Molly were when I came home and why you're always out in the fields all day, and why you texted my son to bring you a rope. Nothing's serious with you. Not even us. I bet this whole month was just a fun fling and I was the available man."

A quiver runs off my lips as the accusation of his words rolls through my heart and pierces it into a thousand pieces.

"Of course," I state calmly. The emotions build behind my eyes, forcing me to realize Rob is just like every other man who sees me through a singular lens.

I lift my chin and swallow it back. "This is what it comes back to. You're always telling me to grow up. Well, maybe you're the one who has to. I've never had to prove myself to someone in more ways than I have with you. Even when I finally had you, I had to dance around your insecurities. You practically ran away from me because I'd made you waffles. They were fucking waffles, Rob. But they scared you because you were so afraid I'd want more than what you could give me. Then, with Cade, I needed to show I wasn't going to jump into bed with him by jumping into bed with you."

"That's why you did it?"

"No!" I yelp and then back away, my hands in my hair. "I did it because I like you, Rob. I more than like you. I like so many things about you, which is baffling because you're also the most closed-minded man I've ever met. I like your smile and the way you don't show it often, so when you do, it's like my entire day is made. I like your vulnerability and the stories you tell about your kids. I like your art and the talent in your callous hands. I like that you took on this house and this land and are slowly making it a paradise for your children. I like our talks and the way you hum when you're just sitting in silence. I like the way you sing when you're outside by the barbecue and don't think anyone can hear you. I liked that you trusted me with your children because you knew I cared about them as if they were my own. At least, that's what I thought because I was blinded."

I brush past him and walk to my room. I take my suitcase out from under my bed and open it up.

Rob's heavy steps follow me. He stands in the doorway, filling it, as he looks down at me while I frantically place clothing items inside.

"What are you doing?"

Sundresses fly off the hangers as I toss them into my bag. "While I like you, I also hate you, Rob. I hate you because I ignored the fact that you treat me like everyone else. Like I'm a loose cannon who can't be trusted. Like I'd buy a kid a beer at a bar because I look like I'd be cool with it. Like I'm an easy woman who will fall for anyone. Trust me, if I wanted any Todd, Dick, or Kyle, I know exactly where to find one. I wouldn't be attaching myself to the one man who doesn't want me. Point taken. I get it. You don't want me."

His brows drop as he swallows. "If you don't want people to treat you that way, you can't pull stupid shit like picking a kid up in the middle of the night and not telling his parents. Or finding out he lied to you about class and keeping his secret so he doesn't get in trouble."

I close my suitcase and rest my hand on it as I gaze up at him. My breath is ragged, yet I take a deep breath to center myself as I look at him. So beautiful yet so distrusting and oh-so disappointed.

"I wanted to be a safe space for Jesse. He trusted me enough to call me. I don't know if it will happen again, and if he ever finds himself in a horrible situation, whether it's next week or next year, I want him to know he has someone he can call who cares about him enough to make sure he's okay. I didn't keep his secrets to hurt you. I did it to protect your relationship with your son. While he has messed up, he's also paid his dues, and he's amazing. The two of you even grew closer, and with every day that passed, I felt better about my decisions. I know they were wrong, but I don't regret them." I pick up my suitcase. "I do, however, regret getting close to you when I know you have nothing to give me in return. I knew you were gonna be a hard man to get attached to, but now that I have and after hearing what you truly think of me, I wish I never had."

I start to walk to my desk, but he grabs my hand and forces me to look at him.

"I told you I couldn't give you what you wanted."

"I thought you meant happily ever after. I knew you weren't good for that. I at least thought, somewhere along the way, I'd earned your respect."

I pull my wrist from him and watch his face fall, along with his hand by his side.

"Where are you going?"

"Home."

"You're leaving?" He shakes his head, as if he just can't believe it. "Just like you did last time."

"Last time, you're the one who said this wasn't going to work out. This time, it's me." I place my laptop in my tote and take the fishbowl box off my desk, the one with Bob swimming around, and carry it through the house.

I walk through the kitchen, through the living room, and out the front door.

Molly and Jesse are on the front steps. Jesse gives me an apologetic look. I place my hand on his and assure him I'm not upset in any way.

"You lied to your parents. You knew this day would most likely come. It's okay. He might be disappointed, but he loves you."

"How do you know that?" he asks.

"You only get that upset when you care so much that you don't know what to do with all the worry you have in your heart."

He eyes my suitcase. "Then, why are you leaving?"

I blow a rogue hair out of my face as I look at him and then to Molly, who has started to cry. I place my suitcase and tote bag on the ground and the fish on the stair beside her.

I kneel in front of Molly and place my hand on her hair, rubbing down her head. "The month was almost over anyway. I'll see you both again, I promise. At your uncle Will and aunt Melissa's. This isn't good-bye. Okay?"

Molly nods as she sniffles her tears back. Her hands find my neck, and she pulls me down to her in a fierce hug. I can feel her body shaking with how desperately she doesn't want me to go. I grip her tight and hug her something fierce.

"I love you, Madam Amazing," she says into my ear, and that's when it happens.

My well breaks, and I start to cry. While I've grown attached to Rob, I also became close to these kids. Both of them.

Jesse places a hand on my back, and I feel his head on my shoulder.

"I love you too," I whisper to them. "Both of you. Very much. It's been an honor to be part of your family even if it was for just a little while."

I stand up, rubbing my tears on the back of my hand. When I look up, Rob is at the top of the stairs, gawking down at us.

I take my fish and hand it to Molly. "Will you do me a favor and take care of Bob for me? I don't think he'll make the drive back safely."

She frowns up at me. "You just don't want him because you named him after Dad and he'll remind you too much of him."

I let out a sad smile at her intuitive assessment of my relationship to the fish.

"Just make sure you don't overfeed him."

Molly nods and hugs Bob the fish in her lap. Jesse puts his hand around her and pulls his sister in for a tight hug.

I walk to my car and put my belongings inside. Like I did a month ago, I storm out of the ranch and watch the dust spit up behind my wheels as I leave the one place that actually felt like a home in a long time.

A family.

My fake family for a moment.

To think, for just a brief second, I kind of thought it could become a real one.

Twenty-Four

"I CAN'T BELIEVE YOU had sex with Rob in a barn," Melissa gasps in a hushed whisper from her seat at the opposite side of the table.

"It's not a barn. It's a shed. But it's not really a shed. It's like a giant wooden garage with large doors, where you house equipment and tools and stuff. Ugh … why does this even matter?!" My head falls into my hand.

"Everything matters when you're overanalyzing your life," Jillian adds from the seat next to me, her glass of water in her hand.

It's annoying that my friends are pregnant because they can't even get drunk or man bash or do something inappropriate, like send a bouquet of penis balloons to him at his jobsite.

Instead, we're sitting at a table in the middle of the outdoor dining room of Café Romano, an Italian restaurant on the waterfront.

It's no doubt that after a woman is ravaged by a man in the best way and then has her heart broken, all within twenty-four hours, she calls an emergency meeting with her best friends. Thankfully, Jillian needed a night out and suggested a refined restaurant. If not, I'd be swigging vodka from a bottle and dancing around a firepit with a voodoo doll in the shape of Robert Bronson.

Jillian has an inquisitive nature to her, so she prods for info. "How did you guys go from arguing all the time to—"

"Romping in the haystacks," Melissa adds.

I correct her, "There was no hay. It's not that kind of ranch." I lift my head and frown, realizing I'm starting to sound just like Rob. It makes me pout, and I let out a heavy sigh.

How did we get from point A to point B? It's simple, I suppose.

"We didn't fight. Once I started staying at the house, we had disagreements, but it worked. I pushed his buttons, and he grunted back. The more time I spent with him, the more I got to like him. He's artistic and kind, funny in his own unique way. He never tried to change who I was. I think he enjoyed the challenge. And the sex ... it was amazing. Out of body and incredible. But he's such a brute. I can't keep up with his multiple personalities. One minute, we're holding hands on the couch, and the next minute, he's yelling because I tried to do right by his kids. He's an animal, and I just can't be around a man like that."

Melissa and Jillian share a look over the breadsticks. It's the kind of look that says they're having a conversation without words. It's annoying, especially since it appears as if they are agreeing with each other and not with me.

"What?" I demand, and I take a swig of my drink. They might be sober, but I am hoping to be so inebriated tonight that I order the balloons myself and then pass out in Melissa's den.

Melissa reclines in her seat and rubs her belly. "You know, Tara, this is kind of what you do."

"Tread carefully before you speak," I warn her.

"And ... there it is," she adds.

I scrunch my face and start regretting asking for a girls' night. If I know one thing about Melissa, she's about to unleash her true feelings of what is happening, and it will come out in a long soliloquy that won't be wrong.

"It's a pattern," she starts and looks almost pained to bring it up. "You meet a guy and over-fantasize about him, to the point that he becomes greater in your head than he is in reality. You build him up so big that he has no other possibility than to disappoint you in some way. It's as if you give him the impossible task to be perfect, which no one is, just so you can cast him aside later on."

"I liked you better when you were reeling from your divorce, didn't believe in love anymore, and kept your opinions of me to yourself."

She smiles. "I'm being serious. You've met some great men over the years, but they never go too deep into a relationship because they do something wrong. They're not intimate enough, they're too intimate, they're rude, they're too sensitive. You even stopped dating that one guy because he wore black socks and sandals out on a date."

"No woman should date a man who would leave the house like that."

Jillian jumps in. "What about the guy who wore the flannel shirt to your birthday party?"

"We went to a nightclub. It was way too hot for flannel. He was sweating all over the dance floor. I couldn't handle it." I make a gagging face.

Melissa tilts her head. "All I'm saying is, maybe you walked out of the house because things were getting serious and you were afraid."

"That makes no sense."

"You were looking for an out. What happened yesterday could have been a fight that was resolved. Instead, you walked out. In fact, you'd walked away from him before."

I point at my chest as I sit up and defend myself to Melissa. "He was yelling at me. He had no right!"

The waiter, who's refilling our water glasses, jumps back at the sound of my raised tone.

As he walks away, Jillian hisses, like the words she is going to say are going to get her in trouble, "He kinda did. You should have told Rob what you knew about his kids. A parent is entitled to know every detail of their kids' lives."

My shoulders fall as I comprehend where she's coming from. "I'm not a parent, but I know parents should know important information about their children. If I found out his child had a horrific disease, I'd tell him. This wasn't malicious." Looking at Melissa, I further explain, "I was trying to be like your mom."

"I know," she breathes. The mention of her mom always makes her melancholy. "Listen, I don't tell Tyler everything that happens with the kids. Sometimes, they need to know they can trust an adult to hold their secrets. I get where your heart was."

Jillian disagrees, "Once you started an intimate relationship with him, you owed him the respect of sharing what you know about his son."

"Wouldn't it have been worse once time had passed?" I suggest.

Jillian shrugs her shoulder and nods her head. "At the very least, you have to admit that he was right to be upset. Whether your intentions were malicious or pure, Jesse is his son. It shows he cares about his children."

My stomach hurts with the notion that Jillian is absolutely correct. "I know he had every right to be upset. I even knew that when he was yelling."

"And you still left," Melissa states. "You walked away because you were scared. His anger didn't scare you. I've seen you stand up to the best of 'em. You were scared because you'd disappointed him and he didn't give you the benefit of the doubt. You walked away because you thought he was gonna end the relationship first."

With my hand on my lips, I look up at the early evening sky.

The moon is there.

It's funny how people only pay homage to the moon in the dark of night when it's bright, but it's there, even in the daytime. It might not be vibrant and shiny, but it's always lingering, ready for someone to notice it.

"Tara"—Jillian leans forward and places her hand on my knee—"are you okay?"

Shaking my head, I digress. "I'm gonna miss that house. It's pretty, and I can already sense it's gonna be drafty in the winter, but it has this comforting charm about it. It's quiet at night, but there's always a creak of the floorboards, like the house is humming. And the property is gorgeous. I've been on more walks in a few weeks than I have in my entire life. I can stare at the mountains all day and pick wildflowers by the bunches for the dinner table."

She leans back and scrunches her brows. "I can see how that house is something you'll miss." She gives Melissa an incredulous look, who just shrugs her shoulders.

I continue, "I should have hugged Molly longer. She was so upset when I was leaving. I'm gonna miss her. That girl has life figured out. She knows the balance between being her own woman and being cool around her friends. She's also a quick learner on how not to be taken advantage of. Jesse, on the other hand, is going through a little of what Izzy went through when you got divorced. He's trying to find his place in this world, and I think he's getting it."

"You were getting close to the kids, huh?" Jillian adds.

"I was," I state with a smile. "I'll miss them."

Melissa bites the inside of her cheek as she asks, "What about Rob?"

I'll miss him most because I was starting to fall in love with him.

"Like you said, I over-fantasized about him, and he didn't live up to my expectations."

Melissa gives a sad grin back. "Tara, that's not what I meant. I think if you just call him—"

I push my shoulders back and give a little shimmy. "It's okay, Melissa. It was good while it lasted, and now, it's over. I'll be fine. I always am. No one can look this hot and be as much of a badass and fall apart every time a man walks away."

She levels her eyes with me. "All true, except for one part. He didn't leave."

I give her the middle finger. Because that's how you respond when your friend levels you with the truth.

Then, I declare, "I have to pee."

The two wave me off, and I have no doubt they'll talk about me when I'm gone. I know my antics have given them plenty to vicariously live through, especially since they're in committed relationships, mothers, and—mostly—sane individuals.

For the most part, my life has been rather exciting with my tales of dating woes. I think I'm starting to realize that I'm tired of exciting.

I'm ready for boring.

As I walk through the dining room, a couple catches my eye. I've met them before under the haze of carnival lights and freshly made cotton candy. Christine and Mike are at a table near a window, holding hands and cheersing with their wineglasses.

I can't help but move toward their table. Yes, I still have to use the restroom, and yet the sight of these two out in the wild, like rare animals, is a something I just want to see more of.

Why? Like I've established, I don't always make the best decisions.

As I step up to the edge of their table, I'm already regretting my decision.

LOVE...IT'S WILD

"Hello there," Mike says as I approach, wide eyes and surprised by my sudden appearance.

Christine is looking at me, befuddled. She clearly doesn't remember me.

"I'm Tara. We met at the fair in Castleton," I remind her.

Mike looks up at me warmly. "Nice to see you again. What a small world to run into you here."

I nod. "Yeah. I'm out with my girlfriends. We have a table outside." I thumb toward the outside patio, as if to further explain where we're sitting.

Christine's mouth opens, as if she just placed me with where she knows me from. "Tara. Yes, the one with the goldfish. You're helping Rob out this summer."

Knowing Rob would hate for Christine to know his personal business, I just nod and don't offer any more info about my helping him—or lack thereof.

"Your kids are amazing," I say instead.

"Thank you. Molly speaks very highly of you," she says, and my heart flutters with the notion that her kid talks about me. It also makes me a little sad. I look at the table set for two and at the half-full wineglasses. "I just wanted to stop and say hello. I hope you have a nice night. Celebrating something special?"

"Our anniversary," Mike states eagerly, certainly proud of his relationship with Christine.

"Congratulations. How many years?"

"Four," Mike says, to which Christine quickly and very sternly adds, "Three."

His brows curve in as he stares at her for clarification. She darts her eyes my way and back to him with a pinch of her lips.

He nods in understanding. "Yes, three years." He doesn't sound happy, having to utter those words.

Now, I know why I walked over here. A woman's intuition is something to be reckoned with, and you should always follow your gut.

"Cut the bullshit," I state. "If you're gonna have the balls to have an affair on your husband, then at least be adult enough to own it. Four years. Happy anniversary. You must be very proud of your infidelity."

Christine's face lights up, as if she's about to launch many words at me, but Mike places his hand on hers and pulls her attention toward him.

"Christine, let it go."

"But she—"

"Don't worry. I won't tell Rob." I stand tall with my hand on my hip, and explain, "I won't tell him that the complaints you gave him for years—he wasn't spontaneous enough or romantic enough or fun enough or plainly just enough of a man—weren't true. It was because you wanted to have sex with someone else."

A woman at the table behind me gasps.

I turn around and let the woman know, "You're gonna wanna keep listening. This is good dinner entertainment."

"Tara," Mike warns, but I keep speaking.

"To have an affair on your husband with a dad from your son's baseball team? Girl, you give housewives a bad name. A man supplies an amazing life for you, works to the bone, and you can't handle that he doesn't have enough time for you."

"I'm not a housewife. I work."

"Semantics." I turn back to the woman behind me and explain, "When people are in the wrong, they always find that one incorrect word you used in your argument and hold on to it for dear life, as if it negates all the other things you said."

The woman nods with me in agreement, so I further explain to the stranger, "The man she left for this guy"—I point to Mike, who buries his head in his hands—"the man I'm talking about, his name is Rob, and he is gorgeous. Like, physically perfect bone structure with the right amount of scruff, and his body is like an Adonis, and his hands are callous from working in construction. You picture what I'm talking about, right?"

The woman fans herself, so I hand over her water glass and then turn back to Christine. "That man is also an amazing father, an incredible artist, phenomenally cool, and a dreamer who had his hopes crushed by a woman who said he wasn't good enough."

Christine throws her napkin down. "Tara, that's enough. You have no idea what Rob is like."

"Yeah, I do. He's a man who bought a ranch with a dream. A

ranch you let him buy so he had a place when you left him. The man can be overpowering because he expects so much from those around him. He has a high moral ground, and when you fall, he can't handle it. Yeah, the man's a dick. He also has a really big dick, which you didn't deserve either."

There are now more gasps and a fork drop or two from people in the restaurant. Is there music in here? Because there should be. It's suddenly very, very quiet. The maître d' starts to make his way over, along with another gentleman.

"He's also a man worth being in love with even when you want to wring his neck and storm out of his house. He's a brute, and imperfect, which makes him everything a woman has ever wanted."

I take a deep gasping breath and then lift my chin. "Anyway, I just want to say happy anniversary, and if you ever mess with my Rob again, I'll come after you in ways that are totally legal yet will ruin your life. I have an Amazon account, and I'm not afraid to use it."

With a pat on the shoulder of the woman behind me, I start to walk toward the ladies' room. Jillian and Melissa are in the vestibule, Jillian with my purse and Melissa with her phone in her hand.

"What are you guys doing here?" I ask them.

"I'm here to tell you we're leaving," Jillian states as if it's obvious.

"And I'm calling Will to make sure you don't get arrested for harassment," Melissa says with her phone to her ear.

Jillian places her hand on my back and ushers me out of the restaurant.

"Where are we going?" I ask them as we walk toward Jillian's car in the parking lot.

"Back to Melissa's house to celebrate," Jillian says, and I raise a brow at her.

When we're all in the car, we close the doors, and it's dangerously silent. That is, until the two burst into a fit of laughter so loud and vibrant that the car shakes.

"That was the coolest thing we've ever seen!"

"Girl, Will is gonna die when I tell him what you said to his ex-sister-in-law!"

Even I join in, the rush of adrenaline from the moment now coursing through my body. "My heart is beating so fast." I place my hand on my heart. "I guess I was more nervous than I thought I'd be, saying that to Christine."

"Nope. That wasn't Christine that's making your heart race," Melissa says as Jillian backs out of the parking space. She turns around and smiles. "You pretty much just admitted to everyone that you're in love with Rob."

"Wow. Maybe I am." My teeth rub against my lower lip as I look up at the sky that's now dark, and my moon is there, hiding behind a cloud. It's kind of like love. You can hide it, run away from it even, but if it's there … it's there. "On a scale of one to ten, how mad do you think he's gonna be at that scene I caused?"

The two of them look at one another in the front seat, smile, and nod.

"Zero!" they say in unison and Melissa adds, "You just told a restaurant full of people that he has a big dick!"

I fall back in my seat. "And I'm the one who gets called out for being childish."

Great, I'm in love with Rob. Why doesn't it feel right? He's mad, but I know this could be resolved if it really mattered. No, there's a gnawing in my gut that's telling me something else.

Telling me that I could love Rob all I want.

Problem is, he won't ever love me back.

Twenty-Five

ROB

BOURBON. A barrel-aged American whiskey. It has a burn that lingers in your throat. Some say it has a red pepper taste. I think it's like a baking spice—sweet and spicy from new, charred oak barrels that release flavors of caramel and vanilla.

Bourbon is a type of whiskey, like the way champagne is a type of wine. All bourbon is whiskey, but not all whiskey is bourbon.

Just like all girls are women, but no other woman is like Tara Parsons.

I kick one of the chairs across the porch. My life was just fine until that woman walked into my house with her catlike dark blue eyes, raven-colored hair, and the sweetest fucking mouth I'd ever seen. Everything about her had the spice of bourbon. From the intoxicating way her lips tempted me to kiss her with every foul-mouthed word that came out of her mouth, to the sweet way she acted with my daughter, to how she moved that body with the vicious sway of her hips, to her too-short dresses that I knew she wore just to tempt me.

The woman complained that I was hard to deal with when it came to my mood swings. But she's the definition of all over the place. An accountant who does paperwork in her room while wearing these sexy glasses and runs through spreadsheets like a savant, but she doesn't know how to keep a room clean. She loves to bake because it has precise measurements. She makes the most delicious baked goods, but can't cook a steak because it's impossible to know if it is still pink inside. She is a beautiful, smart, funny woman who often acts like a child and doesn't know the difference between right and wrong.

The chair I kicked across the porch is on its side. I set it right and take a seat in it. My glass is in my hand, yet I'm not drinking it. I should. It's dependable. No matter how fucked my day is, I can always come back home to the feeling of a glass in my hand, the familiar taste of the bourbon rolling over my tongue, and that burn that eases down my throat.

That's why I like bourbon.

Good old dependable bourbon.

In my forty years on earth, I never thought I'd be sitting on my porch, wallowing. This is the shit you do when you're a teen. Grown men don't drink their sorrows away about a woman who they only knew for a month. They don't replay in their head the fight they had that had her walking out the door over and over again. They don't keep on hearing her laugh and reliving how it made them want to smile, but they didn't always. Why didn't I laugh? I wish I knew.

When I was married, I was a content man. Christine and I had dated a year before I proposed. We were young, but I was the kind of man who knew what he wanted in a short amount of time. We'd met through friends. She was four years older, so even though I was twenty-four when I became a father, she was already twenty-eight and ready to start her life. I wasn't like typical guys in their early twenties. I wasn't in the bars and scoring with different women every night. I liked my comforts. A good day's work. A good drink. A good woman.

When I met Christine, all the boxes were checked. She was pretty as heck and sweet as pie. We made each other laugh and liked to go hiking together. My mother loved her.

Then, she gave me my son, and I didn't think I could love her more. She was funny and had lots of friends. We had them over a lot. Sometimes too much. The kids loved. Especially Jesse.

Jesse … that boy didn't want to come into this world. He made his mom labor for twenty hours and still refused to come out. The doctors had to go in and get him, and then he cried for three months straight. I used to tell Christine the baby was pissed to have been born. She didn't think that was funny.

It bothered her that the baby wasn't this perfect, sleeping child, like you see in the advertisements. Jesse had colic, refused to eat, and only wanted to be held. No sooner did I walk through the door than that baby was placed in my arms and she ran upstairs to get some much-needed sleep.

I didn't mind. I enjoyed those nights with my son. We sat on the couch for hours—him in my arms, baby bottle in my hand, and a game on the television that I couldn't watch because I just stared at him. He was a miracle, and I vowed to do everything in my power to give him a good life.

Christine started to come into her own again just as Jesse came into his own. I wanted more children, but it took Christine some convincing. She wasn't ready to go through the sleepless nights she'd had with Jesse. That's why we waited for many years to have Molly.

Molly … that little girl was born to music. Her labor was so easy. The doctor played Bob Marley's "Three Little Birds" as she came into this world. She was a good sleeper and easy eater, and she always smiled.

If Molly had come first, we would have had ten kids. Until Jesse was born, of course.

My kids are a bit like bourbon. Sweet and spicy. I suppose they get their personalities from living in a home where their mother wasn't happy because their dad couldn't do anything right, and seeing it all through a different pair of lenses.

Life as a parent is hard. You want the cars and the house, the kids need everything they deserve, and it all costs money. I worked overtime and took on extra contracts. Despite the hours, I never missed a game, school concert, or practice. I would have loved to be home more, but Christine wanted to remodel the kitchen, Jesse needed braces, the car broke down, Molly joined a pricey travel basketball team. I put in more hours, started my own company, and got us out of debt. The house always needed work. The lawn mowed, the bedrooms painted, a pipe fixed. Balancing all that as a workingman and a father leaves little room to be a good husband. I came home tired, hungry, and yet I still had to have energy to be intimate with my wife. She, however, was so tired from her day that the thought of being with me was the last thing on her mind.

That's when I started sketching again. A hobby I had when I was young yet put aside. I kept a space in the basement for my supplies. Christine didn't want it near the remodeled spaces upstairs because it looked like clutter.

I've heard the phrase, *Men have it all*. It's bullshit.

I've never had it all. I had the house. I had the job. I had the kids. I had the wife.

What I didn't have was time to spend at my house because I worked so much that I was exhausted from being at my job and away from my family. I loved my kids, but never had enough time with them. And my wife grew distant because no matter how much time I tried to devote to her, it was never enough.

I was never enough.

She was right.

I should've made the time to take her out to dinner. I should have shown her I cared with flowers. I shouldn't have said no to those parties she wanted to attend because I was too tired. I should have taken her dancing when she wanted to slip away for a weekend. I was lost in the routine of life and now I'm sounding like a damn Bruno Mars song.

Still, I loved what I had. I loved my wife. I loved my children.

One day, I came home, and Christine was in our room. She was trying on lingerie. She startled at the sight of me, but the grin on my face must have been enough for her to relax. She looked beautiful, more so because after us being in a rut of just trying to live our day-to-day lives, she was trying to bring us back together, and it made me feel like a fool. A fool for not doing enough for this woman. I made love to my wife that evening.

The next day, I took her out to this ranch and showed her the property I'd been eyeing. It was desolate and decrepit, but I thought it was perfect. It could be a place we'd come to relax and forget the noise of our hectic lives. A summer retreat just for the four of us.

She seemed reluctant. There was so much work to be done, and it was an impossible task, especially for a family who was trying to take on less stress in our lives. She was right. That was why I was surprised when, a short time later, she told me to buy the property. I thought this was a good omen. I was still working a lot of hours, but I was making more money and had the means to give this to my family. We signed for the property and came here for a weekend, and she never returned.

The day after we signed the separation papers, she was sitting next to my friend Mike at Jesse's baseball game. The next game, they were holding hands. By the third, they were officially together.

I'm not mad my marriage ended. I'm mad because it ruined my kids. I'm pissed because I tried everything in my power to give Christine what she needed, and it was never enough. I was never enough.

I swore off love. I swore off women. Swore off happily ever after.

For the past three years, I've been a pissed off walking zombie until, one day, I saw her.

Tara.

It was my brother's engagement party. I was sitting at a table at the backyard reception, watching Molly on the dance floor. Jesse was talking with my parents on the other side of the party. Molly started dancing with her cousins when I looked next to her and saw a woman.

This wasn't any woman.

She was so strikingly beautiful in a black satin cocktail dress that hugged her frame. She had these amazing curves, and her face was like a porcelain doll. Ravishing was the word for her kind of beauty. Her looks were the first thing I noticed about her.

She was dancing with a little girl. I assumed she was her daughter, and I smiled at the sight of them doing these ridiculous moves. Saturday Night Fever type of air pointing to doing the hustle and into the backstroke. None of it made sense, and yet they were laughing and having a great time.

Then, I heard her speak.

"Ainsley, the key to happiness is dancing. Having a bad day? Let it loose in your kitchen. Want to celebrate your aunt getting hitched?

Get freaky in the backyard. And never ever let anyone let you feel self-conscious about your moves because the most irresistible people in this world know how to dance like no one is watching."

"That's silly, Tara. Why would I want to dance alone?"

"If you don't love yourself, who will?" Tara told the girl as she twirled her under her arm. "It's called self-confidence, kid. No one should take that from you."

Her words hit me in the gut. I had to stand up and walk away from the table. I found myself by the bar, getting myself a bourbon. A man and woman were arguing while emptying a box of liquor. I felt more comfortable with the bickering couple instead of listening to the beautiful woman on the dance floor. This, I was used to. The last few years of my life hadn't been hearts and flowers.

I was having my drink while standing at the bar. My eyes still wandered her way. I figured she was married and living a life of false promises that she hadn't realized weren't going to come true. A woman still in the days of a pretend happy life.

Then, I found out it was worse than I'd thought.

"Who is that woman?" I asked my mother as she walked up to the bar to get a chardonnay.

She turned around and pointed rather obviously toward Tara on the dance floor. "That woman is Tara Parsons. She has propositioned every man at this party, and it is quite desperate if you ask me. You see the table of police officers over there? I bet she's run through them like a freight train in the middle of the night."

I nearly spilled my bourbon at my mother's analogy, wondering if she even knew what it meant.

"She's single?" I asked, surprised my assessment of her had been incorrect.

"Desperately so. She'll do anything for a man because he's looking for love and she wants to get married immediately. Mark my words. She's a lot of fun, but a world of trouble. Stay away from that one."

I nodded, almost relieved my mother had squashed the bubble of attraction I had to Tara.

I wouldn't have gone near her if she was taken, but knowing she was single, I might have been caught in her trap. How could I not? She was gorgeous and had sass that oozed from her making you want to see what she'd do or say next.

When I saw her coming toward me, I heeded my mother's words and walked the other way.

I did it the next time I saw her at a family party.

She was wearing pants and an oversize silky blouse this time, so I couldn't even blame the sexy clothing on how I noticed her instantly. She was telling a story to my cousin Kevin and his wife.

"There I was, hiding in the closet in this guy's bedroom because his mother had come home and he wasn't supposed to have girls over. He was twenty-six! I should have known better than to date a man who still lived with his mother, but I never dreamed it would be so bad that he'd usher me into his wardrobe the minute she appeared in the house."

"What did you do?" Kevin asked.

"I stayed there for about five minutes when I realized, Fuck this, I'm an accomplished woman with a killer personality and perfect tits who should be pampered on satin sheets and not crouching next to his Nikes. *I opened that door while they were mid-conversation, flipped my hair over my shoulder, and sauntered my fine ass out of that house."*

I knew in that moment that Tara Parsons was either batshit crazy or the most self-confident woman I had ever seen.

My days of avoiding her were limited when I went to my brother Will's wedding.

I was fixing Jesse's tie when a woman appeared. She had on a rose-pink dress, and her hair was pinned up in a pretty updo that the bridal party was wearing. She was walking through the lobby when Izzy, Will's new stepdaughter, was pacing back and forth with a paper in her hand.

I almost didn't recognize Tara. Once she started speaking, I knew it was her.

"You can't be nervous, Izzy. You got this! You've been practicing your rap-style maid-of-honor toast for months. Here's what you're gonna do. You're going to walk onto that dance floor and picture everyone in shark onesies."

"Huh?" Izzy sounded confused.

So did Jesse and I, and we made faces at one another as we eavesdropped on the conversation.

"I thought I was supposed to picture them naked."

"Takes too much effort. Too many body styles. Just picture them all wearing the same zippered-up fleece shark costume, and you'll suddenly feel all the confidence you need to get through it. And if you can't, no worries. I'll be right by your side. Now, let's go stand by your mom and watch her marry the best fucking man on the planet!"

There was something different about her that evening. The hair, yes. But her body language was a little off. She exuded confidence when talking to people, but when she was by herself, she almost looked … lost.

I knew that expression. I saw the self-doubt in her eyes. The way she took heavy breaths while lifting her chin, as if trying to calm down the negative thoughts in her head. She was better than me because for each moment of low she had, she quickly morphed into this vixen in the ballroom, smiling, flirting, dancing.

I heard they were about to do the garter toss, and there was no way I was standing on that dance floor, being pushed on by my mother, who had recently started talking about me needing to meet a woman. I got a fresh glass of bourbon and walked myself outside.

The smokers near the door were enough for me to head toward the side of the building. A place where it was dark and quiet. Just how I needed it.

I found myself looking up. The moon was big that night. I'd never stopped and stared at it before, but for some reason, that night, I found myself getting lost in its beauty and looking for the face of the man on the moon, the kind kids were led to believe was there.

I was so lost in the craters and wondering if a flag could actually fly up there, and this exact moon was in the sky during the Roman Empire, that I almost missed her.

Tara jogged down the nearby path. I heard her breathing first. It was harsh and labored, like she was upset and couldn't catch up with her feelings. She ran toward a tree and started to climb it. I couldn't believe my eyes as I saw her bunch up the loose dress and hoist herself up. Her strength was evident with the swift way she got up that tree. I walked toward her, mesmerized by the sight of her at the top. She appeared to be looking at the moon as well and talking to herself.

This was a new version of the woman I'd seen. From the sight of her in an oak tree, she was definitely batshit crazy. Yet she was far more relatable in this moment than in the past.

She was unglued, and she was in pain.

I knew I had to stay there. My intention was never for her to see me, but I needed to know she was going to be okay.

And then she fell.

And so did I.

For her.

With her.

In her.

How Tara Parsons had gone from being the woman I ran from to the one I was crawling to was beyond me. I tried to fight it. I tried so damn hard.

I rise from my chair again and walk over to the railing.

I can still picture her crooked grin when she arrived every week, ready to start a new one with us. She looked like she was relieved to be here. Like she was home.

Home.

I liked my home with her in it. I liked the smell of her baking, the laughter that echoed in the house, the way Molly was always talking a million miles a minute to her, how Jesse jingled car keys, ready for her to take him driving, and how I felt when I came home and saw her eyes light up at the sight of my broody ass walking into the room.

Even when she hated me, her eyes gleamed when she looked my way.

Too bad she wouldn't be looking this way again.

Twenty-Six

ROB

"YOU DONE SULKING OVER there, old man?" Will surprises me in my shed while I'm organizing my equipment from the long workweek.

"What are you doing here?" I look him over in his cargo shorts and polo. "Melissa's got you looking like suburbia."

"Don't hate on the khakis. I'm getting into dad mode. Soon, I'll be wearing tube socks and New Balance sneakers."

"I'm a dad, and I don't wear that shit."

"No. You wear jeans in the dead of summer, like a psychopath." He laughs at his own joke as he steps farther into the shed and leans against the four-wheeler parked against the wall. "Lots of gossip going around the Bronson households."

"You don't say." My tone is full of annoyance, as are my actions as I count the drill bits in my kit, getting pissed when I see one is missing, and fling the lid of my toolbox open to find it.

Will seems at ease where he is, even crossing his ankles and folding his arms. "As you know, our family loves to talk. You'd know if you picked up your phone. Don't worry; I've been on the receiving end of everyone calling. I'll just fill you in on the highlights. We'll start with Cade. He said he's never seen you so jealous about a woman before. You were ready to shoot his head off when you saw him rolling on the ground with Tara."

"That kid has always been one for stories."

"He is a bit of a tale spinner. That's why I didn't believe him when he said dinner with you was the first time you looked content and happy in a long-ass time. The way you were in high school when you did that flash mob. Do you remember that?"

I look at him with an *of course I do* stare.

He continues, "I told Cade, there's no way. Rob is the mean one. He's too mad these days to be sated. Tara's too funny and too cool to be a perfect match for his cranky ass anyway."

I grunt at my brother, which makes him laugh. I want to punch his smug face with a sharp right hook. I might if he keeps this shit up.

"You done?"

"I heard there's a ladder in here that leads upstairs."

"Why is nothing sacred in this family?"

"That's what families do. They talk because they care. Mom doesn't know about the shed sex, but she does know something's been brewing out here. She's been calling it for weeks."

"I've been avoiding her on purpose. Tara isn't her favorite person."

"Neither was Melissa, and Mom warmed up to her. Mom doesn't care who we end up with as long as it's true love."

My hands stop before my brain does. I look up at my brother and level him with an intense stare. "I don't love Tara."

"How could you when you don't believe in it anymore?"

I slam the toolbox closed and walk to my metal chest, where I keep spare parts. "Aren't you expecting a baby at any minute? Go home."

"Can't. My wife kicked me out. Said I was hovering too much. She accused me of being a stalker, which, admittedly, I am. I put an app on her phone so I know where she is in case she goes into labor while she's out."

"Hazard of the job, huh?"

"You learn way too much, being a cop." He walks over to my toolbox and opens it. "Since my wife doesn't want me, you get me."

"Can I accuse you of stalking me so you'll leave me alone too?"

"Not a chance. Especially since I have a story I thought you'd want to hear."

"Don't wanna hear it, Will."

"What are you looking for anyway?"

"My damn drill bit. Jesse used it on the job today, and he didn't put it back like he's supposed to. Molly came with us because I had no one to watch her which meant I got nothing done because I was concerned about what she was doing. Now, my drill bit is gone. I like my shit to be where it's supposed to be."

Will walks over to my drill kit and flips open the top. He lifts the drill, and lo and behold, it's rolling around beneath the piece of equipment.

"Found it." He has the nerve to look proud of himself. "Found it right where it was supposed to be. I could think of a few analogies for this. Looking for something, and it's right in front of you."

I take the bit from his hand and place it in the holder inside the kit and close it with a harsh push. "You're an asshole. Tell your stupid story so you can get out of here."

Will, with his smug expression, walks along the shed, surveying my room. He puts his hands in his pockets and strolls around like he's happy.

"Your nanny told off your ex-wife, epically. Christine and Mike were out to dinner where the girls were. Now, I don't have all the details, but apparently, your woman went to bat for you. Big time. Even declared in front of a packed restaurant that you're … well … packing."

It takes me a moment to realize what he means. I conceal the impressed tilt of my mouth as I picture Tara leveling with Christine.

"I'm oddly not surprised she did that. She is crazy."

"Crazy about you. Word has it, she called Christine out on all of her shit. Right down to the way she treated you."

"I don't want Tara sticking up for me." I pick up a wrench and evaluate the steel. It's strong and sturdy yet tarnished from years of use.

"That's the funny thing about loving someone. You don't do things because they want it. You do it because it's what they need, whether they know it or not."

I toss the wrench in my hand. It lands on the floor with a thud. "She lied to me. For a split second, I thought maybe this girl could be something special. Maybe being married to Christine was the fluke, and not all relationships end like that. I let my guard down, and in less than a month, she broke my trust, and she walked out the door. Not the first time either. She'd left the first day she was here. I can't be with someone like that."

"That sucks that she left, but there's probably a good reason she did. Maybe you're not the only one who has a hard time letting their guard down. You push people away. She walks away. Same shit."

"All right, Dr. Phil. That's enough."

He laughs. "I prefer Jay Shetty. A little more modern. Don't give me the accolades. Melissa and I were talking about this all night. Apparently, the two of us are relationship geniuses."

"Says the man who proposed to a woman he didn't love," I say, reminding my brother of his past relationship mistake. One he made out of duty rather than love.

"I got out of that before it was too late, and I got into a relationship with a woman who is mad at me more times than not, yet I can't live without her. Sure, it might not last. Melissa's been divorced. You are. We can name twenty people off the cuff whose marriages didn't work. What does that mean? You gonna die alone because you married a jerk who exposed your negative traits and used it to justify shacking up with your friend? We all know what happened. Only one who doesn't is you."

I run a hand behind my neck and grip the skin, pulling hard to feel something other than the frustration in my chest, paired with the ache in my gut. I hate when my brother is right. He's the golden boy of the family. The hero. And the best man I know. I don't take advice from many, but if I ever did, it would be from Will. I respect the hell out of the guy.

"I'm not an idiot, Will. I know what happened."

"Then, fuck the past. If you don't give it a shot, you don't know what you might miss out on. You think you let your guard down with Tara, but you didn't. Cade said you were like a wild animal when you saw her with him. Like your trust issues were raging."

I look up at the ceiling shed, the one that was the base of my afternoon with Tara. The woman who called me out on the same shit Will is right now. They're not wrong.

"I don't know how to be like you," I say. "Not when I've been hurt before. I'm scared. I hate that I'm fucking scared to be with someone. Men don't get scared."

"Fuck yeah, we do. I was frightened when I thought Melissa wouldn't trust me when we first met. I know Luke was petrified Jillian wouldn't accept him after he left and lied to her. And you don't know how to move on without thinking everything your ex-wife said about you is true and that the next woman will leave you just like Christine did. Brother, you've gotta get your head out of your ass and take a fucking chance."

I turn around and place my hands on head and look down.

Even if I did want to let another woman into my life, Tara wouldn't be it. She lied to me, kept secrets from me, and she left me twice.

"It's not so easy," I say, turning around and going back to my tools.

"You're a stubborn ass—you know that?"

I do. Just another thing about me that will never change.

Twenty-Seven

ROB

THE HOUSE IS TOO quiet. Jesse's been on his cell phone all morning, scrolling through social media. Molly is staring at her fish. Ever since Tara left, Bob the fish has been her favorite thing to stare at. She misses Tara. I know it. Part of me does too.

It's a nice day out, so I urge the kids to go outside. With reluctant steps, they head out the door.

I'm not entirely sure why I end up in the art studio, finishing the portrait of Tara. It wasn't my intention. I came down here for a drink and a mission to clear my head. After too many failed attempts to create something new, I kept thinking about her sketch. I add color, shading, and before I know it, the painting is complete.

Fuck, she's beautiful. Even on a piece of paper, her vibrant personality jumps off the page. I trace the curves of her smile with my brush one last time and then step away.

I can't hang it anywhere. Nudes don't exactly go with the house aesthetic. I'll probably have to burn it. Someday. Maybe. Never.

It's not the first time I painted her. The day Molly and I set up Tara's bedroom, I found myself in here with a sketch pad in my hand. Next thing I knew, I was up until two o'clock in the morning painting the portrait of Tara in the dress she wore to the wedding.

LOVE...IT'S WILD

My imagination ran wild as I pictured what she'd look like dancing in a field with the breeze in her hair. I hung it up in her bedroom and wondered if she'd realize she was my muse.

I look at the time. Four hours went by in the blink of an eye. I wash my hands, then head upstairs, looking for the kids. They must still be outside because they're not in here.

I look outside, but they're nowhere to be seen. I head to the shed and notice the four-wheeler is missing. I don't like them out on it without an adult. Leave it to my kids to galivant wherever they want. They have no respect for authority.

I don't hear the machine, so they're either way too far away from the house or crashed the damn thing.

I head in my truck and pray they're not lying in a ditch somewhere. If they're not, they're gonna get an earful from me.

I'm driving across the grass, probably chopping it up with my thick rubber tires, for a solid five minutes, looking in what I think are the obvious places for them to ride a four-wheeler. They're nowhere to be seen.

I head around the lines of the property, hoping they were smart enough to stay on our land. As I'm rounding a bend, a familiar tower peers out from the trees.

The stone structure was something that caught my interest when I first looked at the property. According to the realtor, it had been built by the previous landowner in memory of his late wife and her love of the children's story *The Secret Garden*. It's half an acre in size with a main tower that's two stories high and a spiral staircase, shrubbery mazes, fishponds, all enclosed by a brick wall. I know all that because I studied the plans for the space, hoping to revitalize it for my family. I made sketches of it exactly as it once had been and then hoped to make the inside a family room with toys and books.

A place to relax, away from electronic devices and the noise of the outside world.

A place where my kids could be imaginative.

Where my family could be a family again.

The tower looks different. It's almost whiter somehow. I start driving toward it, curious about its state. I can only imagine the garden has grown into greater disrepair since I gave up on it.

What would be the point of making a space made for joy when everything was falling apart around us?

I suppose this is where I admit I've been a bit depressed the past few years.

Thank God Will's not here. He'd have a field day, tearing me apart mentally, bit by bit.

I park the truck near the garden and see the four-wheeler parked nearby. I get out and walk around to the opening in the wall.

My eyes can't believe what they're seeing.

I'm so speechless that even my thoughts take a second to reel in where I am.

It's … magical.

I'm standing on a cobblestone path I didn't know was here from the amount of moss that covered it years ago. The path is flanked by two fishponds of water so clear that I can see the bright orange fish swimming around. A frog leaps nearby and brings my attention to the flower beds, full of vibrant wildflowers, thriving in abundance in the sunlight. Some of the plants are so tall that they create a wall between the path I'm on and another on the other side of the flower bed. I walk around, zigzagging through the garden, amazed at its beauty. It's even more ethereal than what I drew in my pictures. I have chills radiating through my bones as a butterfly chases another. I let out a laugh. It's crazy to laugh when you're by yourself, but it's all so surreal that I don't know what else to do.

I look at the tower. The large door is closed. I walk up to it and look at the concrete structure. I run my hand over the door and note the lack of dust and lean forward to smell paint varnish.

I open the door. My mind is completely blown away by what I see. A room, just as I created in my sketchbook, complete with a bookcase, two leather chairs, and a chess table. There are games lined up on the side and photos of me, Jesse, and Molly hung on the walls.

It's brighter in here with light-yellow walls and a yellow-and-blue carpet.

Molly and Jesse appear in the doorway, looking like they've seen a ghost. My presence isn't what they were expecting.

"Dad," Jesse starts, clearly worried about something. "You're not supposed to be here. I guess you can be here. We just didn't think you would … yet." He runs his hands through that unkempt mop of hair. "Are you mad?"

I look at Molly, who is wearing a matching expression. My children are actually frightened of me.

"Why would I be mad?" I ask them evenly.

"Because you hate this place," Molly says, her bottom teeth showing with how she's grimacing. "We remember you coming out here a lot, and then you just stopped."

I nod. They're not wrong. In fact, my kids are more in tune to life than I've ever given them credit for.

Gesturing to the room, I ask them, "Who did all this?"

"We did," Jesse says.

"You two did all this? What exactly did you do?"

They look at each other and shrug, almost as if they don't know where to start.

"I cleaned the outside of the castle. We didn't know there was a spigot out here, so I drove the water buckets back and forth from the house and used dish soap and a rag. It took most of the week, and I almost fell off the ladder a few times, but it wasn't a bad job."

I point a finger at him in disbelief. "You cleaned this entire thing by hand with a rag?"

"It was my punishment for lying to Tara about driver's ed."

A bubble of amusement rises up my chest and comes out of my throat. "She punished you?"

"Yeah. She was pissed."

"Man, Tara is meaner than I am," I joke, and my kids actually laugh. I ask Molly, "What did you do wrong that you had to help out?"

"Nothing. I wanted to help. I cleaned out the pond. It was gross. I threw up twice. Tara said it was good for me. A woman should never be afraid to get her hands dirty and should always know how to do everything a man can. We're the superior species, you know?"

I smile at my daughter's new self-assuredness on life. "You don't say."

"Tara did a lot of this too. The weeding was mostly her, but we cleaned and planted the flowers ourselves," Jesse adds. "She showed me how to trim the hedges with a gas hedger we rented. Don't look too closely because they're not perfectly straight."

"And I learned how to use a leaf blower, power washer, and how to cut corners when painting."

I cover my mouth with my hand as I look at the room again, amazed that my children did all this.

"The furniture?" I wonder out loud.

"Bought from the Salvation Army in town. Tara says we should try to recycle furniture instead of buying new when possible. It's also good for the budget. No need to overspend."

I am shocked by the words coming out of my son's mouth.

Jesse takes a step forward and nods his head toward the staircase. "You should look upstairs. That was Tara's space. She did it all herself."

The wrought iron stairs are small but easy to climb. I follow the swirl of the banister up to the second floor.

If I wasn't shocked before, I am now.

An easel sits by the arched window with a canvas on the wood. On a table in the center of the room, which I assume is so the supplies don't get wet when it rains, are art supplies. They're not what I would pick, but they're all here. Brushes, paints, pencils, charcoal … everything I have in my basement studio, but now, I have a place for myself out here.

There was a time when my art was a burden to my family. A nuisance in the house.

Not only has Tara brought this space back from the dead, but I'm pretty sure she brought me back from the dead too.

"Are you crying, Dad?" Molly's voice startles me.

I wipe my cheek with the back of my hand. "No."

Jesse laughs. "It's okay to cry, Dad. This is really cool. If we weren't part of the process, we wouldn't believe it either. We helped, but it was all Tara. She didn't do this for us. She did it for you."

I place my hands on my hips and shake my head. "I don't understand why. I was pretty mean to her at times."

"Not all the time. You smiled a lot when you were around her." Molly looks like she's making a serious point.

Jesse swallows and looks at the ground. "Dad, she didn't mean to hurt you by helping me. I'm glad she was around that night. I was really frightened, and she raced to get me. I know why it was wrong, but if it's worth anything, if she wasn't around, I don't know who I would have called."

"I know, son. I'm sorry it couldn't be me. I've been hard on you because I worry so much. I'd die if anything happened to you."

Now, it's Jesse's turn to cry. "I know, Dad."

Molly rolls her eyes. "You two are acting like a bunch of babies—you know that? I think we can all agree you've both been boneheads."

I hold my arms out. Molly rushes toward me and hugs me tight around my waist. I nod toward Jesse to come over, and he does, too, slower, but he settles himself against my chest, and I lay my chin over his head, wondering when my kids got so big.

When did they get so smart and strong? When did I stop realizing how amazing they were?

About the time I lost myself.

Molly looks up at me with her bright eyes wide. "All right, Dad, so what's your favorite part?"

"I'd have to say the fishpond. That's really cool. Will they die in the winter?"

"I hope not. They were a lot of work to get in here." Jesse steps away and slides his hands into his pockets. "I like the downstairs room. It's pretty cool. Molly and I were playing gin rummy before."

"I like your art studio, Dad. Think it's really nice here."

I hug Molly tighter. "Yeah. It's great up here. Maybe I'll teach you how to paint."

Jesse takes a hesitant step forward. "I'd like to learn, too, if you don't mind."

"How about now?" I offer and walk over to the table of paints. "We have plenty to get started."

The kids keep their grins on their faces as they walk over to the paint supplies Tara stocked up here, and I stare at them in admiration.

We're gonna start right now.

Not just with painting. I think it's time to begin something new in many ways.

Twenty-Eight

TARA

TONIGHT'S SUPPOSED TO BE my night. When a woman gets an award as prestigious as the Valor County Recognition of Excellence in Accounting and Finance, she goes all out. She wears her friend's dress—a sparkling, hugging ensemble that makes her boobs like those of a twenty-five-year-old and her ass so firm that a quarter could bounce off of it.

My hair is blown out and shiny, looking sleek against the dramatic eye makeup I'm sporting. My shoes are new because I needed some retail therapy to get my spirits up.

I look dynamite, and I mean, if they were casting for a new Bond girl, I could easily get the part. While I look extraordinary on the outside, I'm not quite feeling like myself on the inside.

There's a Michael Bublé impersonator singing tonight. He's singing about having someone under his skin, and it's an annoying reminder of the one who's currently under my skin and taking over every morsel of thought I have.

Nope, I am not going to think of Rob tonight.

Instead, I walk through the room, sway my hips, lift my chin, giggle even, and then look down at the glass in my hand. I ordered myself a bourbon. Of course I did. And so I drink it.

LOVE...IT'S WILD

As it burns my throat on the way down, I think to myself, *Hello, reality. You kinda suck sometimes.*

"Tara," Patrick calls as he sees me standing by the bar.

I let out a deep sigh as I turn to him and put on my airs as he and Victoria stroll up.

"Congratulations on your award tonight."

"Thank you. Congratulations on spending fifteen hundred dollars on a table to impress your friends." I turn to Victoria, who looks stunned. "Sorry, did that come out rude?"

She nods with an uneasy shift of her head, to which I wink at her.

"Good. I meant for it to sound that way."

It's funny how, a month ago, I cared what Patrick thought of me. My looming single status and his pity eyes did something to my psyche that was unhealthy. Now, I think I've completely lost my ability to give a shit what he thinks of me.

Still, Patrick lets out one of those polite laughs meant to defuse the situation. "You're funny. Did you come here alone?"

"I did. It's pretty great too. I can walk around and mingle, drink what I want, say what I want, and go home with whoever I want." I look Victoria right in the eye as I speak.

That comment wasn't meant to be a threat to her, like I'd take her husband, nor an invitation that I'd like her to go home with me. I'm just in a mood and taking it out on them.

And now, I feel awful. They don't deserve my sass. All they did was start a life together, move to the greatest small town in the world to raise their fruit, and happen to have me as a past mistake lurking in their ear.

I blow hard, making my lips vibrate. "Ignore me, guys. I'm having an existential crisis tonight. I wish you nothing but happy days and nights full of orgasms."

I cheers them and walk away from their befuddled stares.

It's really hard, pretending to be fabulous all the time. Sometimes, you're fabu-loss. And when you are, you take a seat and drink your god-awful bourbon, just as God intended.

"Is this seat taken?" a man asks behind me.

I turn to the empty seat meant for Rob, who was supposed to be my date. It's a sad reminder that he was kind of the man in my life for a short amount of time. Then, I do a double take and turn around because I know who just asked that question.

My jaw drops, and my brows rise at the sight before me.

Robert Bronson.

Sweet love of all things mean and good because he's here in a black suit, white shirt, black tie, and looking so ravishingly handsome. His dark eyes bear a secret expression as he looks down at me with one hand in his pants pocket and a smirk on his face.

I've never seen Rob smirk. I like smirking Rob. I like it too much.

"May I?" He points to the chair again.

I snap out of my haze to swallow down my nerves and nod. I have a dazed expression on my face as he sends my pulses spinning.

"I've never seen you at a loss for words."

"I am a gamut of perplexing emotions right now, yes."

He takes the seat. I face the table, but he's angled so his full body is aimed at me. He has one elbow on the table, and the other rests casually on his thigh. I breathe in deeply.

"Hi," he drawls, and I clench my jaw.

Frustration mounts my nerves, along with overall excitement because he's sitting beside me.

"Why exactly are you here?"

"I told you I'd be here on your big night. I'm a man of my word."

"But you yelled at me. You're supposed to be mad at me because I lied."

"And you're supposed to be mad because I didn't trust you. You don't look very mad right now. In fact, I'm honestly relieved that you seem pretty unnerved. In a good way."

He leans toward my shoulder. The heat of his powerful form warms my skin in a way that I get chills for no reason whatsoever.

His breath licks my skin as he utters, "Tara, I'm sorry."

I turn to him. My face is stunned, yet his is stoic and, dare I say, remorseful. His warm chestnut eyes are looking at mine with a glaze of emotion that says he means what he says. There's no facade over them, no hidden purpose that I want to decode. His expression shows he's speaking with blatant honesty.

"That didn't sound like you were spitting knives," I comment, remembering how it once was so hard for him to apologize.

"It's the truth."

I practically melt at his words. I fear I might become a puddle of mush on the floor, and the cleaning crew will have to come in here after hours and clean up the mess.

I shake my head fiercely and wave my hands. "No. You can't do this. You can't walk in here and be all sweet and apologetic. You're gonna make me over-fantasize this to be something that it's not. You're broody, and I'm hopeful. You're mean, and I'm crazy. You're supposed to push me away, and I run as fast as I can because that's who we are."

Rob takes my hand that's practically shaking and holds it in his warm palm. The calluses against my soft skin should be a reminder of how different we are, yet the feel of them makes me stop and take a breath.

"Will you dance with me?"

His offer has me staring at him like he's positively insane. First, he shows up, looking all handsome in his suit and patent leather shoes, and then he apologizes, and finally, he has the nerve—the absolute nerve—to ask me to dance.

"Yes," I say because I'm a glutton for punishment.

Rob rises and takes my hand, walking me out to the dance floor. I follow him and even shift myself into the better lighting of the room because a girl always knows the best place to stand to look irresistible.

He takes my hand and places an arm around my waist. My body pushing into his is so natural. I know this form and what lies beneath the suit. It's gorgeous and powerful and oh-so good at what it does when it's unleashed. I try to blink away the thought of a naked Rob on top of me and focus on the moment.

Our feet move in time to the melody. I'm surprised to find he's not a bad dancer. I mean, he's no Fred Astaire, but the man can keep a beat.

With each glide, I relax into his arms.

He holds me closer.

My head rests against his chest.

His lips find my forehead, and I close my eyes, loving the sensation. It causes me to look up at him in wonder.

Wonder what all this means.

Wonder where this is going.

His eyes speak the same. They brim with tenderness and passion as his heart beats strongly against mine with purpose.

"You're right," he breathes, and I give him my full attention. "I am broody, and you are crazy. But as you said, I need to come up with a few more adjectives. Here's what I have. Stunning—and not just in your looks, but also in the way you light up a room when you enter it. From the moment I saw you, I couldn't keep my eyes off of you, and I think I'll never be able to stop. Tenacious. You have a persistence to you unlike anyone else I've ever met. You keep your ideals and refuse to give up, even when a curmudgeon like me tells you otherwise. Thoughtful. You place others before yourself in a way you don't give yourself credit for. Fun. Strong-willed. Hardworking. Exasperating," he says, and we both let out light laughs at that one. "And wild. Wild because the way you make me feel is unrestrained. With you, I don't have to live behind a wall."

He looks like he's struggling to explain what that wall is exactly, so I tell him, "Veiled steel of emotion. I named it for you. It sounds more romantic the way I say it."

He stares at me for a beat and then ignites into a wide smile.

There's a certain radiance about him, an aura of self-confidence that I haven't seen before. I let go of his hand and step back. We're in the middle of the dance floor, the only couple not dancing, and yet I stand here and look at him with a scowl on my face.

"I'm sorry too, Rob. I was wrong, and I want you to know I'll never lie to you again."

Closing the distance, he brushes a hair that fell onto my temple and places it behind my ear. "I won't push you away again. You won't run again. We'll fight. It'll probably be dirty, but we're gonna try to make it work because I want to give this a chance. Give us a chance."

His strong hands grip my waist, and he pulls me back to him. Our lips are so close, yet not touching as I slide my hands up his chest and then hit him—kind of hard.

"You're so happy. I miss my grump. Yes, I like when you're relaxing on the porch or painting or when you kiss me in the dark hallway, but I want my Rob. The one who did a flash mob in high school, but who was also burned as an adult so he wears all of his emotions on his face. I'm glad your wall is down, but I don't want you to not be you anymore."

That amused grin on his face falls with my words. "I'm still me, baby. Just a little less closed off. Now, let's not forget my original purpose for being here. Where's Patrick?"

I look over my shoulder and point at Patrick and Victoria about fifteen feet away on the dance floor. I happen to look over just as Patrick dances our way.

"He's that guy with the pretty blonde. You want to meet him or something?"

"No, I want to make sure he's looking when I do this."

Rob grips my face and kisses me. A *full-on lips and tongues with a hard erection pressing into my groin* kiss that sizzles as it coaxes every nerve in my body and makes me moan on this dance floor in a room full of people.

The kiss lasts a touch longer than is probably normal. I'd think this was all for show, but from the way we are gripping one another, holding each other tight and pouring every emotion we feel for one another into this kiss, I know it's for real.

When he releases me, I'm slightly at a loss for words.

"You certainly know how to make an ex jealous," I say, coming down from the high.

He takes me back into his arms, and we begin to dance again, his laughter deep and booming. "I could say the same thing about you."

"Heard about that, huh?"

"Only the good parts."

"Well, I had to tell her how amazing you are and my most favorite thing about you."

"My big dick," he assesses with matter-of-fact amusement.

I grin up at him with a shake of my head. "Your art."

His eyes burn with intensity as he looks down at me. The notion that I could love his artistic side is something he never fathomed.

Of course, I let him know, "I am also a huge fan of your cock—not gonna lie. So, why don't we get out of here so I can peel you out of this suit? I think you deserve it, what with the grand gesture of showing up, romantic words, and branding me in front of a room full of my community members."

Instead of releasing me to carry me off into the Newbury sunset, he gives me a twirl, forcing me out and then into his arms and then back to our original pose.

"I have a better idea. My girl is getting a big award tonight, so why don't we stay, dance, eat, drink, hear your accolades, and then we can go home, and I'll let you take this suit off me?"

"Robert Bronson, you sure know a way to a girl's heart."

"I noticed you were drinking bourbon. I saw it at the table. That's when I knew."

"Knew what?"

"That you missed me."

"I did miss you, Rob. Now, get me good and drunk, make me dance till my feet hurt, and then ravish me in the bedroom."

"Yes, crazy. Anything you say."

Twenty-Nine

WE PARTIED UNTIL DESSERT was served and then decided we'd had enough of the Wolfson Manor and were ready to get back to my place. The kids are at Will and Melissa's tonight, which means when Rob parks in my driveway, he gets out, walks to my door to let me out, and then follows me in with a duffel bag in hand.

I eye his bag. "Presumptuous, eh?"

He shrugs as he takes my keys out of my hand and starts to open the front door. "It was either sleep here a happy man or go to Will's and get drunk by the firepit."

We walk inside and turn my kitchen island light on and leave the rest off. I put on some mood music—smooth jazz. Rob puts his bag on the counter and then slides his tie off before taking off his jacket and undoing the top two buttons of his shirt. He eyes my liquor cabinet and kneels in front of it, taking out a bottle of bourbon that has dust on it.

He stands, pours one glass, and turns around.

I stand in the middle of my living room, watching this man, tall and confident and so damn captivating. The contours of his face are accentuated in the shadows of the light. I feel my vulnerability coursing through my veins as he saunters toward me. The man can make me feel powerful and weak at the same time. It's exhilarating and frightening, all at once.

"You never told me what bourbon says about a person," I challenge.

He looks down at his glass for a beat and then back at me, his eyes trained on mine as he takes a sip.

"Bourbon is a strong spirit. It shows a man likes the finer things in life and appreciates all the detail that goes into the things he loves."

I lick my lips as I inhale. He draws closer.

"Second, a bourbon drinker is confident in their taste. They'll spend their hard-earned money on something to know it is going to be worth it. And when they invest, it's for life."

I let out an exhale, my romantic heart drinking in every word.

"Finally, a man who drinks bourbon isn't afraid of the burn because he knows the sweetness that will follow."

He takes another sip and places the glass on the counter, settling himself before me.

"Plus, I have it on good authority that you like the way bourbon tastes on my lips. I'm a man who knows what my woman wants and is willing to give it to her."

I let out a shaky breath. "I could really get used to this version of you, Rob. It's more intoxicating than the liquor."

"Kiss me, Tara."

I bite my lip and smile. "Make me."

Rob doesn't make me kiss him at all. Instead, he places an arm around my back and another under my thighs and carries me to the bedroom. It's not hard to find since it's a small two-bedroom condo. His nostrils flare at the sight of my king-size bed. I have various dresses thrown across the bed, as I tried on a few more tonight even though I knew this was the perfect dress for me. I had to test it out just to be sure.

He places me on the floor, gathers my dresses, and lays them on top of my dresser.

I walk up to him and undo his shirt buttons. One by one, the taut flesh beneath his button-down comes undone. My eyes meet his as I push the shirt over his shoulders. His chest rises. I lean forward and place an open-mouthed kiss over his heart. I leave a trail of kisses on his skin as I move up his neck, his Adam's apple, his jaw, and finally his mouth.

We kiss for what feels like an eternity. We're entangled in a web of lust as his hands glide down my back, releasing the teeth of my zipper all the way down until my dress falls off my shoulders and pools on the floor.

I have nothing on but a pair of Spanx. Rob kneels down and slowly unravels my undergarment, kissing the skin of my thighs, knees, and calves as he makes his way to my toes. I step out and am completely naked before him.

Rob remains on his knees, looking up at me. His hands grip my hips as he stares up at me in admiration. The look takes my breath away.

I take his hand and walk him over to the bed. We stand beside it as I slowly unhook his belt and remove his pants, doing for him as he did for me—kissing his thighs, knees, calves— until he's completely naked.

My hand rests on his chest. He mimics my movement. Together, we let our fingers feather down the front of each other's body. Eyes locked, mouths breathing intensely in unison. I gasp when the tips of his fingers glide over my nipples. He moans when I let mine slide up his shaft and dance around the head of his arousal.

A wave of desire drops to my core, and I clench my muscles at the sensation. I step toward Rob and take his mouth in mine again. We hold each other, skin to skin, heartbeat to heartbeat, as we love each other with our mouths. I feel his erection pulsating against my belly. Together, we move toward the bed. I lie down against the pillows, and he settles himself between my thighs.

"We didn't use a condom last time," I state the obvious. "I know you didn't ask, but I'm on the pill. You're the first man I was with where we didn't use a condom. I'm clean. God, this is so uncomfortable."

He nods in understanding. "Do you want me to wear one? I have them with me. A precaution. We were foolish last time."

"I think the question is, do you trust me?"

He knows what I'm asking. He was married for years while I have a promiscuous reputation.

"Do you trust *me*?" he asks.

I instantly nod. "With my life."

"Then, that's good enough for me."

Rob rolls me onto my side, and we face one another. He takes my leg and lays it over his hip, angling his body so we're wrapped in each other's arms and as close as two people can possibly be. Well, almost.

Rob lines himself up with me, and I whimper when he slides into me. The feeling of him, hard as stone and pumping in and out against my every nerve ending has my gasping out his name.

We press our foreheads together and close our eyes at the sensation that is our union. I'm internally shaking yet I'm still, unable to move from how good he feels.

He moves his head and kisses me slowly as he flexes and pumps in deliciously slow yet potent strokes. "I'm crazy about you, Tara."

I move my hips in unison. "I'm falling in love with you," I dare to admit.

"Me too, baby. I might already be there."

Our mouths come together again, and we are fully united.

There is no foreplay.

No power struggle of positions.

No pushing or pulling. No giving or taking.

We move in harmony. We hold each other with passion.

I gasp as my orgasm builds. He kisses my neck and grips me closer, disallowing me to move away from the impending pleasure that feels like it'll be too much that I might burst.

I look him in the eye and let him know I'm here with him. His forehead creases, and a vein protrudes. He's holding on to me so tightly, chasing his own orgasm and bringing me with him for the ride.

We're fire and ice.

Wild and free.

Basking in the joy of lovemaking and promises of forever, for once, I don't want to run away. In this moment, all I know is, all I want is now. Forever.

Thirty

TODAY, I'M IN MY happy place.

"Come on, people. I want to see you kick the shit out of those bags!"

Keeping the reps to the rhythm of the music, my class gives kicks and jabs to the bags in front of them.

"Right hook, right hook, left uppercut, and an elbow right to the face!"

I have an extra pep in my step today. Running around the room in my sports bra and high-waisted yoga pants, I'm getting the class charged up. I did my own workout before they came in and am living off the adrenaline high.

Kickboxing has always been my workout of choice. When I was asked to teach class one day, I jumped at the chance, and now, I teach one class a week. Jillian and Melissa were coming until they got pregnant. I tried to explain pregnant women could still work out, but they're a bunch of wimps. I really miss having them in class.

Alas, a new student joined today. Rob started in the front of the class. He isn't shy about being front and center for everyone to watch as he follows along with my instruction to a T. His bravado about being able to easily do the workout falters about thirty minutes in. For a man who works in construction, he's a little winded. This is a high-intensity workout, so I'm not surprised.

He, however, looks like he's about to die.

From the red on his face and the sweat dripping down his back, the man is at peak exertion.

At the end of the session, I lead the class in a cooldown in the form of an abdominal series of crunches and ladders, followed by a minute-long plank hold.

"You call that a cooldown?" Rob jokes as I peel him off the mat at the end of the session.

"You had a hard time keeping up, old man." I give him a fierce pat on the back.

"That's a great workout. A bit of a wake-up call. I'm not in shape anymore. I might have to start coming more often."

Jumping up and down, I clap my hands. "I'd love that!"

He gives a disapproving look at my excitement, which makes me do it more overdramatically.

After class, we hit up Beans and Leaves for iced coffees and go back to my condo to shower. Rob has to get the kids and head home while I plan on going to the office to switch out files.

He's making us breakfast in my kitchen when I come out, dressed for the day.

"What time are you heading back to the ranch?" I ask him just as his cell phone rings.

He holds up a finger to let me know he'll answer my question as soon as he answers the call.

My cell phone vibrates with a text. I read it and look at Rob, who appears to be listening to what I was just told via text.

"Melissa's in labor!" I squeal.

Waiting for the miracle of life is one of the most boring experiences—unless you're the woman giving birth, of course. For the rest of us, it's hours in a waiting room as we await Melissa and Will's bundle of joy.

The waiting room is packed. Rob and I are here with the kids, as are Jillian, Melissa's father, and Cade, along with Rob and Will's mother.

We were all told the baby would be here at any minute ... and that was three hours ago. Apparently, your third baby does not guarantee a speedy delivery.

After receiving the text that Melissa was in labor, Rob and I went to the house to get the kids. All four kids went in Rob's car while I hopped into Will's as we caravanned to Valor County Hospital. The contractions were fierce. Melissa's cries of pain were unbearable to hear as I sat in the backseat with her and let her squeeze my hand so hard that I'm still stretching it out to try to get the blood back into circulation.

"Don't ever procreate, Tara. It's like the devil magnifies your cramps by a billion, and the pain spreads through your vagina," she chanted in the car as Will sped down the highway with a police escort.

Cops can be dramatic like that.

They wheeled Melissa into the labor and delivery ward with such a fury that we all thought the kid was about to fly out of her body at any second. Will came out to say she was eight centimeters dilated, and it's been crickets since. We haven't even heard the bell that plays on the speaker when a baby is born. The good news is, all is well. Will has texted to let us know it's just a waiting game at this point.

Rob hands me a cup of coffee, and I thank him, noting the way his mother gives me the side-eye. I've always gotten along with Mrs. Bronson. I've met her many times over the years. I hope she still likes me now that I'm shacking up with her son.

"Did you ask your mom if she wants coffee?" I nudge him, and he nearly spills his.

"Of course I did. She said no. Vending machines aren't her thing. My dad will bring her something when he gets here."

Jesse and Molly ask for money to go to the cafeteria to get a bite to eat. Rob hands them a twenty. I sit back and blow on my steaming cup and look at the ticking clock.

Come on, baby ...

Todd, Dick, and Kyle walk in.

I do a double take at their entrance and then remember they're police officers who work with Will. It's very sweet that they came. Todd and Dick are in full uniform while Kyle is in a T-shirt, clearly off duty this morning.

"Hey, Tara." Todd waves from the other side of the room.

I give him a courteous wave back.

"Hi, Tara," Dick and Kyle say next, and I nod hello.

"Are they part of the Tara Parsons Fan Club?" Rob asks me.

I quietly explain, "I went on a date with Todd once, coffee with Dick, and Kyle and I chatted at a party."

The words are barely out of my mouth when Rob's mom makes an odd noise from her throat. I shrug and take a sip of my coffee.

Jillian leans into me. "Looks like things took quite a turn with you and Rob."

"I have so much to tell you. He showed up at the gala last night and totally swept me off my feet. And then we went back to my place and—"

"Not the place, babe," Rob says loudly from his chair on the other side of me.

I nod with a giggle and see his mom roll her eyes.

I whisper into Jillian's ear, "Is it just me, or is Rob's mom throwing serious shade my way?"

She waves me off. "She's like that with everyone. She's probably annoyed you still haven't announced you're a couple, yet you're sitting here acting like one."

I lean into Rob and whisper. "Do you think we should tell your mom about us? You haven't been returning her calls and she'd probably appreciate you telling her you're shacking up with the nanny."

"Good idea. I'll give you my high school pin you so everyone knows we're going steady?"

"While I appreciate the sarcasm, it's not nineteen fifty-five anymore."

Rob reaches his hand onto the armrest of my chair and takes my hand in his, lifts it to his lips and kisses my knuckles.

"There. We're a couple," he croons, keeping my hand in his and sitting there comfortably.

His mother looks over with a raise of her brows and I grin.

Boys can be so simple. I love it.

The time ticks by.

Molly and I play a card game at a table in the corner from a deck she got from the nurses' station. Jesse is glued to his phone, which he has plugged in by the wall. The officers left, but an extra family member or two have come in and out, all who live locally and wanting to see if the baby has arrived.

I'm declaring gin rummy against Molly when the elevator dings. I don't pay too much mind to it because it's been opening and closing all morning. Molly is trying to shuffle, as I'm teaching her how, when I hear a bit of commotion behind me.

"Don't hit me again!" a man says.

Molly and I grimace at each other and then turn around.

Kevin, Will and Rob's cousin, is backing up toward the elevator bank. Rob is on his feet by his seat in the middle of the room.

"Robert, take a seat right now," his mother scolds him like a child. "Bad enough you ruined your brother's wedding."

"He didn't ruin the wedding. He waited until we were at the hotel to punch Kevin in the nose," Cade interjects in explanation.

"Kevin, I'm saying this one time. Get the hell out of here." Rob means business as he backs up to the elevator.

Mrs. Bronson tosses a hand on her head as she declares, "You're not ruining the birth of his child over some floozy."

My and Jillian's eyes meet.

I point a finger at myself and mouth to her, *Am I the floozy?*

She opens her palms and raises them with the rise of her shoulders as she mouths back, *I think so.*

Rob doesn't seem to be bothered by his mother's glare. He just looks at Kevin. "Leave."

"I didn't do anything wrong. I thought maybe you were drunk, and that's why you hit me. I didn't think you'd still be mad," Kevin explains, to which I make a laugh of indignation, drawing his attention to my corner of the room. Kevin immediately places his hands in front of his crotch. "You're here too?"

I curve my brows. "I'm the best friend. Why are you surprised we're all here?"

Kevin looks down, like he didn't entirely think this visit through.

Cade lets out a loud, barking laugh. "Why are you gripping your balls like that? Oh, right. Rob got you in the gonads too."

"I only punched him in the face," Rob states matter-of-factly.

"I kneed him in the balls," I say with equal measure and then turn to Molly. "We'll have a lesson about men crossing the line when you're older."

"This is abominable! Why is everyone attacking Kevin?" Rob's mom looks positively beside herself.

"Yeah, Kev?" Cade puts the attention on Kevin, and everyone stares at the big guy by the elevator. "What did you do to piss off two people?" The shit-eating grin on Cade's face would be comical if the situation wasn't so uncomfortable.

He looks sick to his stomach as he takes a tissue out of his pocket and dabs his forehead. His voice stutters slightly as he tries to explain, "Can't blame a man for trying. She has a … reputation."

Cade narrows his eyes, as if trying to comprehend.

"Sometimes, couples want to … experiment," Kevin adds.

I lean over and place earmuffs over Molly's ears. Jesse is now completely unglued from his cell phone. Jillian gasps, her eyes wide as she clutches her hand over her heart..

Cade has a wide-mouthed yet shocked expression. "You propositioned Tara for a threesome?"

"Kevin, that's disgusting," Rob's mother yelps and looks repulsed by her nephew.

"What are they talking about?" Molly asks, so Rob takes that as his cue to usher Kevin out of the waiting room.

Rob looks like he could kill Kevin. I'm pretty sure he's going to.

"Out!" He points toward the nearby stairwell and holds the door open for Kevin, urging him down and following him out the door.

Cade jumps up from his seat. "I'm gonna go make sure Rob doesn't literally kill him."

"I'm gonna watch," Jesse declares, but I give him a pointed stare.

"You're not going anywhere," I tell him, and he sits back down.

He seems disappointed, but I don't know what words will come out of Kevin's mouth, and I don't need Jesse hearing them.

I look at Jillian, who gives me a sad yet assuring smile.

This is the hazard of actively dating since you were seventeen. You develop a reputation, whether it's true or not. Now, it's biting me in the ass.

Thirty-One

OLIVIA MARY BRONSON WAS born at 3:56 in the afternoon with a full head of brown hair and crystal-blue eyes. The hospital was packed with visitors, so after giving the baby girl a hello wave through the nursery glass and my best friend a hug, I left and allowed the Bronson clan to enjoy their newest family member.

It didn't matter. I knew I'd get the best seat in the house, which is where I am now—in Melissa's living room now that baby Olivia is home.

"She's gorgeous. Seriously, you people need to procreate more often because this child is beautiful!" I gush.

"Do not bring that up again. My vagina is still screaming at me from labor. This huge-headed child wouldn't come out. I blame the Bronson side. You people have big heads."

Will and Rob both rub their heads, as if to check if they are indeed large. To me, they're a normal shape, but I didn't just push one out of my hooha.

"I could go for a few more," Will states easily before leaning back, away from his wife's evil glare. "What? I'm one of six. I've always wanted a big family. Give it a year or two. You might change your mind."

"I love you, but there is no way I'm having a fourth kid. I'm already thirty-six and was considered a geriatric pregnancy."

Rob gives a hearty laugh. "I don't envy you. Kids are for the young and dumb. They're a lot of work. I commend you for doing it again. This knucklehead has no idea what he's in for."

Will crumples up a napkin and throws it at his brother. "You're the knucklehead." He walks over to his wife and takes a seat next to her, facing the baby that is nursing in her arms. "You know I'm kidding. I was prepared if you said you didn't want to have any. I've always said Izzy and Hunter are enough. But little Livy, she's now the cherry on top of the sundae of life."

Melissa looks at Will, her eyes welling up with tears. "That's so romantic," she breathes, and he kisses her lips gently. "Ouch," she yelps and then turns to her five-day-old baby. "Breastfeeding sucks."

"Why do you do it?" I ask. "This is the same torture you went through with the other two."

"Fair question. Easy answer. Izzy never latched properly. Hunter did it for a little while, and I gave up. I'm determined to make this go smoothly with Olivia. It's like a personal mission."

"It looks so painful," I say as she winces.

"It is at first, and then it's fine. Like labor, it sucks, but when it's over, it's worth every ounce of pain for the joy of being a mom."

"I'll remind you of that when you're up in the middle of the night, complaining about breastfeeding, diapers, your loss of a figure, and unwashed hair," I tease, to which she groans.

"Don't remind me." Melissa burps Olivia, then changes her diaper, puts on a fresh onesie, and goes to put her in her bassinet.

"Absolutely not! Hand that baby over to me," I demand with grabby hands in the air.

She laughs as she places the sleeping bundle of joy in my arms.

"Go upstairs and get your sleep," I tell her, noting the deal we made. "If I come over, then it's your time to sleep. The two of you. I know you're helping a lot, Will. Get on upstairs with your bride and get some shut-eye. Tara and Uncle Rob are here."

Melissa nods as she yawns with a wide-open mouth and arms outstretched. "I'm going to take you up on that. Come, husband. Snuggle with me."

"Yes, ma'am," he says as he gets up from the couch and follows his wife upstairs, but not before giving his daughter a kiss on the forehead.

With the new mom and dad upstairs, I lean back on the couch and look at Olivia. "She's so peaceful right now."

Olivia's tiny head smells like powder and lotion. Rob takes a seat beside me.

I ask him while keeping my gaze on her, "Were your kids good babies?"

Rob puts an arm on the back of the couch, inching close to me. "Jesse was a nightmare. Molly was an angel."

"Their temperaments have been the same since birth then?"

"Pretty much."

I giggle. "Did you ever consider having a bigger family, like the one you came from?"

"Maybe if we had our kids back-to-back, but by the time Molly was born, Jesse was already in school. I knew she'd be the last." Rob pulls me closer and looks down at Olivia. "She's a pretty baby. Hopefully, she's sweet, too, because parenting is a nightmare."

"Nightmare is a bit dramatic."

"I'm not just talking about the baby stage. The toddler years are exhausting. School age is no better with sports, the endless driving and laundry, and dealing with the homework and drama. Jesse is almost in college, and I can see a new set of worries on the horizon. It's a lot of worry. No one prepares you for that. I'm forty and on the tail end of raising my kids, and I can see the light at the end of the tunnel."

"You were a young dad."

"Melissa and Will are gonna be in their fifties with a high schooler while I'll be on my porch, listening to music, because mine will be out of the house and grown. I'll still worry, but it will be with a glass of bourbon in my hand."

He makes a good point. Melissa is going to have a long road ahead of her. When Izzy goes to college, she'll be getting Olivia ready for preschool. She'll be starting the cycle all over again.

I laugh to myself. He nudges me, as if wondering what is on my mind.

"Melissa and I once talked about traveling the world together when the kids were in college. We'd be two single ladies, roaming the greatest destinations on earth. Visiting the pyramids of Egypt and walking the Great Wall of China. Looks like I lost my travel buddy."

"You know, I wouldn't mind going on a trip or two with you. I'm in no means up for the pyramids, but I think it's time I find some balance in my life. My kids are getting bigger, so I can spare some time."

"You'd really travel with me?"

"I would. Slow at first. Maybe the Caribbean."

I moan at the idea of Rob on a beach, running through the sand and then splashing around with me in crystal-blue waters. "You know, they serve daiquiris in the Caribbean. You're going to have to drink one. It's a rule."

"I was thinking more of a peach margarita."

I settle into his side and sigh. "Peach margaritas, canopy beds, and my handsome man on a beach. What more could I ask for?"

His chest rumbles with a laugh. I settle into the hum of him on my back and a heavily breathing babe in my arms. I could fall asleep like this.

My gaze falls back to Olivia.

"Look how precious she is, Rob," I say as I coo at the tiny, fragile bundle. "Olivia is only days old and a masterpiece of life. She has the softest skin against my fingertips and these minuscule fingers and toes. It's a wonder how this tiny life was created and will continue to grow up before our eyes. It's gonna go by so fast. You know, sometimes, I look at Izzy and see how grown up she is and wonder where the time went. She used to stay at my place and play dress-up with my things and called my high heels *up shoes*."

"You really love your friends' kids," he surmises, his head brushing against the side of mine with his stubble rubbing against my hair.

I lift my brows because this is a known thing about me that we established long ago. "They're my babies too. It feels like only a second ago when Hunter was a toddler, crawling up onto my lap and giving me endless kisses. And he had the chubbiest little hand that was always so warm when I held it. I loved going for our walks. He was so inquisitive while Izzy was so insightful. I have all of these memories of her as a baby, who was replaced by a toddler, then this adorable kid, and then the funny preteen, and now, she's this beautiful teenager, who I can talk to. I've loved every stage of watching them grow up."

He gives a harrumph sound behind me.

It makes me twist my body to look at him.

Rob has a blank look on his face as his hand rubs the scruff on his jaw. He catches my gaze, with a peculiar look. He's staring at me like we're strangers who bumped into each other on the street and he's curious if we've met before.

"What?" I place my hand on my mouth, wondering if I have anything in my teeth.

He waits a beat, his eyes narrowing while he searches for an answer or a clue to a question he didn't know he had.

"Why didn't you have children?"

I take a quick inhale, not expecting him to ask that. "I don't need my own."

His mouth purses for a moment before he adjusts his phrasing. "Did you ever want to have children?"

My breath comes out long and low. This is a complicated question with an even more convoluted answer. "I never wanted them enough to settle for just any man in order to have one."

He nods. His looks pensive as he chooses his next question.

"Did you and Patrick plan on having them?" he asks, slow and deep.

I give a nod with a sway of my head.

I let out a frustrated breath. Standing, I place Olivia in her bassinet and cover her with a blanket. She's snug and sleeping with her arms up and outstretched over her head. I walk into the kitchen and look through the pantry and sort through the shelves of boxes.

"Are you baking?" he asks as I take out a box of birthday cake mix and grab a mixing bowl from the drawer.

"Yes. It's Olivia's first week home. She deserves a cake."

Rising from the couch, he heads over to the island. With a quirked brow, he watches me move about the kitchen. "You only bake when you're working through shit in your head."

I point a whisk at him. "Not true. I also bake when I'm horny."

"Drop the whisk, Tara." He takes strong, sturdy steps toward me. "Talk. I want to talk."

"Why?"

"I think it's important that if you and I are going to move forward in our relationship, we both understand what our future could look like."

"I don't need a crystal ball to see how it's gonna go."

He folds his arms and widens his feet. His posture is strong as he looks at me in a way that makes me feel weak with nerves.

The whisk is still in my hand as I explain, "I'll keep my place in Newbury, and you'll have the ranch. We'll go back and forth for a while until we decide we can't be without each other anymore—at which time, I'll spend an exorbitant amount of money on knee-high boots. We're gonna have to turn the bedroom downstairs into my personal office and closet because—let's be honest—you can't handle my mess. My things will need to be contained."

Opening the box, I pour the mixture into the bowl and then walk to the refrigerator for eggs. Rob has a hand on the door, stopping me from opening it. I'm staring at the steel as he closes the space between us, leaning his head down, willing me to look up at him.

I do.

It's unnerving as hell, the way those chestnut eyes sear me with a look that's begging me to tell him the truth.

"You might not be physically walking out of this house, but you are running away right now. Instead of pushing, I'm doing my best to pull you in. You've got to speak to me, Tara. I know you talk a big game, and your confidence is one of the sexiest things about you. Your honesty is my favorite though, so if you'll put down the whisk and talk to me, that would be greatly appreciated."

My shoulders fall. He's doing so much better than I am at this relationship thing. For a girl who waited for love to come banging down my door, I'm doing a half-assed job at letting it in.

My hands rise with open palms and drop as I give up. The whisk falls to the ground.

"When Patrick left me, Melissa went to talk to him to find out why. He said he just didn't see a future with me because I wasn't serious enough. We partied and had fun and dated and traveled.

There was this box of all the places in the world we were going to go together that I'd made for us. He said he realized too late that the life he wanted wasn't the one I was planning for. He wanted to have children right away and settle down in a small town. Ironic, isn't it? He and I are both in the same damn small town while he's raising his kids and I'm loving on Melissa's. Patrick never gave me a chance to grow up with him. I did want kids, and I love this town. Apparently, I didn't showcase that."

I walk away from Rob and move about the kitchen. He places his back against the refrigerator, slides his hands into his pockets, and listens as I pace, fighting the urge to crack some eggs and whisk the shit out of that funfetti.

"I love children. If I got pregnant tomorrow, I wouldn't panic. It's just that the idea of that being a possibility left me a long time ago. I mean it when I say I don't need children to feel complete. Meeting a man was always about love. Connecting with someone and sharing our happiness. If a child came of that, great. If it didn't, fine. It wasn't the endgame. I'm not trying to trick you."

"I never said you were."

"I know people talk. I saw what happened at the hospital. I have a reputation, Rob. Even if I want kids, who wants their mom to be the woman who's slept with half of Connecticut in order to meet someone willing to settle?" I hold my hand up and further explain, "I'm being sarcastic. I haven't slept with half of the state. Believe it or not, my number is far smaller than you'd think."

He crosses his arms and tilts his head at me. "Are you concerned with my number?"

"Not at all."

"Then, I'm not concerned with yours. Nor do I give a shit about what anyone thinks of you. All that matters is what I think."

I stop my movements and bite my lip, half wanting him to say what he thinks and half not wanting him to. "What is that?"

"That you'd make a great mother."

Wells of emotion build up in my eyes as my stomach falls to the pits of despair and this angsty madness rushes through my veins. I shake my head, vibrating as his words set in. I pick up my whisk and start to bake, but there are no eggs, and he's still blocking the refrigerator.

Backing away, I hit the countertop, hard, and so I rub my back and point the whisk at him like a weapon.

"Fuck you," I bite because there really are no other words to say to that.

He doesn't seem offended by my outburst. So, I say it again.

"Fuck you, Rob. You don't get to say things like that. Not when I've made peace with the trajectory of my life. Not when we just started this amazing relationship. Not when you already have your children and don't want any more."

Rob nods his head as he continues to watch me as one would a rabid animal that's been trapped in its cage. Except I'm not in a cage. I'm free, and it feels like he's trying to put me back in one.

"I want to make sure you're not giving up on something you'll regret later on."

"That's unfair!" I say loudly, and Olivia starts to stir.

I wait a minute for her to resettle and confirm she's fast asleep before I yell at him in the loudest whisper I can muster, "That's unfair. It took me forever to find you, and now, you're gonna put thoughts of something in my head that weren't there and make me have to choose. I don't even know if I can have kids, and now, I'm wondering what it would be like to hold my own in my arms and watch her grow up to be this sassy badass. But no. No. This is not how it's supposed to be. I don't want to have a child of my own, and I don't want to have one if it's going to be with anyone but you!"

Fuck. Did I really just say that?

I did.

This is why I bake. If I don't, I let the crazy things in my mind run out of my mouth, and I regret them. Not because they're untrue. I stand by my feelings and my words. It's just never been anyone's business to analyze them, criticize them, or hold them against me.

Maybe it's the way I'm trying to do anything but look at him, yet when I do, I don't see a man frightened by what I just admitted. In fact, he looks rather calm.

"You're freaking me out right now," I tell him. "You're supposed to be angry and annoyed." I wave my hands, as if urging the grumpiness to pour out of him. "Why aren't you being mean?"

He stands there for a while. His head falls as he looks at the floor, his brows curving and his mouth pursing. With a push, he leaves the refrigerator and walks around the kitchen island and over to the living room, where Olivia is sleeping. He stares at her for a while, the tips of his mouth tilting up as he takes in his new niece. A low rumble leaves his chest as he sighs.

"I'm not mad because I always knew if I met a woman and actually liked her enough to keep her around, odds were pretty high she'd want to have a child together." He looks up at me and shrugs. "Then, I met you, and I remember you saying you didn't need children of your own. I pushed it aside, yet I see you with Molly, Jesse, Ainsley, Hunter, Izzy, and Olivia, and you are so good with them. You don't need children, Tara, but you want one. I don't. If it were up to me, I'd close the door on that possibility."

He moves away from Olivia and heads back to me, stopping just a foot in front of me, closing the space between us. My heart is racing and my head is a little dizzy. I swallow hard as I stare at him, my beautiful man who I have a fierce feeling is going to try to end things with me before we even get started because he knows me better than he should.

Rob licks his lower lip and curves his brow. "I just want to know if you'll wake up in ten years, look over at me, and regret me not giving you a baby."

"I won't," I say and then close my eyes to add, "I won't regret you. I could never."

"And I could never let you regret yourself."

I blink up at him, confused.

"I don't want more kids, but I'll be damned if I don't give you everything you want in this life. I'm not saying it's gonna be tomorrow, but if fate decides you and I are fit for the long haul, then I wouldn't say no if you wanted to try for a baby."

My breath comes out as a blast of relief. I didn't even realize I was so worried until this enormous weight leaves my chest and I start to cry. Yes, big, stupid tears fall down my cheeks.

"Really?"

"It's either me give you one or give you up and let some other man love you and give you a baby I was too damn closed-minded to have. I might complain about mine, but if there's one thing I'm proudest of in this world, it's my kids. I'd never regret having another. What I would regret is losing you."

I throw my arms around him and hold him so tight that I might break his neck.

"You got a vise around my neck," he states.

I pull myself up and kiss him. Unlike the night he caught me from the tree and stated that line, I'm not letting him go.

Not now.

Not ever.

"I love you, Rob." I kiss him between words and grip him tight in my arms. "It took me nineteen years of dating frogs to find you, but I did, and it was worth the wait."

His hand grips my head as he pulls me back to look at him. Warm brown eyes lock on mine as he says the words against my lips, "I love you too, Tara. Every crazy, wild ounce of you."

We kiss in the kitchen and get a little handsy, trying not to wake the baby or the sleeping couple upstairs. I'd love to take this man to bed, and I know he wants nothing more than to undress me and ravage me on this floor. But we can't.

Rob takes my hand and pulls me over to the living room. We sit on the sofa, our feet up on the coffee table, my head on his arm, his arm wrapped around me.

Even on a Friday night, babysitting a newborn, we find our moment to just be.

Love.

It's groans, laughs, and a whole lot of yearning. It's ups and downs and fights and make-ups. It's grumpiness and sunshine, sass and crass. It's pushes and pulls and everything in between.

Love ... it's wild. And it's ours.

I'm so happy I waited for it.

Epilogue

MY INTERNAL CRYSTAL BALL was only six months out of becoming real. It was at that time that Rob turned the downstairs bedroom into my very own walk-in closet/home office.

A huge perk of living with a contractor is that he knows how to build things. I gave him my ideas, and he went above and beyond in creating built-ins along two walls of the room with floor-to-ceiling cabinetry to house not only my ranch wear, but my regular clothing too. Against the wall, near the window, is a new desk with a vase of fresh flowers on it.

I'm seated at my desk, looking at the dahlias that Molly picked for me this morning. It's a new plant we added to the castle gardens. One the garden center said would have to be dug up in the fall and placed in the basement, only to be planted again.

I found that to be a lot like love.

You plant it and watch it bloom. When the weather turns, it won't survive unless you protect it. Sometimes, you have to put it away for a while. Times get hard, life becomes chaotic, but it doesn't mean it's not there. You don't stop caring for it. You just wait until the time is right for it to be planted again, watered, and given sunshine, ready to thrive once more.

This time, better and stronger than before.

It took six months for me to move in with Rob, but we kept

my condo in Newbury because my roots are there, as well as the accounting office and gym I still work at. It's nice to know I don't have to drive the hour and a half to the ranch if I'm bone-tired.

We spend some weekends at the condo—with and without kids. When the school year is in session, they are back and forth between our place and Christine and Mike's.

Surprisingly, Bob the fish is still alive and well, swimming in his upgraded tank because he's grown two inches. I think it's because I sneak him bits of pastry now and then.

Yes, I still bake. It's mostly because I'm happy ... nah, who am I kidding? I bake when Rob pisses me off, which is often. It's never anything worth breaking up over. In fact, it's normal couple things, like me failing to tell him I gave Jesse permission to use my car to go out with friends and whose parents we are seeing for the holidays and that one time I went out with my friends in a dress so short that I couldn't bend over without someone seeing my thong. He's a brute sometimes, but I like him for it. Turns out, that's just what I've always needed.

I rise from my desk and walk over to my dressing closet, the one where I keep my dresses. I look at the wall and the painting Rob hung here last summer when he painted the walls a rose color and bought me a new bed. It doesn't quite go with the aesthetic of the room, but I wouldn't dream of replacing it.

After all, the painting is of me.

I didn't realize it until Rob casually mentioned it soon after I moved in. The resemblance is now obvious to me. I mean, the woman is hella gorgeous even if you can only see her side profile. Now, I use it to tease him that he fell in love with me first. He'll never admit it, but he never disputes it. Instead, he grunts.

I love that man.

Yes, it took me six months to move in here since we made us official, and it's been six months since then.

I love this home. I love the family we have in this home. I love everything about my life.

Walking around the house, I see remnants of our year as an official couple. A photo of us from our vacation to Paris. I got Rob to agree to a long European weekend for my birthday. He had a hard time navigating a country where he didn't know the language, and he wasn't too keen on the endless museums, but he did all right when he asked me to dance in front of the Eiffel Tower one night and said it was his favorite part of the trip. Just us. Under the moon.

There's another photo of me, Rob, Molly, and Jesse, taken in Aruba. We traveled there for Jillian and Luke's wedding. Like Melissa, Jillian was pregnant when she walked down the aisle. We'd waited for Olivia to be old enough to travel internationally and then headed to the happy island. Since Luke and Jillian have little to no family, it was really just us friends that filled the seats, and the two looked like they wouldn't have wanted it any other way. Luke's dad was his best man while Melissa and I were her matron and maid of honor. Jillian gave herself away, and Ainsley was the flower girl. Soon after the wedding, their son, Grady Mitchel Incendio, was born.

Next to that picture is another of us from the gala at Wolfson Manor, taken by the professional photographer the night of my award. It's my favorite because that's the night we officially became us.

The house is quiet. Molly and Jesse are nowhere to be found. The basement door is open, and the light is on downstairs. I walk downstairs, through the empty game room, and head to the back, where Rob's art studio is. I peek inside and find an empty room. On the wall, directly across from where he usually works, is the other painting of me he did last year. The one where I sat topless and fought the desire to kiss him. The finished product is more than I could ever have dreamed, and if I didn't already feel beautiful, one look at that image, and I'd be flying high on confidence.

To see me through Rob's eyes is exhilarating.

Oh, and that flash mob video—I finally saw it! Rob's brother, Jack, was saving it for a special occasion. That occasion was my first official dinner at the Bronson household. I got to meet the whole clan over Thanksgiving. I won over his mother's full acceptance by baking three pies and Melissa telling her the story of how I disgraced Rob's ex-wife in a restaurant. If she had any concerns about my intentions with her son, all was good after that. I was rewarded with the video and I was beyond thankful to watch a young Rob gyrating to nineties pop music while wearing baggy jeans and a backward hat.

In fact, I still watch it whenever I need a pick me up.

I exit the basement, turning off the light, and take out my cell phone, texting to ask Rob where everyone is.

We're at the castle.

I smile at his use of the name *the castle* instead of the secret garden. I've always liked my and the kids' name for it better.

Rob and the kids must have taken the four-wheeler, so I walk out on foot. It's a decent walk—a solid fifteen minutes at least. I don't mind it. The mountains in the distance are a gorgeous cascade of brown and green against the lush grass. Rob spent a good portion of last fall reseeding the land, turning what had once been dead into gorgeous turf. It was a labor of love with all hands on deck, but we did it.

I'm in the clearing when I see the ivory tower peeking through the trees. I walk up to it and around the bend. My smile is bright when I pass the flower beds, full and vibrant. I stop by to smell a rose, and a butterfly zooms by. The koi fish are swimming happily, thanks to a filter Rob added, using a solar-powered generator. Again, it's good to love a handyman.

My feet are padding down the cobblestone when Rob steps out from the wooden door. I stop at the sight of him, a bit amused.

He's not wearing his typical jeans and a tee—a look I crave seeing. No, today, he's wearing his gray groomsman suit from Will and Melissa's wedding. I stop and give him the stink-eye, wondering what the hell he's doing.

He just smiles. His dark brows arch mischievously, and he grins in a way that makes my heart race. My man doesn't do suits in the summer. He doesn't dress up for non-special occasions. If he is, that can only mean one thing.

I close my eyes, not wanting to get my hopes up, but fuck it.

"Are you proposing?" I ask and then smash my lips together because I just can't help myself when it comes to speaking.

His perfect teeth make an appearance as he smiles, and his entire face lights up. "There's only one reason I'd wear this thing in the dead of summer, and it's for you."

"How long have you been out here? What would you have done if I hadn't texted?"

"I know you can't go too long without wondering where we are, so we just figured if we waited, you'd come to us."

"We?" I ask and then hear Molly's giggle.

She and Jesse are hanging out the window on the second story of the castle, looking down at their father and me on the cobblestone.

"Now," Rob says, taking a step forward and holding out his hands in offering, "if you don't mind, I'd like to ask you a very important question."

I simply nod and inhale the deepest breath that's possible.

Rob drops to one knee. His hand goes into his pocket and takes out a velvet box. When I see it, I nearly faint at the sight of the most beautiful ring imaginable—a round diamond set against two smaller ones.

"Tara Parsons, you literally fell into my life, and I will forever be a happy man that I was there to catch you. In my wildest dreams, I never would have pictured such a fun, crazy, stunning woman who is fiercely stubborn, insanely smart, and the most exciting person I know, to call my own. I made a vow to love you already, so today, I'm not pledging another promise I haven't said already, other than this: Will you, Tara, not only marry me, but also be a Bronson? Be a mother to my children, a wife to me, and let me honor you and cherish you forever because the state says I'm really bound to you whether you piss me off or not?"

I laugh at his totally insane yet beautiful proposal. "Only if you say please."

"I'm not begging," he says, and I feel a mild disappointment until he adds, "I'm groveling on my knees, asking you to marry me because I need you so damn much that I can't wait to have you as my wife and to love you till the day I die."

I jump up and down, clapping my hands, and squeal, "Yes!"

Rob rises to his feet, and I don't give him a chance to do anything as my hands wrap around his face and I kiss him so long and passionately that the kids start to call from up above.

"Get a room!" Jesse shouts.

"My eyes are way too young to be seeing this!"

Our smiles are pressed against each other. Rob's hands are on my face, rubbing my tears with his thumbs and pulling me in for another kiss.

He slides the ring onto my finger, and it fits perfectly.

"Three stones," he explains. "One for each of the kids. Because you're not just saying yes to me. You're saying yes to us."

"Yes," I say to him again and then shout up to the kids, "Yes, and yes! Now, come on down here and give your stepmother a hug!"

The kids start their way down, and I take one more look at my soon-to-be husband.

"I wished for you. And now, I have you."

Rob grins. "I wished for you too. And I thank the moon every night that you're mine."

Want to read more of Rob and Tara's story?

Check out the extended epilogue for the sexy surprise Rob has in store for his new bride. Read the extended epilogue at https://BookHip.com/GZZZSVW.

LOVE...IT'S COMPLICATED

Read Melissa's romance in the first book in the series.

Anyone who says love isn't complicated is a dirty liar. Ask me how I know...

I used to be a normal wife and mother with a perfectly happy life. Now I'm a divorced single mom who spent a night in jail after breaking into the hair salon my ex's mistress owns.

What can I say? Not my proudest moment.

The only bright spot in that fiasco was the police officer who offered me a sexy, broad shoulder to cry on. William Bronson was a knight in shining armor. A romance novel hero in the flesh.

Then I showed up for work the next day and realized I'd be in charge of planning his fairy tale wedding...to someone else.

And that was just the *start* of my troubles—romantically *and* legally (don't ask).

Now, I need to learn how to navigate my new reality and start building my *own* happily ever after. I have no idea if it will all end in love...or heartache. All I know for sure is that it'll be *complicated*.

LOVE...IT'S MESSY

Read Jillian's romance in the second book in the series.

Second-chance romance only works out in movies. In real life, it's … messy.

I don't need a man for anything.

Love and romance? Pfft. No thanks. Never again.

Between my career as a wedding planner and being a single mother, I barely have time to think about men.

I wasn't looking for a hero when I ended up locked outside a hotel that was engulfed in a blazing inferno, wearing nothing but a robe. I would've eventually saved myself. Too bad he didn't give me a chance.

Yep, you guessed it. Luke Incendio, the sexy firefighter who came to my hotel rescue and the man who had caused me to swear off love years ago, is one and the same.

Now, he says he wants to make amends. He says he's never stopped wanting me. His words are laced in regret as he says he made a mistake.

But talk is cheap—and the tingly feelings he inspires in me are not to be trusted. Because this time around, I'm not the only one who'll get burned if he proves to be unreliable.

And there's no way I'm going to let that happen.

Books By Jeannine Colette

LOVE, EXPLAINED
Love…It's Complicated
Love…It's Messy
Love…It's Wild

ABANDON COLLECTION
Pure Abandon
Reckless Abandon
Wild Abandon
True Abandon
Sinful Abandon

STAND-ALONES
A Really Bad Idea
Just Ten Seconds
Wrecked
Body of Trust

SEXTON BROTHERS
Austin
Bryce
Tanner
Layover Lover

FALLING FOR THE STARS
Naughty Neighbor
Charming Co-Worker
Rebel Roommate
Arrogant Officer
Bastard Bartender
Loyal Lawyer
Heartbroken Hero

Acknowledgments

When I started this series it was with the sole purpose of telling Melissa's story. I wasn't prepared for Jillian and Tara to come to life, begging for their stories to be told. Of the three books, Tara's was the most fun to tell. I enjoy writing angst yet hers didn't call for it. Her past had enough of it, so she met Rob at the wedding I immediately knew this was going to be a joy ride of a love story. It was also important for me to write a heroine who was in her late thirties and unapologetically looking for love. Being married and having babies by a certain age is highlighted so intensely in romance. Tara is the epitome of the strong, single woman who won't settle to meet some criteria we've been set upon. I adored writing her and hope you loved being her for this short time.

I gave myself ample time to write this book but didn't actually do it until I was down to the wire. I would first and foremost like to thank Amazon for their preorder requirements because if I hadn't set this book up to be available for preorder, I never would have finished it! I'd next like to apologize to the laundry, dishes and basic housekeeping that was ignored during the writing of this book. Some people ask how authors are able to do it all. The answer is, we can't. But we sure do strive to!

Now, for the real acknowledgments. To Jovana Shirley of Unforeseen Editing who sifted through the heavy editing of this novel. She is the true hero of this manuscript and without her I'd just be a girl who used too many comas, inserted the wrong adjectives, and made little sense when I meant to be prolific. Thank you times a million for being the best editor on the planet!

To Autumn Sexton of Wordsmith Publicity for beta reading this beauty and giving guidance with every page written. To Lauren Runow who is always there when I need to talk out a plot. To Paramita Patra, Nadine Kilian, Crystal Andrews, and Nicole Westmoreland for your awesome beta notes. To Wilmari who is my final say on everything. To Courtney DeLollis for bringing this manuscript on home perfectly polished!

The dedication of this book is one I've waited a long time to make. Tara McCormick and Nicole Parsons. They two of my best friends who have been emotional supporters, travel companions, venting stations, drinking buddies and overall AMAZING! We hardly see each other since we live in different states, but it doesn't deter the relationship we have. It is an honor to have you in my life and a double honor to name this heroine after you. I miss your face. I love you.

Because this series is about women championing other women, I'd like to call out a few who have been instrumental in my life whether they know it or not. Nanci Weaver, Gwenn Monopoli, Kathy Curro, Dina Pedula, Maria Giuffre, Lynn Distefano, Michelle Worden, Kym Garbartini, Jessica Hertzberg, Jill Meister, Dana Bellini, Diana Gershon, Nicole Lancelotti, Shannon Rinelli, Loriann Kelly, Jillianne Tejani, Kristy Giovanazzo, Anne Marie Foster, Jessica Botero, Marissa Jones, Lauren Costa, Shirley Guirguis, Karen Smith, Nicole Lebovic, and my beautiful grandmother, Marilyn Thompson.

To the gorgeous authors Janine Infante Bosco, Stephanie Rose, AL Jackson, Melanie Moreland, Ginger Scott, Jane Anthony, Carina Adams, Suanne Laqueur, Adriana Locke, Dylan Allen, Katy Regnery, and KK Allen.

To Michael Bass, who finally read one of my books! I'm putting this in here to see if you read anymore. Next, I want to read your story.

As always, I have to thank my husband who reads every story and champions my creativity. To my three littles who I love tucking into bed no matter how old they get. I love you more than all the words in the world.

Finally, to the bookstagram and booktok community. There are so many beautiful reviewers who I adore and love every post, comment, like and story! Thank you for sharing the love of romance!

About the Author

JEANNINE COLETTE IS THE author of the Abandon Collection—a series of stand-alone novels featuring dynamic heroines who have to abandon their reality in order to discover themselves … and love along the way. Each book features a new couple, an exciting new city, and a rose of a different color.

A graduate of Wagner College and the New York Film Academy, Jeannine went on to become a Segment Producer for television shows on CBS and NBC. She left the television industry to focus on her children and pursue a full-time writing career.

She lives in New York with her husband, the three tiny people she adores more than life itself, and a rescue pup named Wrigley.

Jeannine and her family are active supporters of The March of Dimes and Strivright The Auditory-Oral School of New York.

www.jeanninecolette.com